BENDING THE RULES

THE DATING PLAYBOOK, BOOK: 1

MARIAH DIETZ

BENDING THE RULES

Copyright © 2020 by Mariah Dietz

All rights reserved.

No part of this book may be reproduced in any form or by any electronic or mechanical means, including information storage and retrieval systems, without written permission from the author, except for the use of brief quotations in a book review.

Cover Design © Hang Le

❀ Created with Vellum

Learn More About Mariah

Website: www.mariahdietz.com

Also sign up for news, updates, and first glimpses with Mariah's newsletter:
Sign Up Now

Also follow Mariah on:

- Amazon
- Bookbub
- Facebook
- Goodreads

And join Mariah's readers group on Facebook: The Bossy Babes

ALSO BY MARIAH DIETZ

The Dating Playbook Series

Bending the Rules

Breaking the Rules

Defining the Rules

Exploring the Rules - Coming October 1, 2020

His Series:

Becoming His

Losing Her

Finding Me

The Weight of Rain Duet

The Weight of Rain

The Effects of Falling

The Haven Point Series

Curveball

Exception

Standalones

The Fallback

Tangled in Tinsel, A Christmas Novella

1

I never considered myself much of a rule breaker. I wasn't a follower. I wasn't a leader. I was just me, Raegan, queen of naps, lover of sweatpants, and obsessive reader, working to acquire my dream job as a cetologist so I can study whales and dolphins outside of college. And volleying between pretending the man of my dreams will one day realize how perfect we are together and trying to convince myself I'm over him —that is, until I hear his name again.

Everyone has one. A name that makes them pause when heard. A combination of vowels and consonants strung together to create an entire web of memories and thoughts. For me, those letters spelled Lincoln Beckett. And like trying to convince myself that the three-year crush I've been harboring for him is over, I try to pretend the name doesn't cast a spell over me. That I can hear his name and not work to listen to what news follows. After all, thinking about Lincoln is the very worst of bad ideas.

Why?

Simply put, there are at least ten rules against dating your brother's best friend, beginning with the very fact that he's your brother's best friend. Secondly, he's guaranteed to know way too much about your life, your family, and your brother's illustrious decisions. The only thing that might be worse would be dating your best friend's brother—thankfully for me, my best friend's brother is eleven.

Therefore, universal laws, fate, karma, sibling code, and every other fictional or otherwise belief ought to ensure my brother's best friend look okay-ish at worst and troll-ish at best. This was my experience for the first sixteen years of my life. My brother, Paxton, is three years older than me, and his childhood best friend, Caleb, has a red Brillo Pad for hair, two-million freckles, and is so painfully awkward it's endearing. I have no problem wearing a bikini or a facial mask in front of him. If I burp or trip over my own feet, it's not a problem. If I pig out on ice cream, I simply ask him if he'd like a bowl.

Then, Paxton started at Brighton University in Seattle, Washington, where our dad is the Dean of Business, and he was quickly deemed a God because of his skills on the football field as the quarterback.

And my world went to hell.

Fate stuck her big, ugly middle finger up and has been saluting me with it since. Maybe it's because I lied to my mom about the dent in the back of her car that actually *did* happen when I'd borrowed it and illegally drove my best friend, Poppy, to the mall. Maybe it was because I'd pierced my naval when I was thirteen after paying a stranger twenty bucks to sign the release form. Or, maybe it was because fate had taken it easy on me for the first sixteen years of my life and decided I hadn't shown enough appreciation. And the day Paxton brought Lincoln over for dinner, fate waved her 'fuck you, Raegan' flag so high you could see it across the Pacific.

Lincoln Beckett, AKA the President, was not a scrawny gamer like Caleb. Rather, he was tall, and his broad shoulders only enunciated this fact. His biceps were corded, and his dark hair was mussed and perfectly imperfect in the sexiest way possible. And to make matters worse, he was smart, armed with a quick smile and sharp wit that made his brown eyes shine with humor. Seeing him had me forgetting I'd been crushing on senior Michael Porter for three months—hell, it had me forgetting my own *name*.

I was screwed.

To add injury to insult, the day Pax brought Lincoln over, I'd begun my period, and my skin was breaking out. I'd already switched my contacts for glasses, my face was scrubbed clean, and I was wearing baggy sweats to complete my homeless appearance. Had it been Caleb, I wouldn't have even blinked, but the sight of Lincoln standing in the kitchen where I was helping mom finish dinner had me wishing I had an invisibility cloak or at least an excuse to leave.

Paxton moved out a month later, and though he returned home frequently for hot meals and laundry, Lincoln only came by a few times, leaving me to lust after him mostly by memory and occasionally seeing him when I'd stop by the house the two of them rented along with Caleb and Arlo, another teammate who I'd also be fine by Pax being best friends with.

This year, I'm a freshman at Brighton and gone are the days of me fantasizing about Lincoln Beckett, the starting wide receiver and highly acclaimed football player with a killer smile. The man who's so frequently on the news that he's amassed zillions of fans and admirers, my parents included.

Nope.

No.

Not happening.

"Maybe I should have worn the pink shirt." Poppy tugs on her pale blue blouse for the tenth time.

"This is awkward," I say, ignoring her comment because I've already assured my best friend that she looks great a hundred times to no avail. It's obviously not my validation she's seeking. "We're so early. We're going to look like idiots just hanging around and waiting." She's my number one reason for attending Brighton, a University known for football and its legal program. It's prestigious and expensive and thankfully has a strong marine biology program.

"People hang out all the time." Poppy looks around as though to prove her point.

"Yeah, when they have a reason to."

"We do. You have a class in twenty minutes." She looks away, her gaze sweeping across the corridor. "Do you think any of the rugby team will be in our classes?"

"Rugby team?"

Poppy grins, tucking her copper-red hair behind one ear. "They're seriously hot. One look at Blaine Campbell or Nick Carrol, and you're going to be like Lincoln who?"

I laugh. "You've already memorized their names?"

"Oh, Raegan, after you see these guys you won't even blink when you hear Lincoln's name."

I stare at her for a moment, waiting for sense to catch up to my best friend. "You do realize the hottest guy on campus *is* Lincoln, right?"

"The hottest guy on the *football* team, yes, but now we have the entire University at our fingertips." She flexes her fingers, her hot pink polish shining in the bright morning sunlight. "Trust me, in a month, you won't even remember who Lincoln is."

I don't voice my doubts. I don't want to have them. I want to believe my best friend is right, and that this crush will soon be filed away as an embarrassing memory.

We pass a couple of guys who turn as we walk by. One whistles. The other asks for our phone numbers.

"Gross," I say.

An arm slides around my shoulders, and I look up, ready to pull away, but stop when I see my brother's friend and roommate, Arlo. "What's up, ladies?"

"Are all guys creeps?" I ask, ducking out from under the weight of his arm.

"Us? Creeps?" Arlo laughs. "Hold up, Pax and the Pres are behind me. They're just chasing a skirt. Fresh meat on campus." He whoops.

My heart stutters—a standard reaction to hearing *his* name. I turn, trying to catch sight of them, working to remain calm. Then, I straighten my back, replaying Arlo's words. "You really are all creeps." I shove Arlo's arm off again when he drapes it over my shoulders.

"Don't make me kill you, Kostas." Pax appears with Lincoln at his side, pulling my attention like a magnet.

"My hands remained out of the end zone at all times." Arlo raises them as though to prove a point.

"Paws off," Paxton declares. "Otherwise, you're going to be trying to catch the ball with your teeth this season."

"Man, you're going to have your work cut out for you," Arlo says, smiling. "Freshmen are the flames we're moths. You know how it works."

Pax shakes his head, looking at Lincoln. "Poppy and Raegan are off-limits. You guys hear anyone on the team or anyone else saying something you kick their ass." Pax's blue eyes that match mine in both shape and color peer around us.

"Easy, caveman. Remember you've evolved a few hundred centuries. Come out of your cave, lower your stick, and realize times have changed. Women now have rights. We can vote, wear pants, rule countries. And these women…" I point between Poppy and myself, "…will kick your ass if you meddle with who we date."

Pax throws his arm over my shoulder, folding his arm so he has me in what likely looks like a loose headlock. It's something he's done since we were young. "Don't get all huffy. Trust me, us looking out for you guys is way better. These guys are all just looking to get laid."

I shrug. "Maybe we are, too?"

Arlo cheers again to push Pax off the thin ledge his hopes were stacked upon.

Pax sputters, tightening his grip around my neck. "I did not just hear my little sister talk about having sex!"

"No shaming!" Arlo says. "How many girls did you sleep with your freshman year?" he poses the question to Paxton.

I raise my hands, covering my ears. "La, la, la, la, la. I don't want to know. La. La. La. La."

Paxton pulls my hands free. "Probably less than half the number of girls The President banged."

I cringe at the reminder of the third rule I have for dating—never date a player.

Lincoln makes no attempt to disagree, his full lips pulled into a delicious smile that makes my stomach tingle. Good God, I love his smile. Everyone does. And to make matters worse, he knows it and uses it to his advantage, wielding it like a weapon.

"You guys are pigs," I say, shoving Pax away.

Poppy grins. "Don't worry, we won't bother with the football team. You guys can stick to your little cleat chasers. We're introducing ourselves to the rugby team. Did you know they don't wear any pads?"

She raises her eyebrows to let the insinuation sink in. "Talk about *real* men."

The three of them automatically reply, throwing insults and jabs at the sport and the players.

"*Real men,*" Arlo scoffs and grabs himself through his jeans. "I'll show you—"

Lincoln smacks the bill of Arlo's baseball hat, sending it flying.

"You guys are better than asshole jocks," Pax adds.

"Wait. So, you *do* know you're all a bunch of assholes?" I ask, feigning surprise.

Pax grins. "You should find a nice guy. Maybe a tech geek or a book nerd like you?"

"Watch it. I know where you sleep, and I still have your spare key," I warn him.

"Want to use it tonight?" Arlo waggles his eyebrows.

"Don't push me, Kostas," Pax warns. "Your ass will be doing lines today for practice."

Arlo only laughs, undeterred. I'm fairly certain he only flirts with me to irritate my brother.

Poppy giggles. I duck out from under Pax and veer to the left in the direction of the math buildings. "I have to get to class."

"We still have twenty minutes!" Poppy protests.

"I know, but I want to get a good seat."

She frowns, her shoulders sagging. "Soak it up while you can because, after this week, you're going to be a normal college student, slipping into class with five seconds to spare."

I don't even attempt to remind her that won't ever happen. She already knows my aspiration to become a cetologist can't be rivaled with.

"My fingers are crossed that you have a rugby player in your class!" Poppy yells.

I laugh. "You, too!"

Paxton shakes his head. "At least spare me the details."

"Done," I agree.

"Where are you headed?" he asks.

I scrunch my nose. "Math."

Pax grins. "I'm heading over to the math buildings, too, hang on. Pop, if you need anything, just let one of us know." He pauses, his gaze moving between her and me. "I'm serious, though. You guys don't want to get mixed up with any athletes. All they care about is the game and what happens on the field. None of them are looking for anything serious because they're all hoping to either be drafted or possibly transfer to a new school for a better position."

Rule number four feels like a lead weight in my stomach: don't get attached to someone who's going to leave soon. Poppy's ex-boyfriend, Mike, taught me this lesson, and I already know Lincoln will be moving on to bigger and better things—possibly as soon as the end of this year, next year at the latest.

"We're not looking for engagement rings," Poppy tells him. "I don't know why guys always assume girls want to get serious? Have you ever stopped to consider maybe we just want to casually date?"

Paxton's eyes narrow in thought, then he looks at Arlo and Lincoln. "Pretty sure we've seen enough crying girls to prove otherwise."

"Tears of joy," I say.

Pax smirks. "This isn't high school. Here, athletes are practically celebrities. People ask for our autographs and our pictures. Follow us on and off campus. They randomly show up at the house. I've had girls sneak into my bed. I get sexts every damn day, and I've been proposed to at least a dozen times. Trust me when I say there are a lot of girls looking for more than a good time. They want money and fame, and they know that's a possibility if they find the right dude."

"That's pathetic," I say.

His smirk grows as he shrugs. "Is it? Do you know how much a first draft athlete makes?"

"If a girl is only trying to sleep with you because she's hoping to date a famous athlete, then she deserves to shed a few tears," Poppy says before I can consider girls looking at my brother in the light he's painting.

I look at my best friend, and she's cool and calm, her shoulders pulled back, likely because this news isn't sending her reeling, realizing that even without the obvious ten rules for me not to date Lincoln, there's an entire campus vying for his attention.

"Trust me, you guys don't want to get mixed up in all that drama," Paxton says again.

Poppy smiles widely. "We already know to avoid the football team. Our attention is set on rugby. We also have the swimming team. Water polo. Wrestling." She ticks them off on her fingers. "Lacrosse…"

"Lacrosse," Arlo scoffs. "How is that even a sport?"

"Okay, I'm really going this time." I take two steps back, offering a half-hearted wave before turning around.

"Yes," Paxton says. "Focus on school and important shit."

"Like you do?" Poppy asks, sarcasm has her lowering her chin and raising her eyebrows.

"Do what I say not what I do, or however that shit goes." He jogs the few feet to catch up to me and drapes an arm over my shoulders, matching my pace.

"Hey, Lawson!"

Paxton and I both turn at the sound of our last name. Lincoln stands beside Arlo, grinning.

"What?" Pax yells.

"Nothing." Lincoln shakes his head, and then a girl walks past him, saying something to him that I can't hear from where we're stopped some hundred feet away.

He's too far away, and my brother is standing too close to confirm it, but I swear Lincoln's looking directly at me.

I swallow, staring back.

"See," Pax whispers. "Trust me. You don't want to deal with dating an athlete." His arm around my shoulders tightens, and he begins to turn, leaving me to follow him, my head on a swivel as I try to watch Lincoln's reaction.

The last thing I see before I turn toward the math building is Lincoln flashing a smile to the stranger.

2

I should heed Paxton's warning. After all, I know the truth: athletes are as bad as rock stars when it comes to the disposal of women. Too often, they think they're above it all—relationships, school, laws set forth by state and even those we privately enforce with our own company, like decency and respect.

Tonight, I have no doubt I'm about to see all the social laws being broken at our first frat party. I tried to say no, told Poppy I'd rather hit up our favorite Chinese restaurant over on Fifth Street where they constantly play eighties movies, which somehow makes eating drunken noodles all the better. But, Poppy reminded me of my goal for this year, my oath to get over Lincoln, and suddenly I found myself agreeing to come, entering the address into my phone so I'd have directions for when I got home and changed.

I should have waited for Poppy. She had to work this afternoon, but swore she'd get off early and insisted I come and scope it out. She thinks that because I'm a born extrovert, I thrive in these situations. Though now, I'm realizing that sometimes when thrown into the thick of it, I might have more introvert in me than I realized.

"Hey!"

I fight the impulse to turn around. I've been here for twenty minutes and have turned no less than a dozen times when hearing someone yell out a greeting in hopes it's someone I might know or recognize. Instead, I look like a moron, because no one is directing the reception to me.

"Hey!" The voice calls again, and then a hand closes around my elbow.

I turn and discover Arlo, a full cup in one hand and a wide smile on his face. If I didn't know Lincoln, I might have a crush on Arlo. Between his subtle east coast accent, olive skin, and instant smile the guy has all the qualities to be swoon-worthy, except that he gets distracted by every skirt that walks in front of him.

"What are you doing here?" I ask.

His grin is equal parts teasing and mischievous. "Tracking you down. Pax was concerned you guys would get drunk, and someone would take advantage of you."

I sigh. "I figured as much." I stand on my toes, looking around for Paxton. "He's being ridiculous. I don't need a chaperone."

Arlo isn't listening to me, though. His attention is lost in the crowds of people. "I love the beginning of the school year." He rubs his palms together. "Freshmen think we're gods, and sophomores and juniors are struggling with self-confidence and are willing to sleep with any guy who looks their way."

"Boy, you sure know how to make a girl feel important."

Arlo laughs. "Except for you, of course. "

"Of course," I echo.

"What time is Poppy supposed to get here?" he asks, his attention tracing over every female in sight.

"Soon. You can go. Tell Paxton I'm fine."

"That's okay. I'd like to keep my left nut intact."

"Paxton is all talk. Want the numbers of my exes? I promise they're all still alive."

"But do they have all their original teeth and limbs?"

A tall blond guy with dark eyes and a devious grin walks past, his gaze fixed on me so long he has to turn his head.

"Okay," I say, shoving Arlo away. "You're scaring away all the guys. Time for you to get lost."

"Don't give Pax a reason to kill me, all right?" he calls over one shoulder, a brunette already in his sights.

I don't bother with a response because he's already out of earshot. I take a deep breath and wander farther into the house. With my mother teaching at my high school and my brother being an all-state athlete, my aunt being the chief of police, and my dad being a dean, I wear a prominent yield sign around my neck, and the damn thing only lights up when any of my family members are present. Deterrent is an understatement. I've been ready and willing to lose my virginity since turning seventeen, and I'm pretty sure the only way I'm ever going to lose it is to a stranger in another state.

My first boyfriend, Ben Kroger, and I dated summer of my sophomore year. He'd been ready to sleep together, but I hadn't. Instead, I broke up with him, and that fall, I learned he had been dating someone else the entire time we dated.

My second boyfriend was Simon Copper. He was a good second boyfriend. He carried my books, called every night at eight-thirty, and always had good breath thanks to his obsessive need of chewing gum. He moved to Arizona over Thanksgiving break my junior year. I cried. A lot.

My third boyfriend, Jamie Marten, he was, well... a mistake. We won't go there.

My fourth boyfriend, Zach Webb, lived in a neighboring town, my family history unknown and his interest in me high. Unfortunately, his interest dropped like a gavel when my aunt pulled him over and arrested him for drinking under the influence, underage drinking, open container, and reckless intent. It was probably good that he ended things because when my parents found out, they were livid and nearly grounded me because of our affiliation.

And the fifth and final entrant in my dating history is Owen Graham. He was hot but ridiculous and needy like most high school boys. He shoved his hands up my shirt, and grazed my nipples, then pinched them so hard it drew tears. I dumped him the following week, and the very next day, he was working to swallow Brianna Tizznec's face.

My dating history can be located somewhere south of Hell. But this year is going to be different. Better. Epic.

With my chin held high, I stroll past the kegs of beer, pretending I have a purpose and destination, even though I don't.

"Hey," a guy says, stepping forward, his hand loosely circling my wrist.

He smiles when I stop and looks nearly giddy when I grin. "I'm Johnny." He places a hand on his chest, like I need the explanation.

"Raegan," I tell him. "It's nice to meet you."

He leans closer. "Are you a freshman?"

I consider Arlo's assessment of freshman and contemplate lying. Then, I think about the long list of reasons that I'm here tonight, including making new friends, being single, and wanting to make the most out of my college experience—not to mention finding a new path, a fork in the road, or more preferably a freeway to get my feelings and thoughts far from Lincoln. Maybe this guy's smile and hot skin could burn away those harbored feelings, leaving only the remnants of Lincoln's memory in the recesses of my mind. I tilt my chin higher and smile. "I am. Are you?"

Johnny flashes a smile, the dimple in his chin catching my eye. "I'm a junior."

I think I'm supposed to ask him something personal, something flirty, something besides the mundane basics like where he's from and what his major is—something that will differentiate me from every other girl he's met.

Unfortunately, I'm not that original.

"I saw you walk in with Arlo. You guys...?" he smiles coyly.

I return the smile, leaning forward as well. "Are we what?" I know what he's asking. Know that he's waiting for me to deny Arlo and I are together, but I've never been a fan of trailing off sentences. They beg of misplaced apologies and misinterpretations.

"You guys together?" His eyebrows rise with the question.

I study him a moment. Was that a leading question for a hookup? Make sure the other person is single so you can act without regrets.

"Sanders!" a girl screams, stumbling forward. Her tank top is at least a size too small, and her shorts are even tinier. Her hair is striped with shades of blonde, and her cat painted eyes are glassy from alcohol. "I want a piggy back ride."

I take a step back, watching his attention shift to her cleavage.

"You can ride me anytime." He grins like this is sexy.

She giggles.

I frown. Encouragement is the last thing this guy needs. She climbs him like a tree, and his face brightens before he turns and gallops, making a horrible impression of horse sounds.

Is this normal? Was he even flirting with me?

I elect to bury the incident somewhere between that time I ripped my track shorts while trying to hop a fence and my entire freshman PE class saw my underwear and the summer of eighth grade when Evan Springer called every night for two weeks, then suddenly stopped and began dating Kim Kelly two days later.

"Speaking on behalf of all guys, I'd like to assure you he is not the norm. Some of us do have manners, can speak in complete sentences, and won't add crude jokes to every sentence." A guy with dark blond hair and a friendly smile tips his cup toward Johnny. He's cute, not in the same manner as Lincoln, who you picture on the front of a bodice-ripping book, but rather like a guy you'd find on the shiny pages of a magazine, modeling expensive clothes.

"Just some?" I ask.

"Maybe on occasion..." he smiles. "Less occasionally if you're Johnny, I'm guessing." As if on cue, Johnny makes a whining sound mid-gallop and straightens, nearly losing his passenger.

"I have a feeling you're right."

"I'm Derek," he says

"Like Derek and the Dominos?"

He shrugs, the ghost of a smile playing on his lips. "Derek and the Dominos? Do I want to know what that is?"

I shrug. "A who. They were a band. A blip on Eric Clapton's timeline." I shake my head, wishing I hadn't blurted out the original question. No one knows who Derek and the Dominos are except my mom, who plays their single album continuously. And mentioning her right now would make me seem only stranger.

"You're a music buff, and you aren't dating Johnny. You keep getting better and better."

My cheeks pull into a grin that he matches and then raises. His eyes are a caramel brown, freckled with darker hues and curtained by thick lashes that match his mussed hair. His looks are subtler than Lincoln's, but the longer I look at him, the more persistent and prevalent they become.

"I'm Raegan."

"Raegan," he repeats my name. "I don't think I've ever met a Raegan, and I don't know any bands with that name in the title." He chuckles. It's a nice sound, warm and easy. "Would you like something to drink?" He lifts a red Solo cup filled with red punch that has likely been spiked.

I don't intend to drink it, after all, though his smile and laugh seem genuine, I don't know that he wouldn't put something in the cup. However, I'm willing to accept it. Hold it like a promise so I can learn more about him.

My fingers wrap around the cup, but before I can take it, someone else reaches for it and pulls it away, taking my attention as well. Lincoln steps beside me, his gaze on Derek as he lifts his chin in greeting. My heart falters and then begins to skip wildly in my chest. This is the first time I've been around him at a party, and my thoughts are spinning faster than I can process them as I picture him dancing, kissing me, drinking, kissing me, laughing, kissing me. The temperature seems to rise twenty degrees, making the already warm house nearly unbearable.

"Hey! What's up, man?" Derek extends a hand that Lincoln shakes once. It's casual, but too quick. There's tension between the two that distracts me and has me staring at Lincoln for several seconds longer than I should.

"You guys know each other?" I ask.

Lincoln doesn't meet my inquiring stare, keeping his focus solely on Derek. "Our new teammate, transferred from Texas State."

My eyebrows rise and my mouth falls open. "Oh. You ... you're on the football team?"

Derek turns his attention to me, a wide smile gracing his lips and light brown eyes. "You like football?" he asks.

I kind of hate that he appreciates my knowing he's a football player. It only confirms he's more like Arlo and less like my desired boyfriend.

"Derek here is the new wide receiver. The one no one knows about,"

Lincoln interjects, waving his hand with the cup of punch toward Derek, then taking a long drink as he cocks his chin up another notch.

Derek raises his chin, indignation touching the corners of his eyes, which pinch for a second before he laughs. "When your family pays for a new wing of the library, it's tough to get out of the spotlight. Am I right? But, with a new wide receiver on the field, we'll see if you can manage to keep it." He doesn't look at me, but Lincoln.

There's something between them, something that has each of them seemingly lifting a leg to mark their territory, though neither has any ties to me, leading me to deduce there's definitely a feud occurring between them on the field.

"She's Lawson's *kid sister*." Lincoln stands straighter as he punctuates the words.

Kid. The word makes me wince.

Derek pulls his chin back, looking at me again. "Paxton Lawson? I thought you were older?"

I shake my head. "We have an older sister."

He smiles. "You look nothing alike."

"Really? Most people say the opposite." We do look alike, though Pax and our older sister Margaret, who we often refer to as Maggie, arguably look more alike. Our eyes are a similar shape and color, and we're both left-handed. We're told we're expressive, and if I give as much away as Pax does, it means you know most of my thoughts with a single glance. We're both blond, though my hair's a few shades lighter, I missed on the height genes that both he and Maggie inherited. I'm a little on the short side while they're both on the tall end.

"He's just—"

"Going to kick your scrawny ass if you even consider it," Lincoln interrupts him, taking another swig from his glass.

I glare at him. "Don't you have something better to do? Someone to see?" Under different circumstances, I'd be a giddy, nervous wreck to have Lincoln warning a guy away. This is something I've dreamed of for years. Literally *years*. But, this is not how I'd imagined it. Not doing my brother's bidding.

Lincoln shakes his head. "I really don't."

Again, I might be flattered if he were looking at me instead of Derek.

Derek seems to stand taller, returning the same challenging stare.

I don't bother waiting to find out what the two are really fighting about or why. I might care later tonight when my thoughts all roam to Lincoln like they do at the end of every day, but right now, my ego is leading me toward writhing bodies and inviting smiles.

I check my phone again for a text or missed call from Poppy, and when I don't see one, I head for the back door so I can call her. I find a switch on the wall beside the door and flip it on. The area is small, lighting up a fenced back yard that's filled with upside down coolers and a canoe. The air is cool as I step outside, hinting at fall. The days are still warm, but the nights are getting cold. I know I'll be regretting not bringing a sweater on my way home.

Poppy answers on the third ring. "I know. I know. I just couldn't figure out what to wear. I'm sorry. I'm almost there."

"Everyone's going to be drunk by the time you get here."

She tries to laugh, but I know it's not genuine. It's a nervous habit. She's likely struggling with regret and still not happy with what she chose to wear.

"I'm kidding." It's only a half-lie. At the very least, I'll be sober.

"Are there lots of hot guys?"

The urge to tell her about Lincoln tickles across my tongue as I recall the details I hadn't appreciated as they were happening: the savory scent of his cologne, the timbre of his voice, the way his gaze had swept over me. My heart thrums.

"Raegan?"

"Uh ... yeah..."

"You had to think about it?"

"No. I mean..." I clear my throat. "There's a ton of people here. There's a lot of shaggy guys. Crazy hair and long beards. It's still in."

"I'm still not sure I like that look. It kind of spells laziness."

"They're guys. It comes with the territory regardless of the hair and beard."

Poppy laughs. Her little brother, Dylan, is too young to live up to his full lazy potential. "Okay. I just parked." Her car door slams in the background. "I had to park like three blocks away." A cat screeches. "This is kind of creepy."

"It's not creepy. Just dark, and you're nervous. I'll keep talking with you and head that way." I lean forward to look past the shrubs that surround the small porch, locating a gate in the fence.

"Have you seen any rugby players?"

I chuckle, closing the latch behind me. "I haven't studied the pictures you sent me close enough to know who they are." My best friend likes to plan and prepare for everything, which only skims the surface of why she's gone to such lengths to orchestrate meeting the rugby team. Like the Titanic hitting the iceberg, her interest in the rugby team is clear and obvious—it's what's under the surface though that has her so insistent. The broken heart she's trying to nurse and avoid with a six-pack because she refuses to talk about her ex-boyfriend who railroaded her heart.

"Don't fail me now. I was told they're going to be here. Nick for you, Blaine for me. They're best friends. We'll have weddings a few weeks apart, buy houses next door to each other, and raise our babies together. It'll be beautiful."

"Unless he's a mouth breather. I don't want mouth breathing babies."

"Have you seen him? Trust me, you'll get over the mouth breathing."

"Speak for yourself. I'm a light sleeper."

Poppy giggles, and I can hear it echo down the street. She appears beneath a streetlight, and I hang up.

"I should have put on more deodorant," I tell her, rolling my shoulders as she catches up to me.

"I'm nervous, too."

"It's weird. It's like high school but without the fear of parents showing up. And the guys are so much hotter. I'm not sure if that's just because I haven't known them since the paste-eating years, or if guys magically reach a new level of hotness once they hit nineteen."

Her laughter pulls her lips into a wide smile, and then she loops her arm through mine. "Probably both."

"You look cute, by the way."

Poppy stops. "Cute?"

"Good cute. Hot cute. Not babyish cute."

"Do I look like a freshman?"

"According to Arlo, that's a good thing. Well ... kind of." I blink back thoughts of what he'd said earlier.

"Maybe I should..." She begins pulling on her V-neck tee, exposing more of her cleavage.

I reach forward to stop her. "You know me. I'm not going to judge you if you want to have meaningless sex as long as you do it safely. But..." I pause, waiting until she meets my stare. "I think you'll regret sleeping with some guy who notices you for your boobs. Which, by the way, look awesome tonight."

She lifts them. "It's this bra. It's a miracle worker." She sighs deeply. "I just don't want to be seen as a friend or a 'nice girl.' I want to be desirable. Sexy. Mysterious."

"I think you're working against that last one by showing off the twins."

Poppy whacks my arm with the back of her hand. "You know what I mean."

I do. Because I want it, too. This year, I want to shed my neon flashing sign that says 'off-limits' and experience all the fun. And if the first step of that is finding this possible mouth breather who plays rugby, then I'm up for the task.

"Okay, show me what Nick looks like again."

3

"Paxton, Arlo, and Lincoln are playing patrol tonight," I warn her as we round the sidewalk and head down the short driveway.

Poppy slows, her arm squeezing mine as she looks across the yard filled with people in various states. Some are casually talking, others are dancing, and a large group on our left is doing the limbo. A couple of guys are shirtless and manning a grill on the opposite side, cowboy hats and beers in hand.

"It's so bizarre," I say. "Everyone is older, and yet, reverting back to dress up and kid party games."

Poppy chuckles, but it's her nervous laugh. "Well, if the rugby team isn't here, at least you have Lincoln to look at."

I swiftly shake my head. "No. Remember, I am over him. No more Lincoln."

Her smile is shaky, conveying she doesn't believe me.

"Let's go."

We make our way up the concrete steps that lead to the house. The door is wide open, people spilling out onto the small porch. Poppy's arm constricts even tighter as she slows, prompting me to lead the way.

Inside, friend groups are recognizable by matching outfits. There's a small crowd of girls all wearing Catholic school uniforms, their tops consisting of white bikinis. Another group is dressed in red tees with white numbers and names painted on them. It takes me only a minute to recognize Lincoln's name and number printed on three of their shirts, and only another second to find Pax's. A group of guys are wearing sheets and drinking. Another is wearing board shorts and pin-striped suit jackets complete with ties, black hats, and shades.

"There are so many people," Poppy whispers. "How do you know to dress up? And as what? Are these clubs? Popular kids? Are there popular kids in college?"

"I have no idea." My denim cutoffs and black tee seem plain in contrast.

"Say, party!" a guy yells, snapping a picture of us on his phone before turning his attention to others nearby.

I blink away the blinding flash and turn to Poppy. "I'm pretty sure the ratio of girls to guys is at least four to one."

"Seriously," she says, peering over my shoulder. "There are barely any guys here." She cranes her neck the opposite direction. "There's Arlo."

I turn to look in the same direction, hoping to find Lincoln with him. "Did he find the girls in the Catholic school girl uniforms?" I ask.

"He decided to keep things simple and went for the girls in the bikinis." She points toward the back. "Oh, and look, their bathing suits go up their asses. That's lovely."

"Should we wander around?"

Poppy shrugs. "I have no idea."

I suck in a deep breath, searching for the confidence that had me believing this was a great idea. "Maybe we should get some beer."

"Yes. Beer."

I nod. "Okay. Let's just stick together."

We make it through the living room when Poppy pulls on my hand. "There they are!"

"There who are?"

"The rugby team!" she hisses.

A girl bumps into me as I make a sudden stop. She giggles and wobbles, spilling half her drink on the linoleum floor and spraying my feet and legs. I reach forward to catch her arm. "You okay?"

She giggles again, her eyes glassy. "The beer sucks," she says. "It's warm. Warm beer sucks." She belches.

Poppy's nose wrinkles with repulsion as the girl pivots and moves away. "God, I feel like my mother right now," she says. "I'm judging everyone."

I laugh so hard I almost cry. "I wish I'd worn tennis shoes. Flip flops were a terrible decision."

"Hey." A deep voice says.

We both turn, Poppy's hand clasping my wrist, channeling her excitement as we come face-to-face with two guys. They're both blond, one has hazel eyes, and the other light brown. They're medium height and build, but their smiles hold enough confidence to make them appear like they're over six-feet tall.

"They're rugby players," she whispers to me, before she turns her attention to the boys standing in front of us. "Hi," she manages, her voice verging on being breathy.

"How are you guys?" The brown-eyed one asks.

Poppy giggles. My best friend is proficient at flirting, while I remain skeptical of everyone's intentions—even more so now that Arlo shared his view on lower classmen.

"Are you guys freshmen? Sophomores?" Hazel-eyes asks.

My uncertainly grows, silencing me.

Poppy looks at me, soundless questions bunching the skin between her eyes, before she looks at the guys and smiles. "We're freshmen. What about you guys?"

"Juniors," the hazel-eyed one replies. His attention goes to Poppy as she asks him for his name.

"Are you guys here with someone?" The other one asks me, leaning closer as the game of beer pong behind us grows raucous.

As I open my mouth to say 'no,' a clear "yes" is spoken. Heat presses against my back.

I turn around to see Arlo and frown. Paxton is behind him, glaring at the guys in front of us.

"They're possessions of the football team. Sorry, asshats." Arlo shoos them.

The two guys look from us to Pax and Arlo, curiosity and humor visible in their eyes.

"We're not..." I pause and clear my throat, lowering my voice, because my first words were practically screamed. "We're not here with them."

"Really?" The brown-eyed guy steps closer to me, his gaze set on Arlo. A challenge has him squaring his shoulders.

Paxton matches his move, like pieces on a chessboard, his steps are strategic and purposeful.

"I just need to chat with them really quickly," I say to the stranger who doesn't seem deterred at all by the several inches that Pax has on him. Maybe Poppy is right. Maybe there's something to these athletes who don't wear pads on the field. Or, maybe it's just the alcohol that has them feeling invincible.

I put a hand on Paxton's chest, shoving him backward, but he barely budges. I look at Arlo, but his attention is squarely on the guy in front of me. I turn to Poppy, hoping she either runs off with the rugby player in front of her or has an idea on how to deter these two meatheads, both of whom I'm ready to disown.

Poppy forces a smile, but it looks like a frown.

I drop my shoulder into Paxton's chest and face the two rugby players again. "Would you guys mind getting us something to drink? We'll meet you over by the beer pong table in just a minute."

Brown-eyes looks at me, then over my shoulder at Arlo and Pax before looking at me again.

"No, she won't," Pax chimes.

The rugby player looks at me, the left side of his mouth creeping up into a hint of a smile before he shakes his head. "I think you guys have your hands full at the moment. It was nice meeting you." They turn, shaking their heads as they walk away.

I turn back to my brother, ready to slug him. "What was that?" I cry.

"Those two are a bunch of hornballs."

"We just met them. We weren't doing *anything*!"

"But they would have invited you to."

I stare at Paxton for a long second, waiting for my easygoing and reliable brother to reappear and this overprotective and overbearing stranger to vanish.

"You don't want them. They just want to use you," he finally says.

"It's not the who, Pax. It's the what. You can't follow me around, warning guys away. For your sanity and certainly my own." I look from my brother to Arlo. "Same goes for you. No girls are going to come running toward you if they see you watching every step I take and every person I talk to."

Arlo shrugs. "I don't know. Jealousy seems to turn a lot of chicks on…"

"And if you want to have a wing woman one night, you can ask, and *I* will decide if I *want* to play that role. But, you guys can't do this. You're going to drive all of us crazy."

"Can there at least be a couple of ground rules?" Paxton asks.

"Absolutely. No dating my professors. No dating married men. And making sure I am happy." I tick each of the three rules off on my fingers, omitting the most important one: not dating his best friend.

"I'm—" Paxton begins, but I cut him off with a quick shake of my head.

"You don't get to make the rules. I do. I promise to be safe and smart most of the time, but I'm eighteen. I'm supposed to be making mistakes."

His head falls back on his shoulders, and if it were quieter in here, I'm sure I'd hear him sigh. I know his intentions are good. He wants to protect me and ensure I don't get hurt or do something stupid. But, he needs to realize that sometimes the path to getting hurt and being stupid are the most important and memorable ones we can take. "Can we do a check-in system?"

I nod instantly. "Party nights, I'll check in with you. Let you know when I'm home."

"Mom and Dad made your curfew midnight? You goody-two-shoes, I had to be in by eleven."

I shrug. "This is further proof why you don't need to worry about me. I'm the good child."

"And she's got way better legs," Arlo adds.

Paxton throws both of his hands in the air. "*This*. This is why my junior year is going to fucking suck."

"Now, if you'll excuse us, we have some rugby players to meet."

4

On our way over to find the brown and hazel-eyed rugby players, Poppy informs me their names are Chase and Sam, and though I've not heard her mention them, she seems content in modifying our future to include them and forget about the other two she had originally chosen.

"Oh no," Poppy says, coming up short.

"What's wrong?"

She points toward a crowd of moving bodies, a strobe overhead making it difficult for me to focus and threatening to give me a migraine. "Sam is talking to some other chick."

"That's okay. Chase only had eyes for you. You should go talk to him."

"But what are you going to do?" Disappointment twists her lips and creases her forehead.

"I'm going to find some of that warm beer and maybe get some revenge on Paxton and Arlo."

"You mean go find Lincoln?"

Just his name makes my heart skip a beat.

I shake my head. "No. I'm actually hoping to avoid seeing him because the last thing I need to see right now is him making out with someone."

Her lips pull into a line as she attempts to smile. "Why don't I go with you?"

"What? No. Go. Flirt. Giggle. Get his number. Maybe he'll lead you back to the rest of the team, and you can have your pick."

Poppy's mouth falls open as she laughs. "Oh my gosh. Stop giving me hope." She glances back over to Chase and then me. "Okay. I have my phone on. If you need anything—*anything*—just call."

"I've already got babysitters here. I'm good."

She gives me a parting smile, and then her hips sway as she approaches Chase, his smile confirming he notices her.

The number of bodies in here leaves the air humid, carrying a sea of scents: fruity perfumes, a hint of cologne, an underlying of beer all working to compete against the smell of sweat.

Maybe I should move my plan for stepping outside of my comfort zone and dating to next year, after I've mastered the mechanics that come with choppy college schedules, parties, and the idea of few knowing my name after attending the same school for ten years.

I find the keg of beer and a stack of plastic cups, and without a purpose in my way, I head toward it and fill a glass.

"Kelly, right?" It's Derek. He leans closer. His light hair is mussed, like he—or maybe someone else—has been running their hands through it. It's sexy as hell.

Disappointment feels too similar to hope as I shake my head. "Sorry. Wrong girl."

"Right girl, wrong name," he says, taking a step closer to me. "I'm sorry. I'm terrible with names. I literally had to write my coaches name on my forearm so I'd stop calling him Steve. Tell me your name again. I swear, I'll remember it this time."

"Raegan."

"Like the president." He taps his temple, as though storing my name to memory. "Do you remember my name?" He smiles, taking the final step so there's barely a gap between us.

He's flirting with me, and it might be because he's not supposed to, but I cling to the knowledge he talked to me before knowing I was Pax's little sister and smile coyly. "It was David, right? Or Duke? Darryl?"

He laughs. "You're funny."

"Where's your accent?"

He raises his eyebrows, and I take another drink of liquid courage. "My accent?"

"I thought you were from Texas?"

His smile grows. "You do remember." His white teeth flash. "I'm from Rhode Island. I went to Texas for my freshman and sophomore years."

"Really?"

He nods, grabbing a cup and filling one for himself. "What about you?"

"I'm a Seattleite, born and raised."

"Really?"

It's my turn to nod.

"Do you want to stay here after graduation?"

I nod. "I think so. What about you?"

Derek winces. "I don't know. I've got to say, so far it looks way better than I'd expected." He runs his gaze over me, slowly—purposefully, stopping when he reaches my eyes. I feel my heart beating in my neck. "Want to know a secret?" he asks.

I hold on to the facts of him being attractive and smelling really good as I wait for the pickup line I know will make me cringe.

He leans closer, flooding my senses with his cologne, the heat of his body, the fresh scent of whatever product's in his hair. His eyes are expressive, his irises edged by a darker hue that create mazes I'm sure many have been lost in.

"I almost didn't transfer here because I was worried it was going to rain all the time and feel depressing."

Relief has me laughing. "October hasn't begun yet."

"Bad?"

"You get used to it."

He slaps a hand across his chest and throws his head back like I've just skewered his hopes.

Laughter tickles my lips—natural and easy. I want to blame the beer running through my veins for the temptation to lean closer to him. To mold my body against each fold of his in invitation, but that would be a lie since I've only managed a few sips.

"Derek!" A girl appears, her arms winding around one of his. She has long, blonde hair, eyes round and wide as a doe, and a waist that is flat and toned, shown off by the cut off shirt she's wearing.

"Hey." He smiles at her and doesn't try to pull free. "Chrissy, this is Raegan."

He knows *her* name.

"Hi." Her lips are pursed, eyes narrowed. If she had nails that contracted, I'm sure they'd be out and pointed at my throat.

I try to return the diluted smile and glance over my shoulder for an excuse to leave. "I need to meet my friend. Nice meeting you guys."

I turn when Derek yells my name.

"See? I told you I'd remember."

It's ridiculous that I find another smile forming on my lips. Hopeless, maybe, but I'm not shameless, so I lift my glass and continue walking until I'm out of sight and pause, looking around for Poppy.

My chest feels heavy and conflicted. Disappointment from too many interactions weighing me down.

"You look way too serious. You must be a freshman." A guy says, stopping beside me. His hair is slicked to the side with too much product, and he's wearing a yellow polo with blue and white stripes tucked into a pair of jeans with a belt buckle that's the size of my hand. His eyes are locked on my hint of cleavage, making the sinking feeling in my chest careen with a nosedive.

"I'm looking for my friend."

He smiles, his thick neck bobbing as he makes a quick turn of his head. "What's your name, sweetheart?"

"I should go. I..." Am really, really terrible at lying and making excuses, and he knows it, his face brightening with the knowledge.

"I'm pretty sure it was me you were looking for." He offers his hand. "Nice to meet you. I'm Mr. Right."

My laugh is automatic, and though it's not meant to encourage him, he steps closer like it was.

"What? I can't help but fall for you. You keep tripping me with that smile."

"Oh, that one was so bad," I tell him, fighting to stop my smile from spreading.

"Let me borrow a kiss. I promise I'll give it back with interest." He steps forward, and I swallow my laughter as I take a step back.

"You're full of pickup lines, aren't you?"

"Do you know what my shirt's made out of?"

I take another step back, my heel hitting the wall.

Oh boy.

"Boyfriend material," he tells me, standing too close for comfort.

I thank my lucky stars when Lincoln appears next to the guy, his eyebrows drawn like he's bored. Mr. Pickup line doesn't acknowledge him, so Lincoln loudly clears his throat. The sound has Polo twisting. "Oh. My bad," he says.

Lincoln nods. "Yup."

The stranger chuckles like he's undeterred, but sags back a bit, his gaze still on my cleavage.

I look at Lincoln, silently begging him not to leave. "Have you seen Poppy?" I ask him.

Lincoln closes the distance between us, shutting Polo out of my vision. "You just keep needing to be saved tonight."

Indignation has me planting a hand on my hip, ready to repel his words. His dark and obnoxiously perfect tousled hair teases my fingers, and his eyes are filled with alcohol-induced interest as he slides his hand against my waist, wrapping around my hip so his fingertips rest on my butt. My hand and anger fall, along with any pride and sense as I stop breathing. My head's spinning like I've had too much to drink as I realize I could get far drunker on Lincoln than any substance.

His eyes close, and my lungs feel like I've just belly flopped. His lips are hot, dancing across my collarbone, leaving a trail that has me shivering though I'm too warm.

His other hand connects with the left side of my waist, pulling me closer to him. "Pretend you're enjoying this," he growls, grazing my ear with his teeth.

He's doing this for show. An attempt to deter Polo. It doesn't help me breathe any easier. I lift my hands, gripping his shoulders, and he sweeps his lips up the column of my neck, stopping below my ear.

5

Lincoln Beckett has just proven I won't be dying from a heart attack anytime soon.

"You're really making me work for it, aren't you, Lawson?"

I can hardly formulate a coherent thought, much less a sentence.

Someone laughs. The sound too forced and loud to be casual, drawing my attention back to the ogre wearing a polo. He grins, like he knows this is a sham and expects me to call out the farce.

This is ridiculous.

This is stupid.

This is Lincoln!

Shit!

Rule number five of why I can't date Lincoln: I won't date anyone who makes me turn into a shy prude who forgets how to kiss. I want to be with someone who makes me feel empowered, strong, sexy, and when Lincoln is around, I don't feel any of that.

"You're killin' me here, Lawson," he whispers, then straightens.

The quick rhythm of my heart has me light-headed, and his kiss has left me dazed. I start to look in the direction of the ogre again, but Lincoln grabs my hand and tugs me toward the door.

One of my flip-flops nearly comes clean off, getting stuck on something sticky on the floor. I pull my hand free, struggling to get my shoe back on as others step dangerously close to my toes.

A black tennis shoe with dark gray sides boxes in my foot, and I nervously glance up, already aware I'm going to find Lincoln. He grins. It's easy, almost lazy like he didn't just try giving me a hickey—at a party my brother is also at.

I slide my toes between the small piece of rubber that separates my toes and take a quick look around the house, hoping I catch sight of Poppy before we take the remaining steps to the door.

Rain plays a soft symphony outside, hitting everything like it's a target. The air is cold—drawing more attention to how warm my entire neck is from where Lincoln falsely marked me.

"Where's Poppy?" he says.

Emotions and confusion have me clearing my throat, attempting to suppress each of them. I glance back at the house, tucking some of my blonde hair back behind an ear. "Talking to someone."

"Rugby player?"

"Yup." I slowly turn my gaze to Lincoln but can only keep his stare for a second before looking away. I pretend the group of guys wearing sheets is interesting. Like them posing and talking each other up is actually fascinating.

"Well, here's a little insight: the first rule of attending a frat party is knowing who your scapegoat is going to be."

"My scapegoat?"

Lincoln nods. "When you get attention from someone you're not interested in, your scapegoat swoops in and plays your boyfriend to get you off the hook."

I knew it was fake and that he was only pawing at me for show, but the way he dismissively moves on like it didn't matter to him at all stings. "I didn't need a scapegoat. Things were fine."

"You looked like a deer caught in the headlights."

"I *would* have been fine." My words sound more defensive than I intended.

He pulls his head back, his eyes growing round. "Did I hit a pressure point?"

I raise a hand in the direction of the front door. "You guys have to stop. I already talked to Pax. You guys do you, I do me."

The left side of Lincoln's lips tip into a grin that has a dimple flashing. "Oh, yeah?"

"You guys are being ridiculous. I was the only sober person in that goddamn house."

"Since when did little Lawson develop such a potty mouth?"

I growl. Or maybe I shriek, I'm not sure how to describe the sound that climbs out of my throat, expressing my frustration.

"Hey, President!" a girl calls, her tone flirty, airy—the complete opposite of mine. He looks—of course he looks. I'm coming across as an errant child throwing a temper tantrum, not sexy or confident in the least. My heart beats painfully in my chest, regret tangling with frustration. Rule six as to why I can't be with Lincoln: I don't know how to be myself around him.

"What's up?" he calls.

"You coming inside?"

I don't turn around to face the girl. I don't need to add force to the avalanche already crashing down around me, burying me in doubts.

"Yeah, yeah. I'll be in soon."

"I'm looking forward to it." She giggles.

I roll my eyes.

Lincoln smirks. "What?"

"Nothing."

"Oh, that was something. You should probably sit down. You're going to be dizzy after that eye roll."

I shake my head, tempted to roll my eyes again. "Who giggles like that?"

His smirk doesn't lessen. "Like what?"

"Like *that*!" I swing my arm toward the house again for emphasis. "And more importantly, why in the hell do guys find it sexy? Because it's not. It is *so* not."

"Then, what is sexy?"

"Not that!"

He chuckles, and the jealousy in me disguised as anger and offense spreads. "She was just laughing."

"She was not just laughing. That was basically her saying come screw me in the bathroom."

He doesn't refute my words, his calm demeanor serving to make mine a chaotic storm I work to suppress by taking a deep breath through my mouth and blowing it out my nose, something Poppy's mother tells her clients to do when they call her emergency line and are worked up over something.

"I'm surprised it bothers you so much."

"Says the guy who tried to give me a hickey because I was having a conversation with a dude."

"You really aren't going to give me any credit for saving you, are you?"

"No!" I cry.

He shrugs. "Give it a couple of weeks on campus, and you'll realize I did you a favor."

He has no idea how wrong he is. I'll likely be distracted, working to remember every single second and detail of those few minutes. The way his cologne infiltrated my thoughts, the heat of his lips before the scent reached my nose, and how cold my skin felt when he'd worked his way higher on my jaw, like each cell was crying out for him to return.

Lincoln didn't save me. He's likely ruined me.

He chuckles again.

"Why are you laughing?"

"Because I can practically hear your thoughts screaming 'fuck off' at me."

"I'm not..." I release a deep breath, trying to find my footing. I'm in a no-win situation. Admit that's not what I was thinking and risk exposing my jealousy and insecurities that surround him like the Great Wall of China, or allow him to think that's true, and I'm a moody bitch. "I just don't understand why guys think it's cute when girls act giggly and dumb."

"Was she acting dumb? She spoke in complete sentences. Addressed me by name. Were you expecting her to speak in Latin? Recite the Declaration of Independence?"

I sigh.

Touché.

"Okay, look," I say, pointing to where the group of guys dressed with sheets as togas are standing in a semi-circle, a couple of girls off to the side of them dressed in jeans and tank tops, their hair curled. They look like girls from my high school. Girls I'd be friends with. They talk to each other, occasionally stealing glances at the guys. It's obvious one of them or maybe both like a guy in the group. "Those girls have been talking to each other since we came out here, obviously trying to catch their attention, and the guys haven't talked to them once. But, watch this," I say, as two girls with bleach blonde hair wearing bikinis walk by and wave, giggling when the guys call out for them to stop and giggling louder when they make a lude remark. "Boobs and giggles walk into the picture, and suddenly toga boys realize they're not the only ones out here."

"I doubt the giggles did anything. I'm pretty sure that was all boobs and asses."

"You see my point."

"But, why are you mad at the guys. Be mad at the girls."

"Because you guys don't pay attention unless a girl walks in looking and acting like that."

Lincoln tilts his head. "Were you giggling when that guy inside talked to you?"

I pause too long.

He smiles. It's a victorious smile, one that makes his eyes shine and both dimples become prominent distractions. "My point exactly."

I shake my head, my thoughts churning too slowly with his close proximity and my confusion for how this night has gone.

"I thought you were just looking for a good time, anyway?" he asks.

"I am." I nod too vigorously.

"Then, don't worry about it or, you could try it."

"What? Looking like that? No, thank you."

He rolls his shoulders with a casual shrug. I notice he doesn't wince this time. Last year, there were a couple of months where every time I saw him, he'd wince when he moved. It was slight—so much so it didn't feel okay asking about it. "There are no rules or dress codes at these parties."

"As a girl, I have an entire list of rules I have to abide by that you're unaware of."

Lincoln pulls a pack of cigarettes from his pocket and a bright orange lighter. One of the cheap Zippo lighters like the ones Margaret, Pax, and I would pick up at the grocery store as kids simply to try and light them. I never did become adept at using them, but Lincoln has no problem getting it to light with a quick zing of his thumb.

His face glows a warm orange that should be unattractive because I hate cigarettes. I hate the way they smell. I hate the way they look. But right now, dammit if I don't find it warming every inch of my skin.

"Fuck the rules," he says.

6

"Hey, hey! There's my girl!" Mom calls as I make my way into the kitchen. It's Friday morning—or what's left of the morning—and the skies have cleared, unlike my thoughts, which are thickly overcast with memories of last night. My skin still remembers Lincoln's touch, and the farther the hours stretch, the more annoyed I've become that I didn't take every opportunity to play the role he provided.

"What are you doing home?" I ask.

"I'm working from home today," she says. "You getting ready for class?"

I shake my head. "No classes on Fridays."

"Lucky duck," she says. "When you get dressed, I need to take your picture." She's already dressed in a pair of jeans and a black sweater with her jean jacket on and a chunky red necklace, sipping what I'm conservatively betting is her fifth cup of coffee.

"For what?" I grumble, making my way to the fridge in search of leftovers.

A slight wince flashes across her face before she pushes a strand of wavy russet hair behind her ear. "Your first day of school picture."

"It passed."

"I know." Her eyes turn downcast like they do when she discusses her weight and wishes she were forty pounds lighter—something she's eternally uncomfortable with, though my mom's beauty is so far beyond a dress size. I instantly regret giving her a hard time. "I'm sorry. I didn't forget. I had to be at the school early."

"I'm just giving you a hard time. Can we do it Monday? I don't want to wash my hair." It's true what they say about parents taking fewer pictures of their kids as they have more, our walls will attest to it. For every three pictures of Maggie, there's a picture of Paxton, and for every five pictures of him, you'll find one of me. I know it wasn't intentional. Mom and Dad both work but strive to be there for us. When I played softball, they attended nearly every game, and when I sold Girl Scout cookies, Mom volunteered to walk in the rain with me. Dad even finagled his way into meeting the board chair of the local aquarium, which is how I got my volunteer position with the zoologist team.

"I have to leave here at five in the morning for a conference on Monday."

"And it sounds like I'm going to be washing my hair today." I grab a casserole dish filled with chicken and rice from the fridge.

Mom laughs. "If you can get ready by four, that would be best. Pax and his friends are coming for dinner tonight, and if I can bribe you with helping me, we can spend some quality one on one time, talking about your first week at college. I'll be in your debt for at least twenty-four hours."

"Pax and his friends?" I stop shoveling leftovers onto my plate and look at my mom.

"Since Pax made team captain, he wants to start having dinners so the team can bond. Apparently, he forgot the detail about not knowing how to cook, and he's so excited about this year..."

"You're a softy," is what I say, when I really want to tell her this is a horrible, terrible, awful idea. Seeing Lincoln right now with my nerves so frayed is guaranteed to be trouble.

She smiles. "So, we have a deal?"

"Thirty-six hours and a pedicure."

"Deal."

"No. Wait. You accepted way too soon."

Her grin is salacious. "I know. I was going to offer a week."

"You're cruel."

She laughs. "And you call me a softy. Are you working today?"

I return to filling my plate as I nod. "I need to leave for the aquarium soon. Think you can take the picture before I leave? By the way, how many are coming? And where's everyone going to sit?"

Mom shrugs. "I don't know. Pax told me he'd send a head count last night, but he never sent it. I'm going to head to the store while you shower, and I'll call him on the way."

"Maybe I'll go to Poppy's after work."

"Only if you take me with you." She grins. Mom's lips are always tilted upward—an eternal optimist who finds humor in every situation. "Seriously, though. You can't leave me. Invite her over."

"There won't be any room. Their egos will fill every square inch of this place."

She cracks a smile. "Be nice. You know how hard he worked for this. And you should be here. You know your support means a lot to your brother."

"You just want help with dishes."

"I'd be willing to throw in a manicure. I've seen your nails. They would thank me for it."

I glance at my short, bare nails as I retrieve my plate of food from the microwave. "It's the salt water. It eats the polish."

"At least they'd look pretty for a couple of days."

"You're lucky I like you."

She kisses my cheek. "I like you, too, kiddo."

I SHOW up to the Northwest Aquarium of Science fifteen minutes before my shift begins. I've been volunteering four days a week here for the past three years to gain knowledge and to pad my resume, so that come graduation, I will hopefully have an easier time finding a job as a cetologist. I trade my tennis shoes for the heavy all-terrain boots I wear when I'm doing feedings like I've been scheduled for today. My boots have a permanent fish-stench and feel like led weights as I tie them around my calves.

"Hey, Rae!" Jordan calls, her voice chipper as she makes a beeline to the mini fridge and pulls out a sandwich and smoothie.

"You okay?" I ask, watching her fingers tremble as she tears open the sandwich. Her dark hair brushes her shoulders in soft waves, and her dark blue-gray eyes are bright.

"Yeah," she says around a bite. Jordan's been volunteering here for over a year, since transferring to Brighton. She's a year older than me, studying marine biology, and has a passion for sea turtles that is unrivaled.

"Are you on feedings, or are you off?"

She points a finger at me as she finishes half her sandwich. "I'm with you." She flashes a wide smile, filling me with relief. Working with Jordan is easy and fun. We talk about animals, about science, school, the weather, Florida—everything that doesn't relate to Lincoln. "I've just got to get some food into me really fast."

"It's busy today," I say, putting on a blue fleece jacket with the aquarium's name embroidered on the right breast with a couple of sea otters playing in the letters. Hannah steps in from the front observation area, her bottled blonde hair pulled up into a high pony.

"Final vacation rush," Hannah says, heading to where we keep the large inventory of stamps we use in place of stickers to prevent trash.

Even better.

The four hours are swallowed faster than I'd expected, my thoughts of Lincoln and the regret and intrigue from last night only peppering my thoughts during the few brief lulls. Most of my time is spent preparing food for the animals with Jordan at my side, and the rest is spent answering questions and educating guests on the efforts we're investing in to keeps oceans and rivers clean.

I FIND Mom in the kitchen, her hair haphazardly pulled back with a large claw, as she stares at an opened recipe book. She looks up as I get closer, her blue eyes shockingly wide. "Good. I need you. I need to quadruple this recipe."

"Quadruple? How many are coming?"

She shakes her head. "Too many. Ready to start chopping?" Her gaze dances from mine to the produce covering the counter from the sink to the stove. "I didn't use any of the clear plastic bags for produce. It earned me a stink eye from the lady who checked me out," she tells me, pride reflecting in her tilted lips.

"Did you remember your reusable shopping bags?"

"And risk getting a forty-minute lecture from my favorite youngest daughter?" She staples her hands to her hips, but her gaze doesn't provide the same level of confidence as she scans over the vegetables again.

"You forgot, didn't you?"

Her hands slide from her waist, and her chin drops back. "I had them in the trunk. I tried."

I shake my head, trying to hide the outline of a smile I feel my lips sliding into. "What do you want me to start with?"

She makes an apology with her face as she scrunches her nose. "Onions."

"Pax owes me *so* big."

She nods. "I told him he does."

"Where is he?"

"Practice. But he's coming over right after to help."

Mom would do the same for me, so would my brother, and that knowledge leads me to the cutting board where I place the first of several onions and begin chopping while Mom prepares pans and then takes out her own cutting board and begins slicing peppers.

"I like your eyeliner," Mom says.

"Do you? Dylan told me I looked like a raccoon," I tell her, referring to Poppy's little brother.

She tips her head back and laughs so hard her eyes close. "You know better than to listen to boys about fashion or beauty advice, especially ones who can't drive."

"I was concerned because it's the ones too young to drive who are actually honest."

Her laughter grows. "He only said it because it makes your eyes stand out. Trust me, it's beautiful. Next time I have a board meeting, you'll have to show me how."

I nod. "It takes a few times to get the hang of it."

"Is that your polite way of telling me it's tougher than it looks?"

I try to hide my smile with a small shrug. Mom's never worn much makeup. Blush, mascara, and a red tube of lipstick are her essentials. "I'm sure you can do it."

"How much do you think they can eat? Do you think I should estimate each of them to eat a pound?" Her thoughts are scattered to hostess mode, something my mom takes very seriously as everyone who comes into our house always leaves with a full stomach. "Two?"

I shake my head. "I have no idea."

"I should get more bread." She sets her knife down.

"What? Are you really leaving?"

"I've only got six loaves."

"Six?! Mom! You've lost your mind."

"You and Pax eat an entire loaf," she says.

"But we aren't normal."

She pauses, her eyes glazed with humor that makes her lips twitch. "Your words, not mine."

I shake the smile off my face. "Believe me, we'll have plenty."

"I trust you. I just know these guys can eat, and they'll be carb loading. I'll be back." She grabs her purse from the bar. "When you finish those peppers and the squash, you need to put them on the cookie sheets and roast them for thirty-five minutes. The oven's already preheated."

I don't bother trying to argue with her again, knowing the words will be wasted. Instead, I point my knife at her. "Don't forget your reusable bags. Put them in the passenger seat so you see them."

She smiles. "You know me too well."

I focus on finishing up the vegetables and trying to keep the concern of seeing Lincoln on the outskirts of my thoughts as the kitchen becomes far too quiet.

Why couldn't I have just relaxed last night? There's no way he sees me as anything but uptight after my reaction to him. I did the exact opposite of what I wanted to, and regardless of how many times I try to figure out why, I can't.

A heavy sigh breaks through my lips as I run a clean towel over the counter, gathering the small vegetable debris into a pile.

"Hey!" Pax calls.

"Rae Rae!" Arlo follows him into the kitchen, a bright smile on his face, his brown hair combed to one side.

Behind him enters the guy who's been peeling away each of my conscious thoughts—Lincoln. His brown eyes are carefully composed, watching me with so little emotion I can't even begin to surmise his thoughts.

"Mom wasn't kidding when she said I owed you," Pax says. "What can we do? How can we help?"

I blink through the muddled thoughts that have tied my words into messy jumbles and focus on the pile of crumbs I was gathering. "I don't know, honestly. I think we're supposed to start on the sauce. Mom ran to the store. She was worried we wouldn't have enough garlic bread." I turn my back to them, moving to the cookbook Mom moved to the stand Paxton had bought her as a Mother's Day gift several years ago. "We're quadrupling the recipe," I say absently as I scan over the directions.

Pax appears beside me, likely reading the text twice as fast as I am since the words aren't digesting, my thoughts too scattered to absorb anything.

He grabs two large pans hanging over the island, setting them on the stove before turning toward the fridge. Pax, like Maggie and I, is proficient at cooking, a skillset my mom insisted we all learn and then was enforced when he moved out with three guys who didn't know a spatula from an ice cream scoop.

"You coming to our game tomorrow?" Arlo asks.

It takes a few seconds too long to realize the question is aimed at me. And another moment to pull in enough breath to formulate a response. "Yeah. I'm going to be late, but I'll be there."

"Late?" Pax's eyebrows lower.

"Work," I say.

"Coffee shop?"

I nod.

"That place is dead after four. Get off early."

He's right, Beam Me Up is a ghost town most evenings. "Can't. They're running new specials to increase traffic in the evenings."

"Your idea?" Pax asks.

"One I'm regretting. During the summer it seemed like a great idea, but now that I have homework, I'm realizing I should have just brought a book with me."

Pax laughs, stirring the contents he's poured into the two pans as Dad appears, a folded newspaper in his hand. He looks tired, wearing a pair of jeans and a cherry red hoodless Brighton U sweatshirt. His dark hair is silver around his sideburns and starting to weave through the top, more prominent in the beard he recently started to grow.

"You should double major in business," he says. "You have a keen eye for the inner-workings of companies."

I pull in a quick breath, looking skyward for a second to gain my patience. "I don't want to run a business."

"What if you ran the aquarium?" Dad counters, leaning on the bar near Paxton. "I'm just saying you should consider it. It would be a good backup plan in case you decide you want to try other things."

"Aren't you already taking a thousand credit hours?" Pax asks.

"She could fit in one more," Dad says, grabbing a beer from the fridge.

I can't, but admitting that makes me feel like I'm failing, and the year has only just begun, so instead, I pivot the conversation from my impending task list to Paxton's game. "Tomorrow is Eastern Washington, right? They're supposed to have a new defense model. I heard it was pretty good. Did you catch their scrimmage?"

Arlo scoffs. "No. They won't even know what hit them. Their defense is cleaner, but we've got speed."

Pax points his wooden spoon at Arlo. "Exactly. We've got speed, and they've got issues with their teammates, a war for starting quarterback has disrupted their offense. It's going to be a cakewalk."

"Being ranked in the top twenty-five poll you guys are going to get a lot of publicity media attention this year," Dad says.

"Eastern Washington won't know what hit 'em," I say, sensing Paxton's nerves. "They're going to try and slow you down, but Arlo's right. You guys have speed, and it will force them to play your game, which will create mistakes and tire them out."

Dad snaps, pointing his beer in my direction. "Exactly. Make them play your game. Don't play theirs."

"Hey, Dad, what's that on your face?" Pax asks. "It looks like you skinned a chipmunk and glued it to your face." He reaches forward, trying to rub the scraggly hairs that Mom has been encouraging him to shave for several weeks.

Dad leans back, a playful smile pulling his cheeks northward as he rubs his nails against the rough hair. "Don't be jealous of your old man."

"Jealous?" Pax scoffs. "I was trying to give you some helpful advice before they put your face on TV tomorrow during the game."

Dad runs his hand over his chin once more, then rubs along his neck which has been slightly red since he began growing the beard. "How's school going for you, Lincoln? Your transcript's impeccable. I think you'll have your choice of law schools come next spring."

Lincoln drops his head back, the movement so slight I doubt anyone would notice—anyone except those of us who are so well versed in his minor details that the movement seems significant, a population that's larger than I like to consider and heavily female. He clears his throat. My eyes travel over his short hair, scanning over the gray hoodie that's pulled up to his forearms, revealing corded muscles and roped veins that make my heart accelerate and my mind race. "That would be an ideal opportunity."

Dad nods. "Absolutely. You're on the right track." He raises his beer. "You guys help yourself to anything to drink. I've got to get some work in." He spins, making his way down the hall in the direction of his office, a space that was added to the house a few years ago when my parents graduated from only ever having enough money to make ends meet to having more than they'd ever had plus a cushion.

"I should get some homework done. You have everything covered?" I ask, glancing at Paxton.

"I think so."

"Mom should be back any minute." I glance at the clock confirming the fact.

"Need a study buddy?" Arlo asks. "I'll tutor you in exchange for—"

Pax points the wooden spoon at him again. "Finish that sentence, and you're going to be limping tomorrow."

Arlo chuckles playfully, loving the response he evokes so easily with minimal effort.

The doorbell rings before he can add more fuel to the fire, and I take the distraction as an excuse to make a quick exit to the confines of my room where I instantly struggle with a new wave of regret for taking the excuse to be alone when every cell in my body wishes to remain near Lincoln.

My bright yellow volunteer shirt catches my eye in the thick-framed mirror that hangs near my closet, making me cringe as I take in my reflection. I'm still in my clothes from the aquarium, my hair pulled back into a pony that makes me look young and tomboyish. I toss the tee into my hamper and grab a simple gray T-shirt that gathers on one hip. Gray is the starring color of my wardrobe, a hue that often reflects my thoughts and mood as I struggle to ever be on one side of the line or the other, preferring to stay safely in the middle.

Laughter filters up the stairs and through my closed bedroom door, feeding my curiosity and the desire to go back downstairs. I shut it out with my earbuds, flipping on a playlist Maggie sent me recently. I grab my books and sit at my desk, trying to make progress in the heap of homework and reading assignments that have me considering dropping a class.

7

My door opens, Mom appearing with a guilty smile, her steps cautious, making me lose my place in the zoology textbook I've been reading.

I pull out an earbud. "Hey."

"You mind helping us get everything pulled together?"

"I thought we had another thirty minutes?"

She begins to answer then stops, staring at my opened textbook and laptop. "Since when do you do your homework on Friday nights? Are you feverish?" She walks to the bed and places a palm on my forehead.

I bat her away, threatening to add more hours to the time she owes me because I can't think of a sound excuse.

"Come on," she tells me. "I left your brother, Arlo, and Lincoln to finish plating things." She tilts her head in the direction of the door. "Plus, you'll want to grab some food before the vultures eat it all."

I free my other earbud and slowly stand, my muscles eager to move after being stooped over my desk for the past hour. I follow Mom down the stairs and into the kitchen.

"Rae, will you get the bread baskets for Lincoln?" Mom asks. "And then if you'll set some napkins out?" She doesn't wait for me to reply, moving to the table where she maneuvers the extra mismatched chairs around the table again like if she keeps trying, she'll be able to stretch the table. As she moves, she sings to the rock song playing, butchering the lyrics and laughing when Paxton yells over her with the correct version.

There are fourteen coaches and one-hundred-and-eleven players on Brighton's football team. Of those, fifty-five players generally see the field each game, and Pax invited ten of them and the entire coaching staff to our house tonight.

When Mom had told me the number, it bothered me. It seemed elitist and wrong to not invite everyone. Maybe it's because I'm the youngest and was often too young to do the things Maggie could, and, well, too much of a girl to do what Paxton wanted, which was always football. Mom wouldn't let me play, afraid I'd get hurt and dressed me in skirts and dresses as though it would stop me. Dad agreed, saying I was too small. Pax didn't want me to play either, originally. It wasn't until they were a kid short that he lied and told Mom we were going to walk down to the corner market for bubble gum and candy that he took me to play in my first football scrimmage where I did get hurt. Bobby Meyers from down the street tackled me to the ground right as I passed into the end zone, and Pax had to help me clean a sheath of gravel from my shin, but he let me play again the next day, and for the next several years I played with them, learning the rules and setup of the game. I know how hard each of the hundred and eleven players had to work to get on the football team, and each time they don't get invited to celebrations like this, my heart goes out to them knowing exactly how they must feel because, after years of playing football with my brother and his friends, many have forgotten that I scored multiple wins and was easily the fastest player on the field. And when Mom and Dad learned that I was playing football rather than going to the park next to the field and demanded I stop playing, not one of them had my back to say I was as good as any boy. They just whined because they were down a player.

I push those memories into the cupboard where I withdraw the two large bread baskets we only use on holidays and move over to grab the linens that go inside of each. Careful to keep a wide gap between Lincoln and me, I reach for the pile of sliced garlic bread. Lincoln glances at me, his brown eyes mesmerizing as they quickly dart across my face. "Hey," he says.

Rule number seven for not dating your best friend's brother: I want to date someone who I can have in-depth and meaningful conversations with, and when I'm around Lincoln Beckett, I can't think straight. When he licks his lips in a benign gesture, all I can imagine is him licking my neck, growling in my ear when I stood frozen in place like a mannequin. I remind myself to breathe through my nose because I suddenly want to gasp for breath, but work to refrain from being a mouth breather. "Hey." I try to smile, noting how many muscles have to comply with the gesture.

"How was the party last night?" He holds my gaze, the ghost of a smile on his features.

I shrug, matching his stare. "Honestly, I expected more."

His head cocks to one side, his smile spreading. "How are classes going? I didn't hear what you're taking this semester."

In all reality, he knows very little about me, and the same goes for my knowledge about him. This is why I know my infatuation with him has to end this year—it's nothing more than a physical crush, which makes me equally as shallow as those guys at the party calling out to girls who giggle and show their boobs.

Pax palms the top of my head, rifling my hair and deserving the elbow I throw into his gut. "Nerd classes," he says.

"Misogyny isn't a good look for you, Pax." Mom gives a leveling glare, her feminist hat securely in place, though it was absent for those years I wanted to play football.

"I didn't mean it like that," Pax says. "She knows I'm just giving her a hard time."

I could kill them both from drawing every eyeball in the room to me.

"He's just jealous," Arlo counters. "He got the height genes but none of the brains."

Pax grabs a sports drink from the bar and chucks it at Arlo, who catches it without hesitation, a laugh already spilling from his lips. "Don't make me choose because I'll always choose Rae Rae." He winks at me. Arlo stayed with us the summer between their freshman and sophomore years in order to stay and commit to the practice schedule. In those few months, Arlo and I built a friendship I appreciate far more than I'd expected to.

Everyone falls back into a rhythm, side conversations picking up all around. Only six of the guys are here this early, and though I know them by name, position, and a list of stats, I don't know them in the same way I do Arlo or even Lincoln.

"You coming to the game next Friday, or do you have work?" Arlo asks.

"I have to work, but I'll be there."

"You coming to the party on Tuesday? Greek row, baby. It'll be your first toga party."

"I don't know. Maybe? I have class that night."

"Night?" Mom asks. "What class?"

"Statistics."

"Do you know anyone in the class?" she asks. I know where her line of questioning is leading: my safety and the suggestion that I walk with someone to my car after class. Reasons like this remind me why having student loans up to my ears by attending another college I didn't get a full ride to might have been worth it.

"It's still light when I get out."

"It won't be in a few weeks." Mom looks at Pax for backup.

"Football night," I interject. "Tonight, is all about football."

"You're not going to have a social life unless you drop a few classes," Pax says.

"Especially with her awesome multitasking skills." Mom looks pointedly at the half-filled bread basket in front of me.

I reach for more bread at the same time Lincoln does, our knuckles colliding. I quickly withdraw my hand, the heat from his touch stinging like a physical burn. He looks at me, patience and humor twisting his lips into a smile.

"Sorry," I say, reaching for the bread farthest from him.

"Don't worry about it."

Arlo clears his throat. I feel his stare. It's heavy and intentional, and I ignore it as dutifully as I do Lincoln's hand as he helps finish piling up the bread. The baskets are beginning to fray around the edges, well-used over the years, but like many things in our house, they're from the many years that my parents didn't have much in the way of disposable income.

We grew up with most of our friends and classmates having more than us. We afforded living in Seattle because my dad inherited his parents' house after my grandma passed away. My parents both worked as teachers for years. Dad taught middle school social studies for two decades while juggling additional classes to earn his master's degree. My mom being a teacher at a private school allowed us to attend where she taught—a school my parents could never have afforded otherwise. Though there's nothing moral or fair about it, the years we attended private school significantly helped both Pax and I reach our goals. Money has a way of talking louder than principles and values. My parents were comfortably middle-class, making enough so that we never had to worry about having food or clothes, and though they couldn't afford the latest and greatest toys that came out each fall, we always had gifts under the tree and took a road trip each summer. It didn't really make a lot of difference to me—or any of us. Poppy's house is four times the size of ours and everything is dark wood and stained-glass lamps. It reminds me of a library where you're not supposed to touch anything or speak. Our friendship taught me the harsher side of money—the side that few discuss that involves lavish gifts to make up for time they never spend together.

Dad worked toward becoming a dean for another eight years before landing the position at Brighton, and in that time, Mom started going back to school, working toward being a principal. Their salaries pole-vaulted, allowing them to remodel the fifties kitchen we had for much of my childhood, and then more of the house, expanding it so it finally felt large enough for a family of five, though I'm the only one still living at home.

Dad enters from his office, humming an old rock song. "Okay. You guys eat all the vegetables and leave me the garlic bread."

"Oh, this is just the beginning," I tell him, lifting the three reusable grocery bags Mom set back by the dishwasher that are filled with more loaves.

Dad's eyebrows jump. "All right, I guess I'm willing to let them each have a piece."

As I maneuver my way around Bobby and Hoyt, I bump into Arlo. He smiles, wrapping his arm around my neck. "I watched a nature documentary last night about dolphins."

"Did you learn anything?"

"I fell asleep," he admits.

I laugh, and he quickly joins but then stops, his body growing rigid. I look up, cowering on instinct, expecting Paxton to be throwing something at Arlo again, but instead of a hurtling object, I find Derek, a smile on his angular face. His dark blond hair looks like fingers have been pulling at it, and his eyes shine as they dance across my face.

"Hey, Raegan. I was hoping you'd be here."

"Nice to see you, Dean," I say.

His cheeks pull high as he laughs. "How are you?"

"I'm well, thanks. How are you?"

"Better now." His eyes are bright with humor and lust as his attention remains focused on me. The attentiveness is enough to cause an addiction. I can't think of a time when a guy seemed so intent on reading my reactions and was able to block out the rest of the room—a very crowded and loud room, surrounded by his teammates and every incentive to block me out.

Pax moves so he's in my line of sight, harshly shaking his head. Mom watches, her attention slowly shifting between Pax and me before she asks Pax to help her carry some bottles of wine to the table.

"He's an asshole," Arlo whispers, twisting away from me as Derek closes the gap between us.

"What are you doing after the game tomorrow?" he asks.

I shake my head, not having thought about it. I've generally spent Saturday nights with Poppy, and that's the extent of my plans for this week as well.

"There's a party if you're interested?"

From the corner of my eye, I catch Lincoln staring at us, his attention heavy and intentional, making my pulse quicken with curiosity about their feud. "Yeah. Maybe," I say, trying to make my response sound casual and less pleading.

A party with Derek might be the exact thing I need to help recover from my ongoing crush on Lincoln.

8

I pull in a deep breath of the salty air, and pull my coat tighter. It does little to shield me from the cold. I often get tasked with helping with the study of whales at the aquarium. Though our aquarium doesn't house either dolphins or whales, we are partners with several other local organizations and non-profits who study and protect them as well as other marine life. The team at our facility is led by Hans Schrober, and the love and passion he has for his job and helping the animals are so contagious I find myself engrossed with my time and effort spent helping his mission.

He takes a team out to sea weekly, either to the Puget Sound or beyond, and this morning I've been asked to go out to study the very animal that inspired my degree when I was five and my parents had taken us for a vacation down to Sea World, California, where I came face-to-face with an orca whale. I cried. Tears of joy and excitement and an entire plethora of emotions I couldn't label then, and still can't now, because when I get overwhelmed it's like being in a room with Lincoln—words don't come easily for me, and as the feelings build, they begin to spill over and fall down my cheeks. My parents were concerned, ushering me away because they assumed I was terrified. But I wasn't afraid. Not even a little. Meeting that whale had just highlighted a path in my head that assured me I knew what I wanted to do. It took thirty minutes and two meltdowns until I convinced my parents to let me see the whale again, and then they had to take turns carting Maggie and Pax through the rest of the amusement park while the other stayed with me, watching the magnificent creature glide through the water, my mind taking in each detail and questioning them all, making me want to learn everything about orcas. I was torn when we watched them perform, amazed and quickly becoming obsessed with the animal.

Once home with sand still in our shoes and hair and the sea breeze still clinging to our skin, my family began returning to their lives from pre-vacation, but I couldn't. That day, those hours changed something inside of me, and my passion to learn everything about orcas hasn't waned a bit in thirteen years.

Today we're at the Sound. In the winter months, Gray Whales pass through here on their migratory route, and orcas are commonly seen during the summer months. Blue, humpback, and minke whales are also seen here occasionally. But today, our focus is on the pod of bottlenose dolphins that made this their home several years ago, surprising scientists and tourists alike.

"There's Blue," Lois Chavis says, pointing southward.

I stand on my toes, my heart racing with the same drunk feeling I get each time I know I'm going to witness a marine animal. Blue is easily distinguishable from his pod by a long scar marring the left side of his face and body.

Grady Fell, the head of the aquarium's orca research team, leans to grab the microphone and recording device we use to record and study their calls, lowering it into the water, while Lois continues to peer across the horizon, searching for signs of the orcas.

"Anything?" Joe, another researcher on our team, asks, peering through a pair of binoculars across the choppy water beside her.

"I don't see J, K, or L." Lois wipes her hand across her brow, her frown marring her beautiful face. She is part of the tribal team committed to helping the orcas. She joins us regularly in an attempt to count the whales in each pod, affectionately referred to as J, K, and L pods, and prays each time that we'll see them thriving. Mostly though, Lois prays for a baby. The orcas haven't had a baby calf in nearly ten years, and their population continues to dwindle.

"It's the pipeline." Grady removes his baseball cap, flips it forward, and puts it back on. A few years ago, the Canadian government teamed up with an oil company to build a new pipeline which left giant tankers driving directly through the known orca habitat.

"We can't blame them alone," Kenny, a team member from the aquarium, says. "Pollution, contamination, lack of food, over fishing, whale watchers, fisherman..." he cuts the list off there, though I've heard him rattle off at least a couple dozen other reasons in the past.

Lois places a hand on my shoulder, her brown eyes connecting with mine. There's a shared moment of disappointment that fades and is replaced by hope. Orcas have long been a symbol for the tribal community, and Lois is determined to make sense of what's been ailing them so she can help their numbers grow again.

"Let's take some readings," Grady says, lowering the flaps on his Gore-Tex hat that looks like a sun hat but is mostly used to shield out the mist and rain that often comes with living in the Pacific Northwest, unless we go far enough out into the Pacific. Strangely, the ocean is an entirely different beast the farther you get from the shore—one that seems inviting and almost surreal. It can draw you out, exposing clear, calm waters that aren't hit hard by clouds and rain like much of Seattle.

Lois and I move about the small boat to gather the instruments, measuring the noise levels in the water, the temperature, and take a few water samples which Lois will carefully survey in her lab.

BACK AT THE AQUARIUM, I help Greta Alsman, our chief resident marine biologist. If there was ever a woman who should be wearing a cape and mask, it would be Greta. She's a superhero with a mission to save and protect animals. Her vast knowledge and cheery disposition make her my favorite person to be around here at the aquarium.

"I think Snoopy has missed you," Greta tells me, as we stop by Snoopy, our male Giant Pacific Octopus who spends his days shocking the visitors of the aquarium as he gracefully moves throughout his enclosure, rarely trying to hide like so many octopuses try to do.

I chuckle. "That's only because I've been doing his four o'clock feedings lately."

Greta releases a loud laugh. It's one of her trademarks, and it's easily one of my favorite laughs because it's so loud and robust and uninhibited. "And probably because one of the new volunteers called him a squid today."

I fake astonishment. Snoopy is often referred to as a squid, and it's become an inside joke used in multiple references in the aquarium. "How rude."

Greta laughs again. "Did you guys have any luck today?"

"We saw Blue, but he was far away today and didn't come close. Hans seemed happy about it. He's been worried he'll get hurt by all the tourist boats."

She sighs. "It makes our job a lot harder when we can't get close to them."

"We saw some new sea lions, though, and a few porpoises."

"That's excellent. Cara will be happy about the sea lions." She leads me to the otters. They're her passion, and since one of the brothers has been sick, they've been a top priority of hers. "How's school going?" she asks. "I heard you took on some extra credits, and I'm really impressed. The budget proposals were submitted last week, and I submitted a part-time role I think you would be perfect for. It would hopefully evolve into a full-time position once you graduate."

My attention snaps to her, my heart stumbling and tripping over my words as I imagine being able to quit my job at the coffee shop so I can be here and get paid. I don't have time to respond or tell her about the shock of seeing over three-hundred students in one classroom, because our vet, Cara, appears with her medical kit, ready to inspect our sick sea otter, Grover.

"There's my favorite grandkid," Gramps says as I open the front door. "I was wondering if you were trying to avoid me?"

"Apparently, I need to try harder."

Gramps has my second favorite laugh. It's deep and rumbly, like an old car engine, but without the pitch, and like now, it always makes me smile. "You smell like fish."

"You smell like nachos."

He grins, cocking a thumb in the direction of the kitchen. "Your mom's cooking."

"Good. I'm starving."

"They didn't share their fish with you?"

I raise both palms, fingers spread, and reach for Gramps. He grabs a throw pillow from the couch and raises it as a shield. "I was kidding."

With a chuckle still echoing in my lungs, I head for the kitchen in search of nachos.

"Hey," Mom says, her arms buried in dishwater up to her elbows. "How was your morning?"

I take her question as an invitation to sit across from her and unload the weight off my chest, feeling far too close to the overwhelmed breaking point that still leads to tears. "Greta told me that she proposed a new position at the aquarium she thinks I'd be great for."

Mom looks up, her eyes bright. "Seriously?"

I nod, my heart beginning to thump again with excitement.

"That would be amazing! When will you find out more?"

"I don't know. We didn't really get the chance to discuss it, but she said it's in the budget for next year, so it will be a few months at least."

"That's great."

I nod again. "I mean, we have a dozen volunteers—so I really shouldn't consider it mine yet."

"You do so much for the aquarium. Greta loves you. Maybe you could pick up something extra to help pad your resume?"

"I don't know if I can. Dad wants me to add a business class, and right now, I feel like my entire day is scheduled down to the second, and I'm worried that if I continue working with Hans they're going to ask me to be a member of the team studying the whales and dolphins, and I really want to work with Grady and Lois and the orcas."

"You can do this," Mom says. "If anyone can juggle it all, it's you." Her smile offers reassurance, but for some reason, it accomplishes the opposite. "Let's have some lunch, and then you can cash in on your mani/pedi before the game tonight. We can get coffee. It will be fun."

"I can't," I tell her.

"Can't what?"

"I have to work."

"Tonight?"

I glance toward the microwave. "In two hours."

Mom blinks several times, like she's finally hearing my earlier words. "Do you think you took on too much?"

"Probably."

Mom laughs, her brow ruffled. "Should we do something about it?"

"I can't. Hans said I really need to be taking the Organic Chemistry class, and if it could help me get the new position…"

I can tell she wants to say more. It's her inner teacher and mom warring about education and sanity. It's a struggle I've witnessed for as long as I can remember—her wanting us to do our best and put learning first while also wishing to shield us from exhaustion and the stress and anxiety that has become mutually exclusive with the institution of learning.

She kisses my head, her maternal side taking a back seat for now. "Well, let's make some nachos. Grandpa helped me get everything cut up."

Dad does most of the cooking in our house. When I was six, he fell off the roof while trying to repair a leak. He broke his leg and had short-term memory loss that prevented him from being able to teach for a couple of years. He struggled with depression—not feeling like he was contributing or working toward a goal. It didn't help that he'd taken on chores around the house, had dyed or shrunk half the laundry, and that we all complained about eating the cheese and salami sandwiches he made every night for dinner. During that time, Mom and Dad fought a lot. Subjects about how late Mom worked and the height of the grass and how much Mom had spent on groceries began to arise and quickly became hair triggers, bringing a conversation from easy and casual to intense and thorny in a split second.

Maggie moved in with a friend and told them she refused to return until they started counseling. I think they both knew it was an inevitable, and while they might have blamed coercion at the time, they needed it. Dad began going independently first, and then they started going together. Three months later, Dad and I went to the library where he checked out several cookbooks, and within weeks we went from cheese and salami sandwiches to chicken cordon bleu.

Now, Mom still likes to do the cooking for holidays and on weekends, and their balance gets easier as we've gotten older, requiring less of their time and attention.

I fill a plate and follow Mom out to the living room where Grandpa is nursing a beer.

"Where's Camilla?" I ask between bites of chip. Grandpa remarried a couple of years ago to a woman he's known for twenty years through his church. The two are inseparable most days.

"She has a friend in town from Arkansas. The two of them have been shopping and going out to lunch. I think they're getting their nails done today." He shakes his head slightly as if to say he really doesn't have any idea, though I'd bet a free Saturday that Gramps knows exactly where she is. But at seventy, he's still too cool to reveal his soft side.

9

"Do you want something to eat?" Poppy asks.

I glance at her balancing her nachos and tater tots in one hand and her slushy in the other long enough to confirm they're not going to spill on me or the people in front of us. "I'm good."

I'm out of breath from rushing here after my co-worker Rachel offered to close after we had the final rush that came for our buy one get one free coffee special. The parking lot was a zoo, making getting here feel like a marathon. Finding Poppy in the student section was tougher than finding Waldo and his damn little dog's tail.

"Are you sure? I got popcorn, too."

I look at her again, taking a fresh inventory of her lap. "Where?"

She drops her gaze to the bag between her feet. "And some cotton candy." She rifles through her snacks with her eyes. "Oh, and peanuts."

"How much did you spend?"

"I'm hungry," she says. "And everything looked really good."

The skies are clear tonight, making it the coldest night we've had this year. After rushing and walking so far, I'd begun to sweat, which is now making me feel even colder. My cheeks and nose are sure to be red. I tug on the sleeves of my sweatshirt to bring it closer to my skin, wishing I'd have thought to bring a coat or blanket. "It's freezing tonight. It feels like December."

Poppy shoves the nachos at me. "The cheese is still warm."

I shake my head again.

"This isn't even a big game," she says. "They're guaranteed to win."

"I know, but Eastern Washington got Porter this year, and he's one of the best defensive tackles in college right now."

Poppy shakes her head. "Defensive what?"

"Tackles."

"They go after Pax?"

I shake my head. Poppy's been coming with me to watch Paxton's games since we were in middle school and he was in high school, but she's always paid more attention to the concession stands and spectators than the actual game. "They block the wide receivers so they don't get a touchdown or gain yards."

She grins. "It's cute that you're worried about your boyfriend..." Her mouth pops open. "Oh, wait. Which boyfriend are we talking about?" She makes her eyebrows dance, and then smiles broadly.

"Paxton doesn't like Derek. I don't think Lincoln or Arlo do either. It was really tense at a couple of points last night. You should have been there."

"Trust me, if I wasn't stuck with Dylan, I would have. I would much rather have been eating dinner with you and the starting lineup of the football team than listening to him practice his piano lessons. I seriously contemplated putting on a cartoon and setting the alarm and coming over no less than a hundred times."

I grin. "You should've."

Poppy releases a nearly silent chuckle as she shakes her head. Neither of us have a very long history when it comes to breaking the rules. We both excelled in high school, and much to Maggie's dismay, neither of us hated those years. We were never popular. We were also never unpopular. We had each other and would occasionally branch out and spend time with others, but we always came back to our duo, and that was always enough for us. We studied and helped plan the school dances and prom. We joined Leadership and made tacky posters with extra glitter to hang on lockers and Key Club, where we worked with the local Lion's Club to help fundraise coat drives and food drives for the community. We had our moments of being boy crazy, helping each other learn our crushes schedules and interests so we could *accidentally* run into them, or squeal to each other when one of our crushes even looked our direction. But then junior year, Poppy fell for Mike Rio, and Mike fell even harder for her, and our days of chasing crushes and talking about stolen glances ceased.

At the time, I struggled with it because our duo hadn't grown into a trio. Instead, Poppy and Mike often spent time alone together, leaving me at lunch period and study hall. It wasn't until several months later when my relationship with both Maggie and Paxton had strengthened, along with my friendships with others who had been more of acquaintances up until that point, that I realized while I'd missed Poppy, I had gained a lot as well.

Mike and Poppy broke up two months ago. I knew Poppy had been considering it since March when he had been accepted to a school in Arkansas, but the reality of the breakup still hurt her. I spent the first week of their breakup attempting to cheer her up with movies and junk food, offering her enough diet soda to fill a small swimming pool. When that didn't work, I forced her out of her parents' house and brought her to the airstrip out by the airport—a place we used to spend a lot of time before Mike. We'd lie out there and watch the planes and hang from the monkey bars on the playground they'd built nearby in anticipation of families coming. That didn't work either, and so I spent the next several weeks throwing every ounce of effort into trying to make my best friend remember we were fine when it was just us.

I'm still not positive she remembers.

Poppy clears her throat. "Back on subject, it doesn't matter if Paxton likes Derek. It matters if *you* like Derek."

"I don't even know him."

"Do you want to?"

I watch as Paxton breaks the huddle, getting into their offensive set. Both Derek and Lincoln are out on the field. Derek is shorter, his thighs wider. He's strong and fast, making him a favorite for many when he receives the ball. He has bright white gloves on tonight and a sweatband above his right elbow. Lincoln is on the far side—the weak side of the field, a pair of gloves tucked into the back of his pants, and a full sleeve on his right arm. His shoulders are broader, and while speed is an asset Lincoln is famous for, it's his agility that makes peoples' jaws drop.

"So, seriously, who are we cheering for tonight?"

"Don't be ridiculous. We're cheering for Brighton."

"Still Lincoln. Got it."

I'd like to tell her she's wrong. That it doesn't matter who scores, as long as we win, but I'm not that convincing of a liar, so I sit back, my attention glued to the field and Lincoln's jersey—number forty-four.

My voice is hoarse, and my blood is pumping so fast you'd think I had just run the final touchdown rather than Lincoln. The game was incredible. A feat that was expected but not with nearly as high of a point spread, but Lincoln ran circles around Porter, making it look effortless to score against him.

"The parties tonight are going to be insane." Poppy's eyes are bright with excitement. "You should text Paxton and see where they're going."

"I don't know. I think they're all going to get wasted tonight because they'll have an easy practice tomorrow."

Poppy leans forward in her seat. "Come on. It'll be fun. We won't be crazy like the rest of them. We're just going to have a good time. Besides, the only way you're ever going to get over him is by finding someone else you are interested in." She takes a fleeting glance at the field. "Whether that's Derek or not."

"I can't date Derek. He's on the football team, too."

"Yeah..." Poppy lifts a shoulder. "But he's also not your brother's best friend."

"No. Instead, he's his enemy."

She laughs, her empty food containers spilling to the ground as her laughter grows into a giggle, her chin tilting downward and her eyes closing.

"Mmhmm, hilarious."

She clutches a hand to her chest, trying to stop her outburst. "I know, I'm sorry. I'm sorry. But it's a little funny."

"With my luck of exes, I'd date him, then he and Paxton would get into a fight and both would be arrested by my aunt."

Poppy laughs harder—louder. She reaches forward and grips my knee for stability. Slowly her laughter calms. "Rae, we need to go. You need to go. This is college. We are guaranteed to find some nice, single, hot guys. The odds are in our favor."

"Okay, but how about we go to a different party? There has to be a million of them. We could go to one of the dorms or something."

"I don't think that's how this works…"

"Sure it is. Fake it till you make it. It's become my anthem." In more ways than one.

Poppy gives me a pointed look. "Let's just consider the possibility that we go where the team does."

"I already did."

"Raegan Eileen Lawson, stop being a pain in my ass." She shoves a wad of napkins dyed yellow from the fake nacho cheese into the plastic bag at her feet. I help collect more of the garbage spread among our seats.

Poppy straightens when my phone beeps with a text. "Is it Paxton?"

"I doubt he's messaging me now."

"He might be. Maybe Lincoln asked him to."

"Yeah, and maybe I'll win the lottery."

She waves my words away and reaches into my purse, digging till she finds my phone. "Derek?" She reads his name like a question. "You didn't tell me you exchanged numbers!"

My heart rate quickens. "He asked for it last night."

Poppy slowly lifts her gaze, meeting mine. "And you're just now telling me about it? Are you going to read it?"

"Would you let me say no?"

She shakes her head.

"I didn't think so." I slide my thumb across the screen to open the message.

Derek: Hey. You interested in going to that party tonight?

"Is he asking you out?"

I shake my head. "He doesn't say with him."

"No, but it's implied... Right?"

"I have no idea." I stare at the words, reading them again and again. "But regardless, we now have an option."

"Do you think Lincoln and Paxton will be there?"

I shrug. "Doubtful."

"But other football players might, and maybe the rugby team."

"Viable."

"Let's go!"

My thumb hovers over the keyboard, considering how to sound as casual as he does.

Me: Where is it?

"Oh. Nice response. It makes it look like we have options."

"We do," I remind her.

"Not ones from hot football players."

Derek: A house party over on Roseland Ave. Know where it is?

Poppy scrunches her nose. "Do we ask what kind of party it is? I mean, he wouldn't invite us if it was just alcohol and drugs or something, would he?"

"I doubt that's the kind of party he's going to. He'd lose his place on the team if he was caught doing drugs."

She nods. "Tell him we'll meet him there."

Me: I know the area. Text me the address, and we'll meet you there.

"Step one of getting over Lincoln, complete," Poppy chimes.

10

Poppy's eyes light up as she scans the crowd. If parties were rated based on those attending, this party would be given an A+ by my best friend. Not only is the football team here celebrating their victory, the rugby team is here, as well as members of the baseball team and the basketball team.

"There are so many people," I say, gazing across a sea of smiling faces all packed in here ready to celebrate.

"I see Candace." Poppy juts her chin forward toward Paxton's long-term on again off again girlfriend.

"Don't let her see you," I tell her, tugging her back a step. "I can't deal with her drama tonight."

"Good backup option, though," Poppy says. "You have to admit, life around her is never boring. Plus, where she is, usually Pax is close, and where Pax is..." *Lincoln is.*

I chase the ghost of her words away with changing the subject. "Have you heard from Chase?"

Her smile falls. "No. I tried texting him yesterday to ask if he was coming to the game, and he never responded."

"I'm sorry."

"Don't be. He had really short fingers, and while that theory might not be entirely true, I have to admit I was concerned."

"Are we looking for someone else on the rugby team?"

She lifts her shoulders noncommittally. "Maybe?"

I try to smile, but a dose of sadness sits in my gut. Watching her endure heartbreak and work so hard to pretend it never existed now that she can get out of bed, was the biggest incentive and inspiration for rule eight to not date Lincoln: Never date someone if you know they're going to break your heart. Lincoln was sure to break my heart. Maybe not intentionally, but even trying to move past my crush on him sometimes feels painful, and I can't imagine what it would feel like to lose more.

"Three o'clock," Poppy says, squeezing my hand.

I glance over my shoulder, expecting to see dark hair and darker eyes. I scan the area twice before recognizing the blond hair and caramel eyes that she'd been referring to. Derek. He notices my stare, his gaze meeting mine. There's a couple of guys from the football team and a few more I don't recognize and several girls I don't know gathered near him. He lifts a finger, indicating he'll be over in a second.

"He likes you," Poppy whispers.

Derek smiles, his attention still on me as I nod with understanding.

"I'm going to get lost before he comes over here. I'm going to get a beer and maybe find a baseball player to talk to."

"No. Stay. You read people better than I do."

"I've already told you that he likes you."

"But I want you to make sure it's with good intentions."

"Good intentions being naughty intentions?" Her eyebrows dance with insinuation. "Oh. I see Arlo." She goes up on her toes, and I hold my breath, waiting for her to confirm she also sees Lincoln.

"Hey, Rita, right?"

Laughter tickles my lips. "Nice to see you, Dwight."

Poppy looks between us, eyebrows lowered with confusion.

"Derek, this is my best friend, Poppy. Poppy, this is Derek." After feeling like the third wheel for two years, I've realized how important it is to date a guy who likes your friends and vice versa.

He extends a hand. "It's nice to meet you, Poppy."

"Can I call you Dwight?" she asks.

Derek laughs. "I can't promise I'll respond."

A girl stops beside him, placing a hand on his bicep. "Hey. You had a great game tonight."

He gifts her with a smile. "Thanks. I appreciate it."

Her smile grows as she introduces herself, only looking at Derek as she speaks.

"It's nice meeting you. I'll see you around." He takes a step forward and doesn't look back as he threads his arm over my shoulders. "You guys want to get something to drink?"

Poppy smiles at me, but I see past her façade. There's sadness in her eyes as her gaze remains over my shoulder rather than at me. "I'm actually going to meet up with someone. But, you guys have fun." Her eyes finally meet mine. "I have my phone on if you need anything." She shifts her gaze to Derek. "Make sure you aren't the cause, otherwise your nickname will be much worse."

Derek blows out a chuckle. "Understood."

Poppy gives a single nod, then lifts her chin and sets forth into the crowds, a piece of my attention going with her.

"How was work tonight?"

My heart does a somersault as my attention begins to reel back to the here and now and appreciate the hard angle of Derek's jaw, his gentle brown eyes that softly pry at mine, and his short blond hair that smells clean and fresh. He remembered my schedule.

"It was good. Busy. But I was only a few minutes late to the game."

He grants the same smile I've seen him flash a dozen times prior. It's wide and bright—a crowd pleaser, of this I'm sure.

"I bet you second-guessed that decision since it was negative freezing tonight."

I shake my head. "It wasn't that bad. Poppy bought all the hot junk food she could get her hands on to keep us warm."

This time, his smile is followed by soft laughter that wanes as his attention lifts and he begins shaking his head. "Oh, shit."

I turn to see what's holding his attention and spot a couple of guys from the football team making their way toward us.

"Shots! Shots! Shots!" they chant.

His grip on my shoulder tightens, pulling me closer for a second before his touch falls. "I hate them for this. I really want to see you, but these assholes are relentless. Will you be around later?"

A guy I recognize only from the field reaches us first, energy radiating from him as his attention swings between Derek and me. "You joining us?" His attention stops on me.

Shots with the football team at a party I know my brother is at would be suicide for both of us.

"Wait. Aren't you...?" A second teammate joins us. His name is Ian—a defensive linebacker from Mississippi who I've met at least a dozen times, and who still can't remember me. Each time we meet, my ego falls several pegs.

"You guys have fun. I'm going to check on my friend."

Derek watches me, reluctance clear in his gaze, and he wets his lips with his tongue. A grin tugs at my lips as I start to turn, my thoughts scattering like a wave as I hold on to that look and lose the worry of Ian finding me so forgettable.

"Raegan!"

I turn at the sound of my name and come face to face with Derek. His gaze slowly traces over my face, stopping at my lips and then again at my eyes. "This didn't count. This was a blip on our radar. A memory we'll laugh at in five years when someone asks us about how we started dating."

Dating?

Five years?

He grins. "I'll see you later." His cologne sticks with me as he turns back to the others waiting for him, leaving me speechless and reeling at his words.

I need to find Poppy.

I need to decipher these words.

I need to...

A scream pulls my attention to the living room where a group is surrounding a girl with purple and blonde hair facing Candace. The tension is obvious, both girls leaning forward with hands raised like they're about to start pulling each other's hair.

"Paxton," I grumble, weaving through the bystanders, hoping for a girl fight.

"Hey!" I call, my voice too loud and cheery.

"Can you believe this bitch?" Candace asks, pointing at the girl as she nails her with a glare that is both a challenge and a threat.

"You're psycho," the girl says in return. "I don't know what your problem is."

"You were eye-fucking my boyfriend earlier. I saw it." Candace leans closer, provoked by the girl calling her crazy.

"You spilled your drink on me!"

I cringe, ready to stand back, knowing Candace likely deserves getting bitch slapped. If it wasn't for Pax, I'd be drifting back into the growing crowd.

"I'm sure this is a misunderstanding." I glance at the girl with purple hair and try my damnedest to look sincere and apologize before positioning myself between the two. "I'm sure it was an accident that her drink spilled. Parties get so crazy. Why don't we get something to clean it up?"

The girl looks from me to Candace, who stares her down, the challenge still clear in her posture.

"Hey. What's going on? No one wants cops. This is a celebration." Heat tickles my bare arm, then cotton brushes against my sensitive flesh. Lincoln appears behind me. The bitterness of beer mixes in a tantalizing fashion with the sweetness of soap and savory notes of cologne. It makes me drunk, struggling to focus or move as I take another deep breath of him. "Who wants to be on my team for a game of flip cup?" His gaze is on the girl with purple hair, who's smiling at Lincoln like he's Christmas morning in a pair of jeans. His lip pulls up in a cocky and knowing grin, then he steps forward and links his arm around her.

Being forgotten by Ian pales in comparison to being invisible to Lincoln.

11

"Rae, Rae." Arlo appears with two cups, handing me one as he flashes a bright smile. "Have you seen Pax?"

I shake my head. "No, but when you find him, will you tell him he owes me?"

He blows out a laugh. "Hell, yes. But first, I have to find his scrawny ass. He's been MIA since we got here."

"Are you sure he's not in the kitchen?"

"I've checked the kitchen, the front yard, the back yard, the bathrooms, hell, I even went to the damn street to make sure his car was still here."

"That's weird. Did you try calling him?"

"Only a hundred times."

"Stalker."

He laughs again. "He was in a weird place after the game. I just want to make sure he's okay."

"What do you mean?"

"I don't know. Like he wanted to get some space from everything. He and the President are both acting strange lately."

Betrayal has me turning my full attention to Arlo, waiting to hear more about what's going on. Could Pax know that Lincoln kissed me? Does he know the context? Are they fighting?

"Are they mad at each other?"

"Nah. I think Lincoln's just sick of Candace staying at the house. She had friends over last night, and they were being loud as hell."

I should be soaring on a cloud of relief, but disappointment is strapped to my ankle like a weight, pulling me so far into its depths I try to drown it out by taking a long gulp of the beer Arlo handed me.

"This is so gross," I say, wiping my mouth with the back of my hand.

"It's disgusting," he agrees.

A smirk helps push the disappointment away a little farther. "You had a good game tonight. You should be having fun and celebrating. I'll go look for Pax."

"My game was woke."

"Totally woke."

"At least try and sound sincere." He elbows me hard enough to make me sway.

"I did, but you ruined it by raising my compliment with your own."

He hooks me around the back of my neck, wrestling me into a hug. "Go check the front for Pax, I'll go to the back, we'll meet back here in ten." He rolls away, bobbing his head to a new song as he takes a long drink.

"I think he likes you."

I look over my shoulder to find Derek, his eyes brightly glazed as he struggles to focus on anything for long.

"As a friend," I confirm.

"A friend he'd like to see naked."

"Wait, wait. You have a little something…" I lift a hand, wiping a thumb across his cheek, which I examine carefully. "Wait. Is that jealousy?"

He quirks a brow, amusement absent. "What's the deal with you two?"

"We're friends," I tell him.

"Friends who hug?"

"Since when is hugging foreplay?"

"I saw the way he was looking at you."

"Trust me. You misread that situation."

"Did I, or am I misreading you?" His tone is too intense, his eyes too hard.

"You're misreading it all if you think this is okay."

"Raegan," he says, dropping his chin back. "I'm sorry. I'm not..." he blows out a long breath. "I came over here because you looked upset. Forget what I said. Are you okay?"

Asking him for help or even telling him that Pax is missing doesn't sound like a safe idea when I know the two don't trust each other. "I was just looking for Poppy. I'm fine. I need to call her, but I'll catch up with you."

"I'll go with you."

"Derek!" Luck is on my side as Ian appears again, giggling as he tries to tell a story about someone falling over.

"I'll be back," I tell him, smiling in an attempt to make my parting seem friendly rather than an escape attempt.

I keep my eyes peeled for Poppy as I scan each face for Paxton.

"You see him?" Arlo asks, meeting me near where we'd parted.

I shake my head.

"Man, I think he might be hooking up with someone. Finally got tired of Candace's shit..." I don't hear the rest of his likely offensive words because Lincoln approaches us, his shoulders so wide it seems he takes up the entire room.

"You talk to him?" Arlo asks.

Lincoln nods.

Arlo flashes a smile. "Was I right?"

"Maybe."

Arlo cheers, drawing attention that he nor Lincoln seems to notice. "In that case, you go find yourself someone to celebrate tonight's win. I'm gonna get another drink and then lose myself in someone." He scans the crowd, looking for his next conquest.

"We have to find Paxton some pants first."

I cringe. "Pants? Oh God. That's not what I wanted to hear."

"Help me go bust into a room and find some shorts or something for him to put on." Lincoln tips his head in the direction of the stairs.

"You guys can't steal someone's clothes," I say.

"We also can't let the star quarterback of Brighton U show off his baloney pony." Lincoln's brown eyes are startlingly bright and intense, not dulled by alcohol like so many here tonight.

"Where are his pants? Can't we just go get them?" I ask.

Lincoln lifts a shoulder. "Apparently not."

I pull in a deep breath and glance over my shoulder to see if Derek is still with Ian. "It's probably better if less people know what's going on."

Lincoln tilts his head. "Are you using us to avoid dick face?"

"I just figured since he and Pax don't exactly like each other, it's probably better if he doesn't know. I'll invite him to a party happening on campus."

"Negative." Arlo shakes his head. "I'm not going into rooms with the Pres. That's not the rumor I want circulating."

The ghost of a smile skates over Lincoln's features. "Why not?"

"I'm going to play decoy. Hurry your asses up." Arlo turns, looking for Derek.

"Be nice," I warn him.

"Don't ask me to make promises I can't keep." He winks, then raises his hands and gets lost in a crowd.

"Walk in front of me. I'll be able to block you if he's looking for you."

I remain rooted in place, debating if this is a terrible decision.

It's a horrible decision.

Downright shitty.

I'm still trying to forget the pattern his lips made as they crossed my skin.

"Since you seem torn to leave lover boy, why don't I just take care of things." He moves, and before reason can catch up with sense, I move with him, matching his angle and successfully cutting him off.

"It has nothing to do with him. My dread of seeing Paxton without pants was just catching up with me." I swallow. "Let's go."

He doesn't flash a smile or a grin. It's not his way. Instead, Lincoln's eyes prod mine, seeking honesty and validation. I remain still for several seconds, allowing him to search for insincerities that don't exist, then turn on my heel and head toward the stairs.

A hand slides against my back, so gentle and light, I jump.

"Sorry." His touch is gone, tearing a corner of my heart.

"No. I just ... you surprised me. That's all."

"There's a ton of people." He lifts his hand, as though making his action deliberate before placing it on my waist again, this time firmer, each of his fingers connecting with my flesh, the veil of my cotton tee a regrettable barrier.

When we reach the stairs, I take a fleeting glance toward the party to make sure no one's attention is following us. Turning just enough that his fingers run across my stomach, creating an awareness that makes my skin feel too warm and my breaths too weighted.

"Don't worry. Arlo's got this."

"I don't want to make things worse between you and him or with Pax."

Lincoln makes a noise that sounds like annoyance. "Dickhead doesn't pay attention to anyone but himself. He won't notice."

I want to tell him he does. That he's paying too much attention to Arlo. "Is that why you guys don't like each other?"

He takes another step, invading my space, the scent of him a strong hit that leaves me desperate for another. "There are so many things I'd rather talk about. Cholera, the bubonic plague, smallpox..."

"I don't understand why you care. He's not the star of the team. Right now, he's only getting a second of attention from the press." I have no doubt Lincoln is aware of this and likely uses it to his advantage. He knows his role. He wears his fame like a cape, attention following him everywhere he goes.

"He's not a contributing player." He nods in the direction of the stairs.

I go, knowing if I remain still any longer, I'm going to do something stupid like lean closer and take a deeper breath of him, or he's going to head upstairs and call it a solo mission.

A long, dark hallway greets us at the top of the stairs. The walls are paneled with dark wood, empty except for a couple of sconces that aren't on. A guy leans against the wall a few feet from us, one foot propped up as he smokes a joint.

"We're totally going to walk in on someone having sex."

"That's a viable possibility. Just think of it as bad porn."

"I can't believe he did this."

"What? Have a good time?"

My eyebrows lower, hurt pressing on my chest. "Cheated on his girlfriend."

"Candace is like a pimple that can't be popped."

I pull back, ignoring the guy who's blowing out a cloud of smoke and chuckling at Lincoln's analogy.

"Don't tell me you actually like her." His eyes go wide, like there's a conversation being had between us where I'm telling him unicorns really do exist.

"It doesn't matter if I like her or not. It matters that they're dating, and he made that choice. This was a shitty decision, and she has nothing to do with it."

"She's not wrong," pot boy says.

"This is why I don't do relationships," Lincoln says.

12

I struggle to remain ambivalent to his words. I don't need him to know he's just reminded me of rule number nine as to why we could never be together: I want to date someone who has no reservations or qualms about dating—doesn't consider the term to be a four-letter bad word, and Lincoln doesn't believe in dating at all.

"What?" he asks.

"What?" I ask in return, blinking several times because my eyes feel too dry. I think I was staring at him, lost in thought. "This smoke is burning my eyes," I lie.

He snickers. "You made a face when I said I don't do relationships."

I press my lips into a line and shake my head. "Nope. No judgement here."

"Liar."

"I'm serious."

"So am I."

I feel frazzled. Like I need to say or do something that isn't going to make me sound either naïve or innocent. I reach for the nearest door handle and press down on the lever.

Locked.

"I also have no desire to be in a relationship. I have too much going on for anyone to expect or need anything from me."

"Exactly." He practically sings the word, like I'm one of the few who understand him and this idea. His brown eyes meet mine, curtained by dark lashes that are impossibly perfect, just like the rest of him.

A hollow spot in my stomach forms, distracting me from our task at hand and eradicating the positive parts of today.

"We might have to knock if they're all occupied."

I cringe. "That's going to be awkward."

"Less awkward than walking into an occupied room."

"Marginally."

He smirks. "Is it strange that everyone knows your brother?"

I lift a shoulder. Everyone's always expected that it only provides favors, never consequences. "It just is what it is."

"Does that translate to it blows?" He presses down on the next door handle, and this one opens, revealing a linen closet. He turns, eyebrows raised. "We could have him wrap a sheet around himself."

"I'm inclined to say yes, but..."

"But...?" his eyebrows inch higher.

"Him being the only one wrapped in a toga might be strange, especially since this isn't a Greek event."

Lincoln seems to consider this for a moment before closing the door and moving further down the hall. "I bet people have high expectations for you."

"Actually, it's the opposite." I pause at the next door, hesitating as I listen to see if anything can be heard on the other side.

"The opposite?"

I glance at him, noting a faint bruise forming on his jaw, likely from a hit he'd taken in the second half, a hit that only paused him for a second before he'd regained his footing and continued downfield to score a touchdown. "People assume things are handed to me. Like it's the only reason I'm here at Brighton."

Lincoln reaches for the door handle, his hand resting on mine, holding it in place. "Why did you choose Brighton?"

"Because it was expected of me." The admission tumbles out, surprising me far more than it does him. I'm sure of that, because I've tried to shove that thought far, far from my brain, and he barely blinks.

He doesn't say anything, just stares at me. "Do you always do what's expected of you?"

I blow out a laugh I wish were sincerer. "I think you already know the roles we each play."

The corners of his eyes pinch with questions.

"Maggie is the rebel activist, fighting 'the man.' And Paxton is the athlete, which leaves me the role of academia."

His eyes narrow, what appears like doubt tickles his lips. Then, the door in front of us opens, tugging me off balance.

An arm wraps around my waist as someone cries out an obscenity.

"I've got you." The words are quiet, solely intended for me, and they replay again and again with absolute perfection. The deep rasp, the smooth bass, the sureness. My heart has just grown wings the size of an eagle's and is attempting to take flight, jittery and uncertain.

"Sorry. I didn't realize you guys were there," a guy says, reaching to help me get back upright because I'm still suspended, relying on Lincoln to keep me from stamping the imprint of the floor on my face.

"I've got her," Lincoln says as I assure the stranger it was my own fault.

"Sorry again," the guy says, placing a hand on a brunette's shoulder and leading her into the hall. "Oh, and you have to hold the handle up before you try to lock it."

"Thanks," Lincoln says, his hands slipping from my hot and sensitive skin.

We step into the room, and Lincoln closes the door but doesn't move to lock it, his gaze drifting across the room. "Well, we might be stuck with a sheet."

I turn, my heart still too enlarged, pressing against my lungs and making it difficult to catch my breath. The room is mostly dark, lit by a floor lamp in the corner, highlighting the wall next to the bed which is lined with posters of shirtless men flexing.

"Maybe she has a boyfriend?"

Disbelief is etched across Lincoln's face as he stares at me.

"What?"

"This girl's only boyfriend requires batteries."

"How would you know?"

He points at the wall, like I might have missed the decoupage of dudes.

"That doesn't mean anything."

He drops his chin.

"It doesn't. Maybe she just..."

"Is single?" he says.

If I were Maggie, I'd be able to articulate a well-versed explanation as to why his words are offensive and grossly inaccurate.

"Guys don't want to see that their girlfriend is fantasizing about other men, especially so blatantly. It makes us question shit. We're fragile creatures." He winks.

"Or, maybe she's really confident in her sexuality and just likes to look at hot guys." I stride the few feet to the closet and slide one half open. Inside is chaos. Torn boxes reach my waist and clothes are wadded and shoved on the top shelf, nothing hanging but a couple of naked wire hangers.

"She's a female Arlo." Lincoln peers across the mess and then turns as soon as his gaze moves to me.

"The dresser might be easier," I suggest.

"That's like saying Nero might have shown pity to the kind Christians."

My traitorous heart thumps obnoxiously in my chest. Hearing him make a historical reference is hotter than watching him peel his shirt off and reveal his impressive abs which defy human anatomy because I've seen the segments and counted each defined muscle, and Lincoln Beckett has an eight pack rather than the average six. He would because there's absolutely nothing average about him.

"I don't think we can compare someone's messy room to a Roman Emperor who lacked a conscious."

He shrugs, a playful smile teasing my heart and distracting me from paying attention to what he's doing.

"Bingo," he sings.

"Oh, good." I walk forward, relief quickening my pace to step next to where he's standing beside the bed. I stop when I realize what he's looking at.

"Lincoln!" I hiss. "Close the drawer."

"I told you her boyfriends required batteries."

"That means nothing."

His smile turns knowing. "You have a collection?"

I'm grateful the room is darkened so he can't see how quickly my embarrassment spreads from my cheeks to my entire face. Maybe he thinks it's hot or funny that he asks such a forward question, but it's neither, and when he laughs, I have the urge to slam his fingers in the drawer.

"Wouldn't you like to know." I stare at him, waiting for him to realize I don't find his comments to be flirty or even appropriate.

"Um, excuse me…"

Before I can consider all the reasons my stomach feels like it's tied into knots, I turn and forget every single one of my concerns as a girl with long, dark hair stands in the doorway, a small duffle hanging from one shoulder.

"It's bad enough my roommates had a party without me, but a whole other level of shitty to discover people are using my bed to boink. I'm Kate. You should probably know that before you complete the deed…"

"Oh, we weren't," I assure her.

She stares at me, disbelief sitting heavily on her lowered brow. "Sure you weren't. Then why is my bed a mess."

"That was the last couple," I tell her.

"So, my room has been used as a goddamn brothel. Awesome."

"The blankets are rumpled. Headboard in place. Pillows still at the top. They probably had boring missionary sex that he lasted all of two seconds for."

Kate turns her attention to Lincoln, trying on a coy smile that looks well-rehearsed. "Let me guess, you think your stamina would have broken the bed?" There's a challenge in her stare.

"Actually, we didn't even make it to the bed," I quickly say. "In fact, he ended up getting a little too excited, if you know what I mean. We were actually looking to see if you had a spare set of shorts or pants that he could borrow."

Lincoln's attention cuts to me like a knife, sharp, fast, and demanding of attention. "That's not exactly—"

Kate sighs heavily, cutting him off, her lips falling south. "So much for dreams of a broken headboard. Guys are all talk." She drops her bag and moves to the dresser where she opens the bottom drawer. It's old and painted white, covered with different stickers that are impossible for me to make out.

Lincoln's stare becomes heavier.

"What size do you need to cover your oatmeal blister there, champ?" Kate asks.

Laughter bubbles in my stomach, making my lips twitch.

"My oatmeal blister?" he repeats, offense taking the humor out of his tone.

"Do you prefer wood booger?" she asks.

I have to press my lips together and look away so I don't laugh out loud. Lincoln is still staring at me, shaking his head in fractional inches. He takes a deep breath. "If you have a large, that'd be great."

"Well, you're in luck. My ex never came and picked up his shit, and I've been too lazy to pack it up for donation." She tosses a pair of mesh shorts at us.

Lincoln catches the black material. "My lucky day."

"Thanks," I say. "We really appreciate it."

"Yeah, well, considering your position and mine, you might still be having a worse night, so it's the least I can do."

Lincoln's fingers graze my waist, his touch so gentle I have to glance down to ensure I'm not imagining it. He tilts his head forward, suggesting we leave.

"Thanks again," I say as we clear the doorway.

Lincoln pulls the door shut behind him. "You owe me. You owe me so big you don't even know it yet." Lincoln's voice is a deep rasp that sends chills down my arms and across my neck.

"Paxton owes you. I got the shorts."

"We should have taken a damn sheet."

I shrug. "Maybe next time you won't act like a caveman."

"Hey! There you are." Poppy appears, her eyes bright as she clutches a plastic cup in her hands. "Arlo told me you guys were up here. What are you doing?" She looks between Lincoln and me, and then slowly draws her head back as a smile consumes her features. "Don't tell me you guys..." Her jaw drops. "I knew—"

I vigorously shake my head. "Paxton lost his pants."

Poppy stops, her eyebrows soaring high on her forehead. "Come again?"

I lift both shoulders. "I don't know. I'm not going to ask. Well, I am, but I'm not... We came up here to find some pants for him so he doesn't have to do the walk of shame out of the house."

"How does one lose their pants?" Poppy asks, following us to the end of the hallway, where Lincoln stops at the base of the stairs that lead up to the attic.

"We'll wait here," I say, linking arms with Poppy.

Lincoln glances between us, that same cocky expression from earlier returning. "You're sure?"

"Positive."

He climbs the wooden steps two at a time. The house reveals its age, creaking under his weight.

"So ... you and Lincoln hanging out, huh?" Poppy's eyes grow bright.

"Hardly."

"What happened? Did you guys like ... do ... anything? Hold hands? Accidentally rub up against each other? Fake choking so he had to give you mouth-to-mouth?"

"Better," I tell her. "He acted like a cocky jerk, and I acted like an uptight prude. It was awesome. Romance in the making."

She gives a silent look that screams 'yikes,' then grins. "So, how exactly does one lose their pants?"

I shake my head. "You can ask Paxton that yourself. I'm not sure I want to be around to hear the answer, though, so be sure to censor his response for me."

13

Poppy leans her head on my shoulder. I tried to convince her to go downstairs with me after Lincoln went to meet Pax with the shorts, but she insisted her feet hurt and that she needed to sit down, so against my better judgment, I sat with her. We dissected my interaction with Derek, she told me about making out with a guy who she didn't even ask for his name, while I bit my tongue and tried not to pass judgment because a small part of me understands that constant ache in her heart.

"He kept doing these really short kisses, where he like shoved his tongue in my mouth and then pulled back and breathed really heavy. Maybe I'm a bad kisser?"

"Was he a mouth breather?" I ask.

Poppy leans into me further, laughing. "I knew you were going to ask that."

"Well, maybe he couldn't breathe while he was sucking on your face."

We're both laughing when Lincoln comes into sight, closely followed by Pax.

"Rae needs to know if the story is PG before I ask for details," Poppy says, sitting up.

"It's boring," Lincoln warns.

"I think we'll be the judge of that," Poppy argues. "I know I've never heard a boring story that ended with missing pants." She looks at me. "Have you?"

"Technically, it's ending with pants." I motion to Pax, taking in the mesh shorts that are far too short and tight. "Really *tight* pants." I cringe, looking back at Poppy. "I think I'm going to have nightmares."

Poppy bursts into giggles.

"You guys found the smallest dude in the state of Washington to borrow clothes from."

"Actually, those are now yours, courtesy of the ex who never claimed them. You're welcome." I stand up to avoid being eye level with things I don't want to see from my brother. "On this note, I think I'm calling it a night."

"What? It's barely one." Poppy juts out her lower lip.

"Yeah, but by now people are going to either be drunk or passed out. That's always what happens at this time of night."

"Some are both," Lincoln adds.

"See?" I say, looking at Poppy.

"We could go back to our place?" Lincoln looks at me, like the invitation extends beyond him and Pax and the small caravan of girls that are sure to leave with them.

I stare at him for several seconds too long, attempting to read more from him, though I know it will only lead me farther down the tunnel of confusion and hope I've been falling down for years.

"I'll buy you shakes and fries if you both promise to never talk about this moment again," Pax adds.

My attention returns to my brother, the reminder of what brought him to wearing the ridiculous pair of shorts to the front and center.

"I know, I know," Pax says.

"Do you?" I ask.

He nods. "It was stupid."

"It's okay to be stupid. Stupid we can recover from, but regret is a whole other beast."

"I know. You're right. Lincoln already laid into me."

I glance at Lincoln, surprise hitting me like a cold blast of wind. He doesn't acknowledge me, though.

"I know I was being a selfish bastard, and I'm sorry you had to be involved," Pax continues his overly rehearsed apology, making me roll my eyes.

"I don't care about that. I'm your sister. I'm always going to help you, regardless. But, I'm going to say this, and then I won't say anything again: you're better than how you acted tonight. You aren't the kind of person who cheats, so don't start now."

Poppy nods. "Cheaters suck really big, hairy balls."

"It won't happen again. I promise." Pax draws an 'X' across his chest.

Downstairs, the party is surprisingly active. I'm expecting Poppy to point this out and suggest we stay, but instead, she points out where Arlo is charming a girl.

"You want to leave him?" Lincoln asks.

"Last time we left him to his own devices, we didn't see him for three days," Pax says.

"Three days?" Poppy looks at me, eyes stretched with surprise and shock.

"He didn't regret it," Lincoln says.

Pax shakes his head. "I sure as shit did. Coach was livid."

"Then go and get him, and let's go. We'll meet you outside." Lincoln tips his head toward the front.

"I think we're just going to head home," I say.

"No. Come over. You guys can help me figure out what to do about this Candace situation," Pax says. "Because, I don't know what to fucking do anymore."

I wrinkle my nose. "Gosh, I hope someday a guy refers to me as a situation."

Pax glares at me. "Are you going to ride my ass all night?"

"Are you going to be sensitive all night?"

"I'm just saying..."

"That you're going to get me onion rings and a chocolate milkshake. Thanks. We'll meet you at your house."

"Can you just wait five seconds?" Pax asks. "There's all kinds of drunk dudes looking for someone to go home with."

"And I'm really good at saying no." I flash a smile that is neither sincere nor friendly.

"And they're really bad at listening. So, just hang out for a few." Pax turns to Lincoln, a silent request to have his back.

I want to tell him he's being ridiculous and point out the fact I've been out plenty of times without him and was able to find my way home safely.

"Oh, there he is," Poppy grips my hands. "See him? The one with the lip ring."

I scan a group that is passing a large bong around, spotting the guys she's describing. He looks too much like Mike, the same shade of hair, same skinny build, and permanent frown.

I glance up, feeling Lincoln's stare. His face reveals so little, it's impossible for me to know what he's thinking, and before I can think of something to say, a girl starts to approach, her intent obvious.

"President! You're here!"

He turns toward the blonde who's dressed in a low top that doesn't hit her naval and a pair of jeans. The moment he faces her she throws her arms around his neck and hugs him. "Your game was epic tonight! So good!"

Poppy's hand engulfs mine, squeezing as a reminder she's with me.

"Paxton!" The blonde screams, launching herself at my brother. "What bet did you lose?" She laughs, checking out his shorts.

"She's a groupie," Poppy whispers. "She'd take any of them."

"What are you guys doing here?" The blonde asks Lincoln and Pax.

"We're actually leaving," Lincoln tells her.

"What? No. Stick around. Andrea and I just got here." She stands on her toes, scanning over the crowds.

"Not tonight," Pax says. "We both have practice in the morning."

The blonde pouts, and I hate her a little more because even her pout is beautiful. "Forever the responsible one."

Lincoln turns as the blonde hugs Pax again. He goes to where Poppy and my hands are joined, forcing a larger gap as he drops a hand around both of our necks.

He's using us.

I eye him, defiance causing my shoulders to drop.

"Oatmeal blister," he whispers in my ear.

The reminder has me stopping, a chuckle growing in my chest.

"I'll call you, Pres," the blonde says.

In response, Lincoln pulls Poppy and me closer to his chest.

"I've always wanted to be someone's fake girlfriend," Poppy says, feigning wistful.

"Trust me. You aren't. You're feigning someone's hookup," I say.

Poppy fans herself. "Oh. Be still, my heart."

"You want the top or bottom?" Lincoln asks her.

"Always the top," she says. "I like control."

Lincoln turns his attention to me, his eyes shining with humor and something that makes the breath fall from my chest. "I guess that means you're on the bottom."

Poppy grins, pulling the front door open. "Oh shit. It's freezing," she says.

I welcome the cold, desperate for it to coat my hot skin and create a stinging sensation of discomfort.

"Where'd you guys park?" Pax asks, reappearing with Arlo at his side.

I look at Poppy for help. I can barely remember my own middle name right now, let alone the location of my car. She stifles a smile. "Two blocks that way," she says, pointing to the left.

"Are we going to discuss what just happened between you and Nikki?" Arlo asks, looking at Lincoln. "I'm pretty sure we need to drive you to a hospital. You must have hit your head tonight because when a fine lady like her asks you to stay, you stay."

"You never heard that story?" Paxton answers.

"Obviously I didn't, or if I did, I was drunk." Arlo shrugs.

"She gave him an ultimatum. Wanted to be exclusive," Pax explains.

We reach the edge of the sidewalk, and as we step down, I duck out of Lincoln's touch, needing the embrace and anonymity of the night.

Arlo chuckles like what Paxton said was funny. "Okay, okay, so she *does* want you."

"She doesn't know what she wants," Lincoln says harshly.

"Well, she. Is. *Fine*. I'd hang around and let her figure out what she wanted if I were you."

"Be my guest."

"You wouldn't care?" There's doubt in Arlo's tone.

Lincoln shakes his head. "You don't need my permission. Go."

Arlo looks back at the house. "I'm too lazy and buzzed, but next time…"

Paxton chuckles.

"Wait, so you didn't date?" Poppy asks.

Lincoln shakes his head. "Nope."

"But she wanted to date?" Poppy continues.

"I already said she didn't know what she wanted."

"What does that mean?" Poppy remains in sync with him, making it impossible for me to see her face, but I can feel her looking past Lincoln to ensure I'm paying attention.

"It means I fit her agenda," he says.

"Could you be any more cryptic?" Poppy asks.

He sighs. "She liked me because I was popular. Because I started appearing on the news and reporters were calling me."

"Does that scare you guys?" Poppy asks. "That people aren't going to be genuine?"

"All the fucking time," Lincoln admits.

"Well, I hate to tell you this, but we only hang out with you guys because we're hoping it makes us popular. And of course, to date hot guys—obviously." Humor coats Poppy's words.

"Obviously," I echo.

Poppy giggles.

Lincoln weaves, bumping into my side. I ignore him, my emotions too heightened. We continue a few more paces, Pax and Arlo falling behind as they discuss details of the game. Lincoln bumps into me again, this time hard enough I have to take an extra step to catch myself. Then his arm encircles my shoulders again. He shakes me. It's juvenile at best, but my traitorous body clings to his touch like he's the sun.

"This is us," I say as we near my black Civic. I pause, waiting for him to pull away, and when he doesn't make a move, I turn to gain some footing on this unfamiliar ground we've stumbled upon.

He's looking at me, his eyes dark pools of questions that, like the ocean, are deceiving in their depths and intentions.

I grin and duck out of his touch again, making a beeline for Paxton. I jump on his back, and he catches my weight easily. He runs forward several feet, then comes to an abrupt stop and leans forward so far I swear we're both going to lose our teeth on the sidewalk.

"You win. You win!" I call between giggles, gripping his shoulders so I don't fall on my face. Pax easily stands. The move is rehearsed, something we've been doing for years.

I'm still laughing as my feet hit the sidewalk. "I seriously was inches from the ground. You almost dropped me this time."

Pax shakes his head. "I had you. You almost lost your grip this time."

"We'll meet you at your house. Don't forget the onion rings." I move back to my car, fighting the jealousy I feel at my best friend being stapled to Lincoln's side.

"What's that?" Poppy asks, pointing at my windshield.

I glance at my car, squinting in an attempt to see more clearly. I have to take several paces to be close enough to discover the small paper crane under my windshield wiper, which I free with a quick tug.

"That's cute," she says.

I toss it to her. "Merry Christmas."

She laughs, catching it with Lincoln's arm and attention still focused on her.

14

"He likes you."

Poppy's words hit me like a semi-truck, hope slamming into my lungs and denial colliding with my heart. "What are you talking about?"

"You know what I'm talking about."

"Derek?"

"Lincoln!" she cries. "I'm serious, Rae. He watches you. Like, watches your reactions, your movements."

"You clearly hit your head tonight."

"Raegan, I'm not even joking. He likes you."

"You told me Derek likes me."

"He does."

I shake my head, trying to dispel her words from clinging to hope. "Lincoln doesn't like me. He can't."

"Because you don't think you guys should date?"

"Because he *doesn't* date," I remind her.

"I thought you don't want to date?"

Her words bristle against my spine. I lower my foot on the clutch and shift, going faster, wishing I could outrun these thoughts and feelings. "I don't."

"Next time, try making eye contact. It's always a dead giveaway that you're lying when you won't look at me."

"He doesn't date," I remind her again.

"Maybe not, but he certainly is wanting something from you."

Her words fester in my thoughts, distracting me from the many thoughts that have been filtering through my mind for days. Ones about the aquarium and my class load and Derek.

When we pull into Paxton's driveway, Caleb's car is next to me. Freshman year, he went out with Pax and Lincoln every time, but last year he started going out less, so I'm not surprised to find him in the living room with a gaming remote in his hands. He turns, pushing his black-rimmed glasses that are sliding down his nose back into place. "Hey," he says, turning back to the TV. "What's up? Hi, Poppy."

"Hey, Caleb." The two are still formal with each other. I blame this on Caleb always having his nose in a remote or another piece of tech, and Poppy refusing to take the lead in their friendship.

"Oh, you know. We just got off a night of crime." I plop down next to him on the couch while Poppy takes the time to remove her shoes before sitting beside me.

"Yeah? Straight gangster, huh?" Caleb asks, his eyes still glued to the screen.

"You know it."

He smiles, his thumbs moving rapidly over the remote.

"How have you been?" I knock my knee against his. "No party tonight?"

His smile broadens. "I'm partying it up right here."

"I like your style. At least you get to be comfortable," I tell him.

The front door opens, and Paxton comes in carrying two drink trays, followed by Arlo with two large white bags. Lincoln follows, carrying another white sack. He grins as he steps inside, asking Caleb about the level, but his gaze never goes beyond the TV. I glance at Poppy as though to say, 'you're wrong,' but she dutifully ignores me. Being an only child for nearly half of her life makes it difficult for her to accept defeat.

Arlo takes the bags, setting them on the dining room table that sits in the corner of the room. It used to be our family dining table, but Mom took the opportunity to get a new one after Pax lived here for a full year without one. Arlo tears open the sides of the bags and creates a large paper surface, then stacks piles of chicken nuggets and fries. "Okay, Rae Rae, tell us, is it acceptable to break up with someone through text?" he asks.

I look from him to Paxton. "No. Definitely not. Especially when you guys have been dating so long."

"You know she's going to go nuts." Paxton tries the victim role for a full minute as I stare him down.

When he doesn't back down, I cock my head to the side, working to remain patient. "Don't be a douche, Pax. You know that wouldn't be right."

"Would it really be that bad?" Lincoln asks. "I mean, come on, Lawson, they break up every other day through text."

"Which is partly why they are where they are, and also why if you're really done—" I pause, waiting for the word to sink into my brother's head because he's told me more than once that he's done and never is. "Then you need to face her and make sure you both understand."

"She has a point," Arlo says, stabbing a straw into a drink.

"I have lots of points. Want to hear more?" I ask.

Paxton grabs a fry and chews on it while considering my offer. "Like?"

"Like, you need to decide *soon*. Before you go out again, soon. Because you can't pull what you did tonight again. You're going to get caught, and then this isn't just a tough breakup, it will be a really ugly breakup, and you're going to have to explain to the next girl you date that you're a cheater, and let me tell you that word makes even the hottest, smartest, nicest guy sound and look like an asshole. Cheating creates an entire landmine of red flags."

Paxton munches on a chicken nugget.

"*And*, you need to go change. Those shorts are way worse than you think they are. Change, and then burn them."

He throws a fry at me, but a smile breaks the look of despair that was consuming his features. "I'm going to keep these babies and wear them to your graduation, and then to your wedding."

"Great. But for tonight, go change."

He snickers, but turns and heads toward the stairs.

"We should bring those shorts to practice. Make whoever's late wear them," Arlo says, shuffling through the different dip sauces.

"Caleb, you hungry? Arlo's going to eat all this if you wait until your game is over," Lincoln calls. I hate that he addresses Caleb. Hate that he's become good friends with him because, in high school, Paxton's football friends were always complete tools to Caleb, acting like they were too good to hang around him.

"Yeah, just…" He glances over at us, and grins. "You guys are killing my score."

"But we're worth it," I sing. "Get over here."

Caleb removes his headset, revealing an indent in his hair, and sets his controller down.

"This one's yours." Lincoln hands him a soda. "No ice."

"Thanks, man."

"No ice. When did you turn European on me?" I ask.

"I've got a tooth that's been bothering me. I see the dentist on Monday."

That sting in my chest becomes a burn, and when Poppy juts her elbow into my side to ensure I heard, I make the first excuse I can think of to gain some space and perspective. "I'll be right back. I need to go grab my charger from my car," I say.

"You want me to grab it?" Caleb asks, setting his drink down.

"No, I'm good. You eat."

Poppy starts to set her drink down as well. I shake my head. "You, too. They'll clear all this in five minutes flat. It will only take me a second."

The cold air helps clear my thoughts. I step off the cement stoop and take slow strides though my body is tense from the temperature. I open my driver's door and sit inside, taking a deep breath as I replay the night. Poppy's assurances of Derek. The quick spark of Derek's temper when he saw Arlo and me. The maze of Lincoln and I trying to find steady ground and topics while finding those shorts for Pax. Poppy telling me Lincoln likes me—watches me.

Lincoln watching me—liking me—the words becoming a soundtrack to the reel of memories.

It's stupid and dangerous to have thoughts like this, to be considering if he might actually like me and what that would mean. It leads to hope, hope leads to disappointment, and disappointment hurts so much after harboring this crush for three long years.

We shouldn't have come over. We should have stayed at the party. We could have called Derek to see where he was. We could have gone back to Greek Row and checked out what was going on there, because at the beginning of the year with rush happening, it seems there's a constant party at each of the houses.

I sit long enough for each of my thoughts of Lincoln to be sorted into realities versus desires, long enough to make a plan for tonight and the rest of the quarter. I'm not going to keep doing this to myself. That girl who wanted to date him was gorgeous, confident, and so put together. She looked like a life-sized Barbie, perfect down to her shaped and polished nails, and toned and tanned arms. She is what all of us girls have been taught by social media and marketing that we want to be and should work to become. If he can't commit to dating her, there's no way in hell he would have interest in me. I'm not trying to be a martyr, it's simply the truth. And after three years of holding onto my heart in hopes that he would want it, seeing her tonight gave me the realization that even someone perfect can't get him, and therefore I need to avoid Lincoln and get over him once and for all.

"What are you avoiding? Or should I say who?"

The voice startles me, and then there's the quick zing of a lighter, and cigarette smoke fills the air. Lincoln stands near the hood of my car wearing a black hoodie shadowing most of his face.

I hate that my heart quadruples in speed, especially when I just made the commitment to quit him. "No, I was just..." I shake my head. "...thinking."

He nods a couple of times, then slowly saunters toward my door. "About what?" He blows out another breath of smoke.

"Why do you smoke? They're going to slow you down."

He takes another puff. "There are always obstacles. I figure if I create some of my own, at least I get some say in my life."

"That's stupid."

He pulls his head back, like my words were an assault.

"You're self-sabotaging. Why make life harder?"

"I keep asking myself that same damn question."

"Then quit."

He stares at me, his gaze intense and heavy as the soundtrack of Poppy telling me he watches me—likes me—begins to play again. I swallow, steeling myself, recalling all the reasons and proof that he doesn't. I grab my phone charger from the USB port and get out of the car, closing the door behind me so the street goes dark. "Or don't. Be your own obstacle." I shrug with indifference and take a step to move around him when his hand catches mine, the movement so fast it nearly startles me. I look down where warmth radiates from his fingers to my skin, and catch the spark from his cigarette hitting the pavement beside us. His tennis shoe covers it, then his other hand goes to my waist, his pinky and ring fingers sliding below the hem of my sweatshirt, finding my bare skin. The roughness of his fingers and warmth of his touch creates a contrast that makes my heart feel like it's hiccupping.

He stares at me, and I stare back. Where I'm fairly certain his eyes are searching for permission, I'm seeking understanding.

"Stop me," he says. "Tell me this is a terrible idea. Tell me to go back inside because you're not interested."

My mind is spinning, reasons and thoughts tangling and knotting, impossible to separate. His lips part and he leans forward fractionally, pausing so that he's still too far away. His fingers constrict around my waist, and then his thumb pushes my sweatshirt higher, resting against my flesh. The faint scent of cigarettes still hangs between us along with the clean and masculine scent of his cologne that leaves a cool and spicy feeling in my nose.

"It's a terrible idea," I tell him, reaching forward and fisting his sweatshirt. "A really terrible idea." I try to pull him closer, but I'm fairly certain I'm the one moving.

He nods, his breath falling like a warm caress across my skin. His fingers slip under my sweatshirt, each digit pressing into my skin. It's gentle and yet sure—his touch confident like he is on the field.

My heart is still hiccupping in my chest, and I can't stop staring at his mouth, memorizing the outline of his lips, the fact that the right side is pulled slightly higher.

He leans closer at the same time he presses me backward, my hips falling against my car, the cold seeping through the denim of my jeans barely registers against the heat of his chest pressing against mine. His heart beats against my chest—as loud and unsteady as my own—and his breaths move him closer and farther in unmeasured breaths.

He's so close I can taste the flavors of his breath, the salt from the fries and sweetness of the shake, the bitterness from the cigarette. The sound of the front door is a distant thought, and then I feel the loss of Lincoln everywhere. He pulls me forward, and I stumble, but his hand catches mine, holding me up and grounding me until it too falls away, and he takes several steps back, facing the house.

"Everything okay?" Paxton yells from the stoop, the interior lights glowing around him, making his face dark.

"Yeah," I call back. "I just needed Lincoln's phone for the flashlight. I dropped my Chapstick."

"Clutz. Did you find it?"

"Yeah." I glance at Lincoln. His chest is still rising and falling too quickly, but his eyes are on Paxton. "Yeah, I found it.

15

The next two weeks pass by at a crawl.

I've picked up three extra shifts at work because the flu has been going around, and my professors seem to be trying to outdo one another with the amount of reading and homework they each assign, warning about pop quizzes that have kept me up past midnight to ensure I don't fail. We also still haven't seen anything from the J, K, or L pods, and with less tourists coming into the aquarium, things have been slowing down.

And Derek has texted me four times.

I haven't responded to any of them.

I also haven't seen or heard anything from Lincoln.

"Where are you off to?" Mom asks as I pull on a hoodie, scrummaging for something to eat in the pantry.

I grab a granola bar and unwrap it. "Pax asked me to come by. All that porn he watches has infected his computer."

"Raegan." She closes her eyes as though attempting to wipe the possibility. I laugh. "He mentioned things with Candace weren't going very well."

"I think they're going to break up," I tell her.

She pulls in a deep breath. "So do I."

"What are you doing? You're home late."

A smile graces her face, one wider than I've seen in a long time. "Well..." She goes over to the wine rack that sits on the counter next to the fridge, a gift from Gramps. "December is our twenty-fifth wedding anniversary." She uncorks the bottle. "And I'm surprising him with a trip to Greece."

"Greece? You guys are doing it?" My parents have discussed taking a trip to Greece for as long as I can remember, always moving it to the back burner due to other expenses and goals that took priority.

"You only live once, right?" she says, her expression a mixture of hope and question.

I nod, smiling. "Mom, I'm proud of you. You guys are going to have the best time."

"Are you worried?"

"About what?"

"Well, you'll be alone."

"Mom. I'll be fine. The house will be fine."

"I'm more worried you won't eat or sleep. You've barely breathed lately. I'm worried about you."

"It's going to be fine. Everything will settle down soon."

"I know. But..."

I shake my head to cut off her words of concern. "Tell me about your trip. Athens? Corinth? Where are you guys going?"

Mom's unease evaporates as her excitement for the trip takes precedence. She finishes her glass of wine and tells me about the museums and landmarks she's planning they visit before Dad arrives home from the weekly basketball game he attends with a couple of friends and sometimes Pax.

He sets a paper bag on the counter, and the aroma of tomatoes, basil, and garlic waft from the top. "I brought you dinner," he tells Mom, pressing a kiss to her temple.

Mom closes her eyes and smiles. It's a peaceful look, one that helped inspire my own set of rules for dating.

"I'm going to take a shower, and I'll be right down," he says. "I got extra breadsticks for you, Rae." He winks at me.

Once he's upstairs, Mom leans closer. "He's going to have a heart attack about being off work."

"No, he won't. I'm going to Pax's. Make sure Dad doesn't eat my dinner. I fully intend to eat that as my second nighttime snack." I kiss her cheek and make my way outside where the sun is starting to lower, the shadows of the trees appearing like skyscrapers on the pavement as I head to my car. I pull open the back door, tossing my book bag in, then settle into the driver's seat, cranking the engine and stopping when I notice some paper tucked into my windshield wipers.

I glance at the road, looking both ways for anyone walking or outside who might have left it before I get out of my car and reach for the notebook paper carefully folded into the shape of another crane, my thoughts traveling back to the party and the crane we'd discovered and haven't spent a second thinking about.

I twist the paper in my hand, wondering if it was there earlier and I missed it? And questioning who put it on my car?

My phone rings, the sound making me jump before Maggie's face appears on my screen, distracting all my thoughts as I answer the call I know will only last a few minutes due to her intermittent internet.

"Mags!"

"Hey!" she cries, her voice vibrant and warm.

"How are you?"

"I just finished an entire bottle of wine and don't have to wake up until noon tomorrow. I'm fantastic. How are you, baby sis? How is college treating you?"

"It's good. You know the drill."

There's a brief silence—one that has become more frequent as time continues passing, our days separated by a vastness neither of us seems capable of articulating. My tasks and problems are so mundane and simple compared to her daily experiences living in a third-world country where she works to educate young girls whose country doesn't promote the simple and weighty right. She releases a chuckle several seconds too late, an attempt to cover the stretch of unease neither of us knows how to navigate. "It's fun, though, right? Lots of new people and a new setup."

"Yeah," I say, thinking about my classes and the few people I've made an effort to speak to. In all honesty, I've done a horrible job expanding outside of my small circle, focusing most of my time and energy on Poppy and getting over Lincoln.

"You're an extrovert, Rae. Soak this up. Make friends and get out of your comfort zone."

"Don't extrovert and comfort zone seem like contradictions? I'm pretty sure I fall directly under introvert."

"Not even close." I hear the smile in her voice, and closing my eyes, I imagine my sister's bright blue eyes playful as she leans forward to contest my words, an entire arsenal of logic and examples ready to fire at each of my points. "You like people, you just get stuck in your routine. Mom said you're taking like twenty credit hours. You need to drop some of those, Rae. Enjoy being a freshman. Meet people, stay out too late, party, be dumb."

I think of the last two parties I've attended and how neither has made me feel confident or even interested in going to more. Granted, both have led me to Lincoln, but those instances both seem to have brought out the worst in maybe both of us.

"Trust me. These are the years to do it. Break promises and hearts and just have fun."

"Black widow style?" My tone is teasing, verging on mocking.

Maggie responds with another laugh that populates a hundred memories, watching her as she belts out the sound. "Promise me you will have fun this year and won't just focus on school?"

Though her words evoke a chain reaction of oppositions, I know she's right. I also know I've been failing at pushing outside of my norms, just like she accused.

I PULL into Pax's driveway, regret sitting on one shoulder, desire on the other. I should have asked him to come home or meet at Beam Me Up, the coffee house where I work—anywhere but the scene of the crime. My only relief is that no one is home—even my brother. I grab my biology textbook and sit on the front porch, hoping I can get enough studying in that I might see the back of my eyelids before the date changes again.

. . .

I'M READING the notes in my used textbook, working to decipher if I'm that clueless or if the person who previously owned this textbook was a genius, when an engine directs my attention to a black truck pulling up next to my car.

Lincoln.

"Hey," he says, climbing out of his truck. He's dressed in a pair of jeans and a collared shirt.

My stomach twists, instantly turning sour.

He's dressed up.

For a date?

But he's getting home early, and alone. I pull in a deep breath, hating myself for every second spent thinking entirely too much about him.

I sit straighter, closing my textbook, willing myself to stop analyzing the situation. "Hey."

"Everything okay?"

I swallow, looking at the driveway, the yard, the house across the street—at everything but him. "Yeah, I'm just waiting for Pax. He said he needed some help with his computer."

"I think he went to meet Candace."

"Yeah, he mentioned that. But, he said he'd be here at eight."

He glances at his watch. "You've been here an hour?"

I cringe, feeling the judgement of waiting outside on their front porch for an hour. I'm sure he assumes I was waiting for him. "I wasn't really paying attention to the time."

"Don't you have a key?" He moves past me, unlocking the door.

"Why would I?"

He shrugs. "Why not?"

I slowly stand, gripping my textbook like it's a shield capable of disguising the emotions that are multiplying so fast I'm worried they're written across my skin, exposing my vulnerability and exactly how undone I feel when he's near.

"You want something to drink?" he asks, flipping on lights as he continues into the kitchen, leaving me to trail slowly behind him.

"That's okay. I should probably get going."

"Don't leave on my account." He pulls open the fridge and grabs a beer.

"I have a class at seven."

Half the contents of his beer vanish in one drink. It's then I finally look at him and actually see him for the first time in two weeks. His jaw is hardened, his eyes distant and angry. Each visible muscle is contracted—even his free hand is balled into a fist at his side.

"Are you okay?"

His eyes swing to mine, his intensity rising. Lincoln has always invaded every space he's occupied, like he's too much of everything to be contained. Too good of an athlete, too much masculinity, too much *him*. "What does everyone expect from you?"

I blink back my surprise, hearing his question on a loop as I work to process the direction of the conversation. "People don't know I exist," I tell him. "The expectations I have are mostly theoretical."

"What does that even mean?"

"Someone thinks that if Paxton has a brother or sister, they shouldn't get doors opened for them. I'm an *if* in a hypothetical situation most of the time, and the other times..." I hate trailed off sentences, but going down this path feels too raw and unexplored, especially to travel it with Lincoln.

"Why do you constantly censor yourself?" His words are a bite. An accusation.

"I wasn't."

"You were." He finishes his beer and shakes his head as he turns away.

I pull in a deep breath and hold it while my thoughts pass by on an internal freeway. "If I tell you that by just being a female has a large majority believing I'll fail, you're going to roll your eyes at me and assume I'm a crazy feminist with an idealistic agenda. If I say my mom wants me to consider taking some courses as a backup option and tries to disguise the suggestion with comments like I might enjoy or it might be fun, you're going to think I'm crazy for assuming it's anything more than support. If I say my dad didn't allow me to do anything or watch anything until I memorized the periodic table when I turned thirteen and randomly quizzes me in attempt to stump me, you'll assume he's trying to motivate me." I press my lips into a thin line. "My sister wants me to date around but doesn't believe I can, and Paxton doesn't want me within fifty feet of a dude. And my best friend took a mallet to the heart this summer, and I don't know how to help her." I shake my head. "But, even to my own ears, these 'expectations' sounds so ridiculous and petty when I've been given opportunities many could only dream of. I mean, Maggie's in a country where girls aren't even able to get an education, and I'm complaining about…" I shake my head slowly. "…things that really don't matter."

"So, you think because others have it harder than you, you can't feel badly about the way others treat you?"

"That's the thing. No one's treating me badly."

He stares at me, his own thoughts passing on a silent freeway, one he doesn't pause or make any attempt to express. I don't have the balls to call him out. His eyes aren't windows, they're walls.

I think about their game schedule, attempting to ascertain if that could be a contributor. The team was out of town for a game this past weekend, and I missed their last home game and the dinner my parents hosted because I had to work, but I watched the highlights, and both games were blowouts in our favor.

I rub my lips together, the strawberry balm I applied an hour ago still fragrant. I have no idea how to help sort through whatever demons or expectations he's struggling with, and based on his empty stare, he knows that.

"Are you worried about the scouts? School?"

He laughs, but it's mirthless, and his gaze somehow becomes more distant before he opens the fridge and pulls out another beer. "How was your *date*?" He stresses the T sound.

I pull my chin back, wondering how we managed to get to this side road and why. "My date?"

Lincoln tips his head back, the beer pouring down his throat, revealing what I fear might be another bad habit that would likely fall under self-sabotage. "Derek."

Apprehension has my thoughts speeding up.

Is he mad about Derek?

Jealous?

"What did you guys do?"

"We didn't."

He lowers his beer, surprise cocking his chin as he looks at me. "You told him no?"

"Why does it matter?"

"He's a dick."

"I'm pretty sure the same question applies."

He takes another drink, closing his eyes like he's searching for joy within the act. "Because he's a dick. If you want to sleep with the rugby team, do it, but don't fuck things up for Pax by sleeping with Derek. You'll make things worse."

Blood whooshes in my ears. Anger building with regret. Something twinges in my chest, something far too similar to embarrassment, which feels more unfair than the regret.

His eyes narrow. "Stop censoring your fucking words."

"You're an asshole."

"You knew that, yet you were still willing to hump my leg."

Disgust sets in, making my voice louder and my tone accusing as blood pumps ferociously, making my muscles limber and warm while my mind ushers the fastest escape routes and excuses. Pride keeps me glued in place for a moment, waiting for his own reasons to catch up—for some semblance of kindness or remorse to grace his features.

Neither appear.

"I didn't hump your leg. For the record, that was you. That was all you."

"I was just giving you what you wanted." He finishes his beer.

"You're disgusting."

"Disgusting, but honest."

I grip my bag and turn toward the door, swinging it open so hard the edge of it cuts painfully against my wrist. I slam it behind me and make a beeline for my car. Anger has tears forming in my eyes, blurring the street and my ability to speed away as I'd like. They fall down my face, fat, hot pools that coast down each of my cheeks, leaving chilled paths in their wake. If anger hadn't always made me cry tears of frustration, I might be worried about the brittle feeling in my chest, but years of trying to stop this reaction assures me it's my pride and patience that's fracturing.

16

I spend the fifteen minutes it takes to get home taking deep breaths and counting out of order, a trick Poppy's mom constantly suggests to her patients. The strange order and lack of sequence distract you enough to break whatever evil loop has taken center stage in the mind. My lips and cheeks both feel swollen, but my vision and nose are clear. I climb the five porch stairs in two steps and enter the key code into the door.

The living room and kitchen are vacant, allowing me to pocket my prepared excuse. A note on the fridge reads:

I put your food in the fridge. I'm having an early night because I have to get up early. Dad ran to the campus to get some extra work in. Call us if you need anything.

Love you, Mom

The beginning of each semester is a constant zoo for each of them. I crumple the note and toss it into the trash, my appetite gone.

I turn to head for my room when a sound roots me in place. My thoughts cease as I listen closely, then the door from Dad's office bursts open, and he appears. His wide smile freezes and his eyes grow as he notices me. "You startled me, kiddo."

"You nearly gave me a heart attack," I tell him. "Mom left a note saying you were at Brighton?"

"I brought my work home. They were cleaning the carpets tonight." He stops at the fridge. "Were you able to get Paxton's computer fixed?"

I shrug. "He never showed up."

Dad's brow lowers as he clears his throat, turning away from me. "That's weird. Did you call him?"

"No, I took advantage of the extra hour and did some biology homework."

"You know, I spoke with Professor Bachman, and she said she'd allow you to transfer into her Business Management class if you're interested."

"I don't know, Dad. I don't know how I'd make time for it."

"Well, think about it. It's a great opportunity." He plucks a green bottle of wine with a yellow label from the fridge. "What are your plans for the evening?"

"I'm going to go call Poppy."

"Are you going somewhere?"

I shake my head. "I don't think so."

He nods. "Well, I've got to get back to work." He reaches for a wine glass. "Think about the offer, though, okay?"

I nod, watching him retreat several paces before flipping on each switch to guide my way to my room where I listen to Poppy's phone ring three times before she answers.

"Are your ears burning?" she asks.

"Should they be?"

"I was literally just about to call you. What do you know about definite integral rules?"

My throat grows tight. Hearing her voice makes me want to deposit the contents of my heart into her lap and see if she can make sense of the pieces. "If you come over and bring Oreos, I'll teach you everything about definite integral rules."

"Rae? What's wrong?"

"Nothing."

"Are you crying?"

"No. I'm fine."

"You don't sound fine."

Her compassion makes my bottom lip tremble.

"What happened?" Her voice is rushed—urgent.

"Nothing that Oreo's can't fix."

"Who do I have to cut?"

I chuckle, leaning back against my white paneled headboard. "We'll discuss it when you get here."

"You want me to stay on the line with you?"

"No, I'm fine. I just need my bestie."

"I'm on my way."

"Drive safe." I hang up before she can ask more questions. I need a couple of minutes to compose myself.

A stray tear trickles out the corner of my eye. Frustrated, I swipe it away and stand so I can change into sweats and the warmest pair of fuzzy socks I can find to warm my feet. Fashion had me sacrificing socks all day, and the thin canvas of my shoes did little to shield the cold.

Fifteen minutes later, a muffled knock on the front door has me shuffling down the stairs. Poppy's on the other side of the glass panes, her head cocked, attempting to read my expression before I can even get the door open. Her hands are full with two packages of Oreos in one and a drink tray with iced coffees in the other.

"You didn't have to get coffee, too."

Her head tips further. "I think the last time you asked me to come over because something was wrong was sophomore year when stupid Aaron Grandy told everyone he had sex with you."

"He was a vile human being," I say, taking the drink tray from her and closing the door.

"The worst."

"Lincoln Beckett is trying to be a contender as well."

Poppy is silent, only her eyes revealing her surprise for several seconds. Then, she points to the staircase, ushering me forward.

I shuffle back to my room with Poppy on my heels. "What happened?" she whisper-yells.

I close the door before I turn to face her, taking the drink with whipped cream and removing the lid. "You know that party we went to two weekends ago?"

"Yes…"

"Remember how we went to Paxton's afterward?"

"Do you think I've come down with amnesia? Yes. Of course, I remember."

"Well, do you remember when I went out to grab my phone charger?"

She's silent, tracking the correct memory. "Yeah…"

"Well, Lincoln went outside, too." I suck in a deep breath, then release an even longer one. "At the party, when Lincoln and I went to find pants for Paxton, we kind of had this strange moment—"

"If you guys had sex and you didn't tell me, I need to prepare myself so I'm not upset." She pulls in a deep breath and closes her eyes, both hands extended, signaling for me to wait. "Okay, did you sleep with him?" She peeks at me through her long lashes.

I shake my head.

She frowns. "That was anticlimactic." Disappointment rings in her voice as she leans back on my bed, grabbing her coffee. "Continue."

I tell her about almost kissing him. About *him* almost kissing *me*.

"Ohmygod. Ohmygod. Ohmygod." She shakes her head in tight little jerks. "This was not what I was expecting. So, why are we mad at him?"

"Because Pax asked me to go help him with his computer tonight, and he totally ghosted me, and Lincoln showed up. I don't know what happened to him, but he was in a dark place and was all over the map, and it led to him accusing me of humping his goddamn leg. I mean, this guy's ego is literally the size of the Pacific Ocean. It would have taken Magellan twice as long to cross it."

She blinks slowly, and I know she's trying to understand how things ended up where they did as well. "What did you say?"

"I don't know. I was so mad, I can't even remember."

"I don't understand." Poppy reaches for the top pack of Oreos and pulls the resealable plastic back before passing it to me. "I don't know if these are going to be strong enough for tonight."

Tears prick my eyes again, and these ones aren't from anger or even sadness, but caused by her sympathy. "That's why I called you."

Her smile is a thin line of hope that falls as she wraps her arms around me. "Guys are so stupid. I love you, Rae."

I lean into her, resting my forehead on her shoulder. "Maybe we should do what Pax said and forget all athletes. Maybe they really are just a bunch of douchebags."

17

"Raegan. Be careful." Lois watches me carefully. Reluctance has her reaching out to me, though she's thirty feet away.

I smile in response and lean a little closer to the water. We've stumbled upon an illegal drift net that got tangled in the engine of the boat. Hans is attempting to reverse the engine in hopes it will untangle, while I gently lead it out of the way. One of the reasons I know cetology is right for me is my ease out on the ocean. Many come out here and freeze, hating the cold dampness that enrobes you and the choppiness of the water, which causes many to feel sick and off-balance. Out here, things make sense to me. The water, the waves, the tides—there's reason and explanation for each, unlike the rest of my life.

It's been a week since I left Lincoln in his kitchen to drown out whatever demons he was facing. A week since I allowed Poppy to realize my crush on Lincoln ran deeper than she'd realized. Seven days since I've been able to sleep a solid stretch.

"There! You got it!" Joe yells as the engine fires rather than cutting like it has a dozen times before. I use both hands to tug the rest of the net free and pull it into the boat, hopping back over the rail and into the body of the boat where Lois grabs hold of my shoulders and Joe helps further pull in the net.

"Shit." Hans appears, our shared relief not stretching to his expression.

One glance out at the net confirms why. Several animals are caught between the large holes, many aren't moving, likely dead.

"Let's pull the rest of it in. Maybe a few can be saved." Joe pulls harder and faster at his own instruction, and we follow suit, the sound of our hearts breaking with each thump as another animal falls into the base of the boat.

It's dark by the time I get home. Within a month, it'll be dark by the time I leave class. Living this far north, summer nights stretch on, but during the winter months, the days become painfully short.

I head into the house, my body aching from being cold for so long. It took us all day to pull in the entire drift net and work to save the few animals that were still alive. Another two hours to wait for the coastguard to arrive, and then we had to transport a young seal back to the aquarium to get medical attention. Greta tried to see the positive side, focusing on how we found the net before it could do more damage, and how we were able to save some of the animals impacted. Hans and Joe refused to see the positive in the situation, though. With more than thirty years between them, they've grown skeptical about things ever-improving. Too many illegal drift nets and poachers, too many failed and unenforced laws, too long between sightings and positive stats are blows that continue to beat them into a constant stupor of negativity.

"Oh my god!" Mom is out of her chair and rushing toward me before I can get the door closed. "What happened?" Her eyes are frantic and wide as they rake over me, her hands both outstretched, waving like she doesn't know where to place them.

There's commotion, shifting, and movement as I look down at my sweatshirt and sodden jeans. I'm covered in dirt and blood from today. "It's not mine," I tell her. "I'm fine."

Mom shakes her head, her eyes raking over me again and again, not believing my words. Her attention stops on my hand, which she pulls into her grasp. "You're hurt."

I fight a wince because my take home of the day is a deep cut from a fish hook that got caught on the top of my hand between my thumb and forefinger that tore my skin a full inch before I even realized I'd gotten cut.

"You can't do this," Mom says, keeping my hand pinned between hers as her eyes meet mine. Hers are several shades lighter than mine, tinted red because, like me, she gets teary when feeling overwhelmed. "You promised. This was a part of our deal."

"I didn't," I tell her.

"Raegan." Her tone is a warning, a threat because my omission of truths last year created an entire web of lies that has her still doubting me.

"I swear, Mom. I was with the Aquarium team. A huge drift net got stuck in our engine, and we just pulled it into the boat. This is from a seal pup that was caught in it." I wave to the blood covering the front of me.

She stares at me for several more beats before accepting my honesty. "We should probably get this stitched."

"It's okay. It's not that deep." She's not listening to me, though, and the thin scab on my hand hasn't had enough time to set, leaving a slender trail of blood to stain much of my hand and wrist.

"Jesus," Pax says, appearing beside Mom. Beside him are Lincoln and Caleb, and I realize the motion I'd seen when Mom screamed was Caleb leaving, likely to get Pax.

Lincoln's lips are parted, his brown eyes raking over my torso again and again like he's trying to make sense of the scene before meeting my gaze. A silent question hangs between us as Pax fires off questions as quickly as Mom had.

"I'm going to take a shower," I tell them, disregarding the entire lot.

"Are you sure you're okay?" Mom asks.

"I'm positive. I wish I could say the same for the seal."

Mom's shoulders fall, reading the defeat I'm currently drowning in.

It takes me too long to untie my boots, my fingers stiff and sore from rope burns and small cuts I endured because I'd removed my gloves to get better traction after the net had continuously slipped from our hands. My boots fall with a thump, and then I peel off my layers, shedding the dirty clothes and leaving the only traces of my day on my hands.

The spray burns initially, my body still too cold for several moments before the warmth infiltrates and spreads over me.

Once dried, even my hands barely show any evidence of today's events. My cut, though wide, isn't half as bad as I'd feared. It still insists on bleeding, but with so many tendons and muscles in hands, I made off easy.

I clutch my towel, listening to ensure the others aren't near before I open the door and make a quick escape to my room, where I pull on a pair of yoga pants and a tee that says 'I love naps.' I should blow dry my hair. It would probably make me feel warmer, and I know it would make me look a step up from the drowned appearance I'm currently sporting, but with my intention to get over Lincoln still fully intact, I dismiss the thought and tie the strands into a quick knot. I go to hang my towel up and gather my dirty clothes to shove in the washing machine.

I rip off a paper towel hanging over the sink in the laundry room, pressing it to the cut on my hand, grab another to clean up the smears I left on the washing machine, and turn to find Pax staring at me.

"What happened? The unedited version."

"Nothing, I swear."

"Rae..."

"Paxton, *I swear*."

Lincoln appears, his attention shifting between Pax and me before he lifts a small tube. "This what you want?"

Pax grabs it, glancing at the label before tossing it to me. "If you're..."

"I'm not. I didn't do anything."

Pax blows out a long breath. "Do you need help?"

I shake my head, gripping the small tube of super glue he tossed me. "It's not that bad." I switch off the light, heading toward the bathroom. Pax veers off, heading back to the kitchen, but Lincoln follows me.

"What happened?"

"Oh my gosh. How many times do I need to tell you guys? It was nothing. I got cut on a fish hook."

"I mean what happened that has them so off balance?"

"It was nothing," I mutter, grabbing the small medical kit we keep in a tub under the bathroom sink.

"Then why don't they believe you?"

"Why do you ask questions and expect answers when you don't answer any of my questions?"

"What questions have you asked?"

"What had you so upset the other night? Expectations?"

His gaze drops.

"Exactly." I begin to turn, stopping when he takes a step into the small space, his presence once again consuming every inch of space.

His eyes rebound to mine. "My dad wants me to quit football and become a corporate lawyer."

I pull my chin back, shock still radiating like I've been slapped. "What? Why?"

"Because in his eyes, that's what I was born to do. To take over the legacy he's built."

"But you're too good to quit. You'll be a first-round draft pick. Easy."

He scoffs, his gaze travelling around the small bathroom painted a light blue to match the new gray tiles that were installed two years ago when the bathroom became solely mine. "I spent nearly half of last season out because of my shoulder. The only way I'm going to get drafted is if we win every game this year and next."

I pull my shoulders back, unable to make empty promises, no matter how badly I want to. "Did you know that sixteen thousand whales are killed each year? Sixteen *thousand*," I say the number again because it's a fact that deserves to be heard a dozen more times. "And it gets worse. The numbers get bigger. Sharks? Over a *hundred million*. Every. Single. Year. Slaughtered. And those numbers don't even account for the thousands dying from pollution. From drift nets." I pause, realizing I'm starting to get on a tangent that I could easily go on for hours about, sounding more like Joe than Lois or Greta, who teach with hope and care.

"I wanted to stop the numbers from growing, so last year, I met a group who wanted to save marine animals. We collected information, helped count different species, and checked on them. A few times we'd come across illegal hunters or poachers, and we'd report them, but it never made them stop. They'd move on, maybe getting fined in the process, but they made so much that it didn't matter." I sigh, considering the damage they caused and the high sums they collected while doing so. "One day, we came across a boat that was trying to separate a baby whale from its mother, and we knew there was a good chance that the authorities wouldn't get there in time or even come at all, so we intervened." I think back to the moments that escalated so much quicker than I could have anticipated. "A guy on our boat got hurt really bad. Several did."

His jaw grows tight as he turns his head a fraction. "Were you hurt?"

"We couldn't just walk away from it all. We were so tired of watching them make their own rules."

"You almost needed a lawyer," he says the words like he's dusting off a memory, one I wish he'd have buried a bit deeper.

"I didn't need one. My parents were just paranoid."

"You broke your arm," he says, his eyebrows lowered as he dusts off another corner of the past. "I had no idea it was related."

I shrug away his concern, but his gaze is on my arm, tracing the edge of the scar that peaks out under my tee, a reminder of that day and my choices. "One of them had a fillet knife, and I got too close."

Lincoln's eyes flare, an angry war taking place that keeps me silent for a full minute.

"He wasn't trying to hurt me, not really. He was just trying to scare me because I was cutting their net. But it was slippery, and there was a lot of pushing and shoving, and it just got ... really intense."

"And they thought you were out again today?"

I nod once. "I didn't. I wasn't. Today was nothing." Admitting this doesn't feel good. Last year, I promised my parents I wouldn't associate with the group—wouldn't fight a war I didn't understand and was ill prepared for. Yet, every day I see the carnage of the side we fought against and I continue to keep my distance, though it feels like I'm allowing them to win each time I do.

I twist off the cap of the glue with my teeth, but Lincoln intercepts the small silver tube. He takes my left hand in his, folding my wrist to give himself the optimal angle. His eyes meet mine. I swallow back memories from that night a year ago and more from only a couple of weeks ago—both of them inflicting pain and neither offering a resolution. His gaze moves to my hand, squeezing a thin line of glue along the wound.

"You, Raegan Lawson, are badass."

"I'm a coward."

"That's bullshit," he says.

"You quitting football is bullshit."

He stands opposite of me, his eyes raking over my face. It feels like we're exchanging another conversation where I again don't know the subject or even the language. And it ends too soon, as Pax reappears, a box of butterfly bandages in hand. He stops in the doorway, his attention volleying between Lincoln and me before his brow creases heavily with accusation. "What's going on?"

"My hands are sore," I explain, extending them to reveal the many rope burns and nicks.

Pax turns his attention to Lincoln for confirmation, but Lincoln doesn't say or do anything except stare back.

"Thanks for the bandages," I say, grabbing the box from Paxton. I open the lid and rip one open using my teeth. I fumble with the edges, folding one half of the bandage before getting the protective film off the other side.

"You're a train wreck," Pax says, taking the bandage from me and tossing it into the trashcan.

"You want to stop judging and help? Lincoln picked up your slack, but you're about to be fired."

He snickers, plucking the box from my hand and making quick work of applying two small bandages across my cut.

"Are you guys having another team dinner tonight?" I ask.

Pax shakes his head. "We were gonna watch some tape. Coach Harris gave us a damn cassette, and the only people I know with a VCR is Gramps and Mom and Dad."

"You should have chosen Gramps. He likes to watch tape and Camilla's been baking cookies to test for their church's bake sale next month. She's determined to have the best ones."

"Yeah, well, I was kind of hoping you'd be interested?" he says, wadding up the small amount of trash and shooting it at the garbage.

Pax and I haven't watched tape together since he moved out. "Why?" I don't mean to sound so abrupt, but the question catches me out in left field.

"Because it's Colorado State, and Coach is worried."

"I'll tell you what. I'll watch film with you if you can get your football team to clock hours next week for a beach cleanup. It would give you good community service, and it would help the ocean."

"There's no way they're going to agree to that," Pax says.

"Convince them, team captain."

"How many hours?"

"Two."

"Seriously?"

"I will move the event around you guys, and I'll even make sure two news stations are there."

Pax sighs. "Deal." It's a begrudging agreement, but the whisper of a grin confirms he would have done it for me regardless. "And no naps while you're watching the game," he says, pointing at my shirt.

"If we're raising the ante, you might have to feed me."

"I blame Mom for your negotiation skills."

"That was all you and Maggie."

He laughs, his eyes drifting to my hands, his smile sobering. "You good?"

"You'd think I was fragile or something." I turn, setting the first aid kit back under the sink. "Let's go."

PAX SITS UPRIGHT, tracing the skin around his mouth with fingers, again and again. He's nervous.

Lincoln is next to him, a backward baseball cap covering his dark hair. Mom and Caleb are on the opposite couch. Mom's going over resumes for an open teaching position, and Caleb keeps alternating between watching the film and playing a game on his phone. I'm in the recliner which sits empty until Mondays when Gramps visits.

"They're physical," Pax says, watching another play where Colorado takes down the offense like a bunch of bowling pins.

Lincoln's silent, watching as wide receiver after wide receiver is leveled by their defense.

"Wait," I say.

Pax hits pause, looking at me for direction. "I recognize him. Play that again."

"He's a sophomore," Pax tells me.

I turn to my phone, searching his name, and see the face that looks more familiar, the one at least twenty pounds lighter with shorter hair. I spin my phone so Pax can see it. "Recognize him?"

Pax pulls his chin back. "He played for Arizona two years ago."

I nod. "He was kicked off his high school team for excessive force after he caused a kid brain damage. It says he changed his name last year after his parents had an ugly divorce, and he transferred. Red shirted it last year."

"Shit," Pax blows the word out.

"Hey," Mom calls, nailing him with a glare.

My attention cuts to Lincoln, who's watching the film again as the player in question levels another player, leaving him immobile on the field.

"Looks like it's going to be hunting season for Lincoln," Caleb says, turning back to his phone.

"He's fast," I say. "But he always plants on his right knee. I'd bet a hundred bucks he's either nursing an injury or they don't make him practice going left because he's fast enough to recover nine times out of ten." I stand up, walking to the TV. "And this guy is his insurance." I point at the player sprinting down from midfield.

Pax runs his hand over his mouth, leaning his shoulders back against the sofa before looking at Lincoln. "They're hella fast."

Lincoln nods, his attention on the TV, all his defenses raised, making him impossible to read. I have no idea if he's concerned or if he's masterminding ways to avoid being added to this player's list of targets.

We continue watching film, Pax filling several sheets with notes until he gets a call that has him standing up. "I've got to get this. It's Candace."

"How are things going with them?" Mom asks.

Caleb shrugs. Lincoln doesn't hear the question, his attention on the game we're watching for a second time.

Mom sighs. "I'm going to order some pizzas." She sets her stuff down and heads toward the kitchen because my parents might be the only two people in the state who still use a landline.

Lincoln's attention doesn't shift from the game, even when food arrives, he's absent except for thanking Mom and taking several slices.

18

I stare at the red line on my hand, the one separating lucid and sane from the madness I keep edging toward.

"This is amazing," Greta says, shaking her head as she smiles.

"They're like local celebrities," Jordan adds.

It's true. I called Greta the morning after dissecting Colorado's tape with Pax, asking her to share that Brighton U's football team would be at Beach Day, and it was shared over ten thousand times in less than twenty-four hours. We generally struggle to get more than a dozen volunteers, and this morning we have well over three hundred. Four local news stations are here, and two newspapers are interviewing the team and are scheduled to meet with Greta and Hans afterward.

The football team is walking on air, eating up their celebrity status as people ask for autographs and pictures.

"Where are we with hating Lincoln?" Poppy asks, blowing into her cupped hands. "Do we still hate him?"

I take another gulp of my lukewarm coffee. "We probably should. Seems safer."

"What about Derek? Do we hate him?"

"I'm pretty sure he might hate us. I never replied to his last message."

"Anyone else we should be avoiding?"

"I don't know. Anyone on your list?"

"I hate everyone." Poppy shrugs.

Laughter bubbles out of me, and I'm grateful my best friend was willing to trade shifts so she could be here with me today.

"Uh oh. Warning. Eleven o'clock."

"Who?" I ask, glancing over my shoulder.

"Wrong eleven o'clock," she says.

"What?" I turn to look over my other shoulder.

"That's three o'clock," she hisses.

"For who?"

"Me!"

I swing back around in time to see Derek, a smile stretching across his lips. "You're supposed to say the time based upon the person you're telling," he says, winking at Poppy.

I look at her, sharing a silent 'I told you so.' Because I have so many times.

"Hi, Derek," she says.

"Hi, Poppy. Raegan."

"I'm going to get some trash bags." Poppy points in the direction of the setup table, though I know full and well she has two bags shoved in her pockets because I handed them to her.

Derek shoves his hands into his pockets, his blond hair shorter. He looks at me, going up on his toes. "How have you been?"

"I haven't been ignoring you," I tell him.

His brows pull upward. "No? That's good to hear because I was a little worried that I might have crossed the line back at that party when I asked if you and Arlo have something."

"You kind of did, but that's not it. I just..."

"Bad breakup?"

"Something like that." It has been, and though it's only been a one-sided breakup, I've learned over the past couple of weeks that recovering from a crush can feel awfully similar to a strained heart.

"But there's nothing going on between you and Arlo?"

I shake my head. "He's like a brother to me."

"Should I heed that as a warning?"

A smile pulls at my lips. "Depends on your intentions."

"Initially? To convince you I'm different. Then, to make you forget about whatever asshole failed to be good enough."

My heart accelerates, beating so loud and hard I can hear it in my ears.

"What are you doing next week?"

"Next week?"

He nods, his smile gentle and patient.

"When?"

"Any day. We can go out and talk. Hang out without a party and a million distractions."

"Monday? We could meet around two?"

"Sure." He flashes a smile that is equally beautiful and cocky, his attention so intent I find myself forgetting the rest of the beach and the entire purpose of today.

"Did you get roped into coming by Paxton?" Derek asks. "This place is colder than hell. I don't know if I'm going to be visiting the beach again while living on this side of the country."

"It's actually pretty nice today," I say.

"Nice? You're not supposed to have to wear your winter coat to the beach. The Atlantic is warm. You wear a bathing suit and swim in the water, lie on the shore and tan. It's nice. Relaxing."

"But, you can't see an orca."

He laughs. "I'll take you to the Outer Banks and show you the wild horses and the dolphins."

"Ladies and gentleman," Hans says, addressing the hundreds of volunteers gathered on the shore. He gives a compelling and touching speech about the partners the aquarium works with on a continuous basis and the mission statement we strive for each day. It's a heartfelt message that I hope will sink in a bit farther than today alone.

Then Greta takes the mic, a wide, prize-winning smile in place. "We want to thank you all for joining us this morning. We know it's cold, but we promise, once you get moving, you'll appreciate the breeze. And you volunteering today will help save sea turtles, dolphins, whales, birds, and so many more animals. We want to sincerely thank you for volunteering and want to remind you of the various events we run over the course of the year.

"While I'm up here, I also want to give a special shout out to one of our own. Raegan, where are you?" She lifts a hand like a visor, peering among the crowd.

"Rae Rae!" I hear Arlo yelling, followed closely by Paxton.

Joe is just a couple feet away and spots me, waving an arm in my direction. Greta laughs, her eyes finding me. "Raegan is one of the smartest, most motivated young women I've had the pleasure of meeting. If you haven't met her, be sure to chat with her today. She's probably the kindest person you'll ever meet, and though she won't admit it, she's rather funny. So, stop by, tell her she kicks ass, and give yourself a pat on the back for saving animals and keeping our water and Earth a little cleaner."

Applause breaks out, and I'm grateful I can blame the wind for my rose-tinted cheeks.

"You completely let me put my foot in my mouth, didn't you?" Derek asks, his lips climbing into a grin before he shakes his head. "Let me guess, you love the beach?"

My smile is instant, enjoying the scratch of unease I see on his perfect exterior. "It's my favorite place."

He nods a couple of times. "Well then, I retract everything I said and plead ignorance because this is where I plan to spend *all* my time." He lifts his shoulders with a slight tremor of a shiver. "Once I get a new winter coat for subzero weather, that is."

My laughter is immediate and genuine, only tapering off when Arlo and Paxton wander over.

"Look at you, all-star," Pax says, throwing his arm around my shoulders.

"I know. Can you believe all these people came just to see me?" I tease, striking a pose.

Arlo laughs, but it's censored, his attention split between me and Derek. Pax grins, poking me with an elbow.

"Don't get such a big head that I have to roll you home," he warns.

"I don't know. I might have exceeded that point."

"Years ago," he adds, his blue eyes filled with humor. "Listen, I've got to catch up with Candace, but find me before you leave, okay?" Pax glances from me to Derek, giving a tight jerk of a nod that I'm fairly certain is an olive branch, albeit, a fragile one.

"Make sure they're actually picking up garbage," I say, referring to the team who all seem to be impressing someone at the moment. "The celebrity factor is great, but I still need the beach cleaned."

"Always the hardass."

"You know me."

"Unfortunately."

I flip him the bird, but my motivation slips as I catch sight of Poppy in the distance, talking to Lincoln. A smile that looks both kind and patient making him more handsome than the broody look I trace each night before going to sleep.

"You ready?" Derek asks, shaking out his garbage bag.

Poppy laughs at something, and Lincoln follows, shifting the gray beanie concealing most of his dark locks. If there was ever a hope for superpowers, I'd wish I could hear their conversation. To know what's happening. Because, try as I might, my jealousy right now is aimed solely at my best friend.

"Yeah," I say, turning to face Derek. "Let's go."

"So, you're the youngest of three?" he asks.

We pass several people here to help clean up, going against the wind that pulls at our coats and blows my hair into my face. I pull it into a quick knot so it doesn't become a massive tangle and nod. "I am. What about you? Do you have siblings?"

"A younger brother."

"Yeah?"

"He's a sophomore in high school."

"Do you guys get along?"

"Not like you and Paxton," he says. "I mean, we're cool, but we don't talk much. He's trying to do his own thing and hates if we're compared."

"That's normal. My sister's seven years older than me, and with Pax in the middle, I think it made it easier on us in some ways because people were less inclined to compare us. Especially since his thing was always football."

"What's your thing?"

I think of telling Lincoln how I always felt forced into academia, but now I'm not as sure. I don't feel sure of much anymore. "I don't know," I admit. "I don't really have a thing."

He chucks a thumb back toward the crowds. "I think you're lying, because that lady listed off at least four, and though I barely know you, I can tell she's hardly scratched the surface." His stare is consuming and demanding that I acknowledge his words. "You have no idea, do you?"

"No idea of what?"

"How amazing you are."

I chuckle. The response necessary to lighten the mood that he's made too intense with a few words that construct an entire castle of thoughts and hopes that are both too large and grand. "You worry me."

"Why? Do I make you nervous?"

Probably. Sometimes. "There's always purpose behind your words, but I'm not sure I always understand the intention."

"I'm trying to make that really clear."

"But are these words this easy to find for everyone you talk to?"

He flashes that cocky grin he's getting known for as the season progresses. "Are you asking if I'm a flirt?"

"I'm asking if you're genuine."

He stops, pivoting so he's facing me. "No bullshit. I like you. There's something about you that just makes me feel good. I want to know you. I want to know everything about you. I want to find out if you're a bed hog and what you like to eat for breakfast. I want to know who your favorite band is and if you sing along in the shower."

"I don't know if I'm ready for that," I tell him, hating myself for feeling so broken when these are words I've dreamed of hearing since I was six and fell in love with fairytales.

He grins, this time it's softer, radiating more warmth than force. "I didn't say it has to happen next week. Consider us a radio station. We start off with a slow tempo, and we keep going, changing the beat, changing the pace." Caramel eyes scan mine, searching for understanding—hope.

"I sing in the shower and the car," I tell him, trying my best to convey I'm willing to try.

His smile climbs, staining each of my thoughts.

19

"Where's the controller?" Gramps asks, interrupting the pregame as they discuss Brighton, breaking down their year as well as several players, evaluating stats and strengths. They're focused on Derek right now, discussing how impossibly fast he is.

"Rae," Gramps says. "You ignoring me?"

"I'm just ... listening."

"Yeah. I'd like to as well," he says. A throw pillow hits me in the face, falling to the floor. I glance back at him sitting in the easy chair. "I need that pillow, too." He points at the offending pillow he threw.

"Anything else, your highness?"

"Just your love." He smiles smugly, sitting back in his seat and crossing his arms and ankles.

"You're ruining your chances of that." I warn him.

"It's not my fault. I'm sore from all that walking yesterday. Camilla and I filled two garbage bags. Think of all the turtles we saved."

His words fade as I turn my attention back to the TV where they're talking about Derek again, showing a highlight reel from the previous games.

Grandpa clears his throat. It's a loud and exaggerated sound. I lean forward, grabbing the pillow. "How come you're watching that pretty boy? You fancy him?" Gramps asks.

I swallow, handing him the pillow. "He's a friend."

"I bet Paxton's not happy with that," he says, chuckling as he shifts and gets comfortable.

"What doesn't Paxton like?" Mom asks, coming in from the kitchen with a plate filled with cheese and crackers.

Grandpa nods in the direction of the TV. "Derek Paulson."

Mom turns her attention to me, her eyes twice their normal size. "Really?"

"We're friends," I tell them both.

"That's what gramps said up until the day before he and Camilla got married." Mom reminds us.

"We're not getting married."

"He's cute," Mom says.

"A little arrogant," Gramps adds.

"Dad, I dare you to find one on the team who isn't," she counters.

Gramps laughs again, his deep rumbly laugh that transports me back in time, to memories of sitting with him on that same chair, watching football games and cartoons together.

Dad follows, the crock pot in his hands, the scents of vinegar and brown sugar making my mouth water as he presents the little smokies he makes for each game day. "What are you guys laughing about?" he asks.

"What do you think about Rae dating a football player?" Gramps lifts his eyebrows, his intention to wreak havoc clear.

"I'm *not* dating a football player."

"Which one?" Dad asks, looking at Mom.

"Paulson. Derek."

Dad pulls his chin back. "I didn't think Pax liked him."

"Are we done?" I ask, grabbing the remote and turning the TV up so Gramps can hear.

"I thought we were talking about Derek?" Mom asks.

"We weren't."

"You guys did look cute yesterday," Mom tacks on.

Gramps snaps. "That's right. You guys were together on the beach for a while. But then he was doing those interviews." He sits back, absent as he tries to recall the specifics. "He liked the lime light."

Dad looks pale. I think he dreads these conversations more than I do.

"He has a nice smile," Mom says as they flash a final picture of Derek, moving onto Paxton and his story, showing pictures of my brother when he was young, playing football and film from his high school games. Gramps cheers, Mom claps, and Dad and I sit back, soaking up each words of praise they add to his long resume of accomplishments.

They use Pax's friendship with Lincoln to segue into Lincoln's highlights, showing several videos of him weaving down the field, his agility and speed equally impossible. They cut to his injury from last year and more of him working on his recovery, including a short clip from tonight getting his ankles taped and his shoulder stretched by the trainer. His face is stoic—broody. He doesn't flash smiles at the camera like Derek does, and it only seems to draw the camera crews in, waiting to earn a glimpse when you see joy hit his face and spread to his eyes.

Mom places a hand on her chest. "He's a special kid."

Thankfully, the game starts, and with Brighton on offense and Pax on the field, conversation ceases as we focus our attention on the game. My heart hasn't been beating evenly since I woke up this morning, a nervous energy after thinking entirely too much about this game and the possible outcomes. Pax is caught on camera, his fingers laced through Lincoln's helmet as he says something to him. I pray it's a reminder of the steam train that's going to be headed right for him. Lincoln nods, and then Pax does as well, and the two break apart, lining up.

Play after play. Hit after hit. We're silent, watching one of the most physical games in the history of Paxton's career, flinching and gasping each time one of our players is laid out.

"Damn," Gramps remarks, opening a beer. "This game is practically a wrestling match."

I don't comment. I can't afford to look away as Pax completes a perfect throw, the ball sailing into the hands of Derek, who races down the field to complete a touchdown.

Mom's clapping, and Dad and Gramps are reliving every touch of the ball, but I'm noticing Lincoln pull off his helmet, his jaw tense as he approaches Pax, saying something that looks far too similar to anger than celebration. Before they show Pax's response, the camera focuses on Derek, catching him run a hand through his short hair, smiling as he jogs back to the huddle.

The announcers spend halftime comparing Derek and Lincoln. I loathe each second of it.

"Oh man," Dad says, filling a small plate with crackers. "I think I'm team Lincoln," he says.

I roll my eyes. "I think you might be a little biased."

"You have to admit it, he's a better player."

I shrug, attempting indifference. "I don't know. Derek is having a strong game. He's got speed on his side."

"Lincoln's got those Velcro hands though," Gramps says. "I've never seen that kid drop or even fumble a ball."

"And he practically dances out there. He's so smooth. It's like he's skating." Dad reaches for more cheese.

The wound on my hand winks up at me, the ghost of Lincoln's lips on my neck, his hands on my waist. My chest feels tight as I frantically work to chase every last detail—including some I'm fairly sure I'm fabricating.

The doorbell rings, scattering my thoughts. Relief curves my lips, but reluctance and regret make it difficult to breathe. For several weeks, I've lost entire hours obsessing over the details, desperate to understand each motive and touch.

"Hey, Poppy," Mom says, swinging the door open wider so she can enter.

"Hi," we call, waving from our seats.

"You're late," Gramps calls from his chair.

Poppy stops at his side, kissing his cheek. "I know. I had to work this afternoon." Poppy works part time for her mom, organizing files and rescheduling appointments. "How are they doing?"

"Up by two touchdowns," Dad says. "Hungry?"

"Starving," she says, sitting beside me, her black slacks and floral blouse a stark contrast to my yoga pants and red Brighton U hoodie. She fills a small plate and sits back, her arm brushing mine. "This was on your doorstep," she says, dropping a folded crane in my lap. I stare at the paper for a second.

"What is it?" Mom asks.

"A paper crane," I tell her.

"That's odd. Where did it come from?"

"Didn't we see one of these recently?" Poppy asks absently, kicking off her shoes.

I move the crane to the table, my attention pulled back to the game as they span over the team.

"Intense game?" Poppy asks.

I nod. "These guys are out for blood, and Brighton needs this win."

"Here we go," Dad says, announcing the start of the second half.

We watch in silence, Poppy gripping my hand when Pax is taken out, and sharing a breath when he stands. She re-fills her plate twice, complimenting dad's cooking and offering to get me a drink when the silence stretches too long for her comfort level.

The intensity lessens as Brighton switches to defense, Dad joking with Poppy. Mom talking about the cold front, until we return to offense. They don't work to include me. They know after too many years that I don't like to chit chat during games, my focus on the field and the players, studying each play like it's a new theory which I dissect and separate into facts and schemes.

Pax counts, his steps too short. He's hesitating. Several states away, I can sense his trepidation, causing my back to go rigid. His release is perfect, drawing a defensive tackle. The cameras follow the ball into Lincoln's fingers.

"No," I whisper. "No." But it's too late, and he can't see the player creating a solid wall that he hits with enough impact it makes the defensive player fall as well.

He lies on the field, the ball still clutched in his hands, the only small piece of comfort.

"Ladies and gentleman, what a hit. I have a feeling Becket is going to be seeing stars after than one," the announcer says.

Time seems to stop. I can't breathe or think or even hear anything as I stare at the TV, hating the fact they're cutting to an ad when we're several states away.

Poppy grips my hand, her fingers pressed so tightly against mine, a dull ache surfaces. It's a welcomed reprieve to the current hurricane that's stirring in my chest, immobile and wreaking absolute havoc.

"It was a low hit," Dad comments. "I hope his knees are okay."

"It's the concussions that always worry me. They're kids, playing a sport that could injure them for the rest of their lives." Mom reaches for her glass of wine.

The ad cuts, returning to the game, showing the same hit twice with different angles, and then it goes to a current shot, showing Lincoln still on the ground, Pax and two medics from Brighton at his side.

"He's talking," Poppy says.

More importantly, he's also starting to move. Pax leans over him, grasping his hand and helping to haul him up.

Gramps claps. "There we go. There we go. That kid is one tough son of a bitch."

Lincoln rolls his shoulders, moving his neck side to side, before moving the rest of his limbs as though confirming they still work.

This is the problem with Lincoln: I don't feel anything small when it comes to him. Everything is bigger and more intense. It makes me lose my footing and my thoughts, and sometimes I worry that if he ever noticed me as something more, I'd lose myself entirely.

I'M SUCKING down my second Dr. Pepper of the morning on my way to my math class which, has become the bane of my college career. I stayed up past 2 a.m. last night, my thoughts focused too much on Lincoln's injury, making digesting any of the homework I had practically impossible.

They're flying back this morning, and I'm struggling to stop making excuses to go visit to ensure Lincoln's really okay. I know it's the very last thing I should be considering, especially since I have a date this afternoon with Derek.

"How fast does your mind go?" The familiar voice hits me like a cold wave, clearing my thoughts and making me stop in my tracks. Lincoln grins. It's lazy and slow, a confirmation he knows how much he affects me.

I look past his smile and bright eyes, scouring his body for any sign of injury.

"Go ahead and feast," he whispers, leaning closer.

"Are you okay?"

"You watched the game on Saturday?"

I roll my eyes. "You know I did."

He shrugs. "You've been busy."

"How's your shoulder?"

"You probably read the play before it happened, didn't you?"

"I had the advantage of seeing the entire field."

"And you can read plays like you're in their heads." I'm fairly certain I see admiration shining in his eyes.

I don't know what to say. Intuition is urging me to flirt, but that doesn't feel right. Not now. Not after thinking about my impending date with Derek. Not after the way Lincoln spoke to me in his kitchen.

"How's your beach?" he asks.

"How's your shoulder?" I ask again.

"You're relentless, aren't you?"

"This is hardly being relentless."

"How's your hand?"

"You're hurt," I say quietly, trying to keep my tone from being accusing.

He presses his lips together, closing his eyes a fraction too long to play coy. "It'll be fine. I wasn't stabbed." His tone is flippant as his gaze refuses to meet mine, but then he reaches forward, his finger blazing a trail across my skin, following the crooked path of my scar like he can see it beneath my sweater.

"Why does weakness scare you so much?" My question is a lit match dropping in a dry field, sparking a reaction I should have seen coming. I can see his reaction instantly, the squaring of his broad shoulders, the defiance in his clenched jaw that is confirmed as he pulls away from me, the harshness that makes his eyes appear icy.

"See you, Lawson." He starts to walk away.

If I were braver, I'd push him with more questions and accusations, force him to give me something besides an easy copout that his him going in the opposite direction. But I'm not, and he's already walking away.

"What's with you?" The words leave my mouth before I can stop them. It's the very definition of word vomit. Embarrassment creeping over my skin, wishing I could take back the mess and be sure no one heard it happen. And dammit if my feet aren't following the disaster, leading the trail right to Lincoln.

He turns, indifference etched across his features. "You'll need to be more specific."

"You're always playing games. Like it would be so terrible for someone to actually know what you're thinking. I can't tell if you like me or if you tolerate me or if you're simply bored and looking for a few minutes of entertainment because everything is meant to amuse you. Sometimes it seems like this is your world, and we're merely existing in it."

He laughs. It's mirthless, and I know in every particle of my being that I should heed his warning and walk away. Ignore the mess and chalk it up as an embarrassing moment that I look back on and cringe, refusing to admit I ever broached the gauntlet I've just laid.

"If only it were that simple," he says, staring at me with a million silent words kept behind an indestructible dam that I'm beginning to believe others don't even see. Likely because defiance masks it so well.

Later today, or likely in a week—a cunning remark will pop into my head. But right now, I can't think of anything to say that won't exacerbate my vulnerability and highlight his don't-give-a-fuck stance. So instead, I turn, allowing the mess to remain out there, muddling the very thin definition of a relationship we've constructed.

"You're his sister," he says.

I flip around so fast my head spins, hoping to catch something more obvious on his face than his words have exposed. He's standing still, his dark hair a teasing mess of perfection. "I'm way more than that."

He purses his lips and shakes his head. "You can't be."

20

I park at the coffee and wine bar Derek had asked me to meet him at. It's a twenty-minute drive from campus. The parking lot sparks a sense of familiarity, but the memory doesn't seep in until I open the front door and hear a poem being recited. I came here twice before, both times with Maggie while she was dating Jeff Sievers. They had dated for nearly nine months—a record for my sister. It began when she was a junior in high school, and Jeff was one-year post graduation—our parents had lost their shit. Maggie, in true Maggie-fashion, rebelled against each order and rule they set in attempt to keep the two apart. After a couple of months, Dad insisted he come over to the house so they could meet. It began as a blatant attempt to break them up—Dad talking about lawyers and coercion, Maggie freaking out and crying, and Mom filling in all the blank spaces by talking about all of Maggie's ex-boyfriends—I never knew if that was in attempt to remind Maggie about other love interests or try to scare Jeff away—regardless, it was memorable in a worst-date-ever kind of a way, ending with Maggie slamming her door and crying, Dad slamming their bedroom door and yelling, and Jeff telling Pax, Mom, and me that he had a mentally and emotionally unavailable wasteland of a heart, filled with broken promises. He proceeded to cry, and in that moment, realization dawned upon Mom to stop fighting at keeping them apart, realizing that was only forcing them together. Over the next couple of weeks, Maggie bribed me to go with her—her girlfriends from school refused after meeting Jeff only once. We had sat in the front, drinking hot chocolates and chai tea, listening to Jeff pour what he referred to as his twisted soul, often crying during his performances.

I move farther inside, automatically sweeping over the stage and tables to see if Jeff is still here.

"Hey." A deep voice pulls my attention from the stage to Derek beside me. His blond hair is freshly cut and his caramel eyes look like the color of steel with a dark gray team sweatshirt stretched across his strong chest. He smells good, and looks even better, smiling at me.

"Hi." Air fills my lungs, surprising me. I'd been considering canceling up to the second I walked through the door, my thoughts so tangled and consumed with Lincoln that it didn't seem fair to either of us for me to come. But, Poppy encouraged me to try, reminding me that the only way to move forward is by actually trying. I'm shocked to realize Derek's presence brings a sense of calmness and ease.

His eyes shift over my face, and then he cracks a smile. "I kind of thought you weren't going to show me up."

This shocks me more than my ease with him, my eyebrows shooting high. "Oh my gosh, what time is it?" I look at my watch, which confirms I'm ten minutes early—something I'm not sure is good or bad.

His smile broadens before he dips his face. It's a shame because I'd like to study his features longer, memorize this side of him that seems so far from what Pax and the others assume about him. "No." He shakes his head, and then sucks in a deep breath and meets my stare. "I figured your brother would talk you out of coming."

His words run through a long course of reasons, stretching them for truths and snark, then for passive aggressiveness before settling on what I think is an admission. "Did you want him to?"

Derek lifts his chin. "No. Definitely not. I was really hoping you'd come, I just was trying not to hope too hard. Rejection from you seems like it would be a tough sack."

It's not the most eloquent compliment—still, my heart speeds up and my lips begin tilting upward into a smile.

"Have you been here?"

I nod. "Yeah. Kind of. It's been a long time. My sister used to date a guy who performed here."

"Yeah?"

I find myself nodding again, words suddenly farther than Maggie as I stand in place, thinking far too much about where I should place my hands—at my waist, crossed over my chest, bent? Awkwardness and nerves manage to successfully swallow me in one large gulp.

"You want to get a coffee, or some wine?"

"I'm only eighteen," I admit.

"Oh, yeah. Yeah. Sorry." He shakes his head, his eyes blinking rapidly. "So, coffee?"

"Sure. Coffee's great."

We spin at the same time, my left foot kicking his right, making us both stumble. My trip is accompanied by a small shriek which has numerous people turning our way.

"Sorry," we both say. His eyes are narrowed in the corners, a frown marring his face like he's embarrassed.

I shake my head, hoping to dispel the sudden hurdle that seems larger than the Great Wall of China, and try on another smile. "Let's start again."

He licks his lips, then breaks out a grin. He gestures forward with one hand, and we fall into line. On stage, a girl is crying, thick black lines of makeup staining her cheeks as she talks about stabbing someone's tires like they stabbed her in the back. Derek twists toward me, silent questions sitting heavy on his brow. "My roommate suggested this place when I asked where to take a smart girl on a date. He said this place would impress you. But, if this isn't your scene, we can totally go."

"Do you like mini golf?" I ask him.

"Mini golf?"

I nod.

"Depends. How badly do you hate losing?"

My smile turns genuine. "Oh, prepare your concession speech."

"I might consider it if I had any experience with losing."

Laughter hits as quickly as the awkwardness did. "Let's go."

"Just for the record, I have nothing against people crying or poems or..." he trails off as we reach the parking lot. I'm about to tell him that it's okay, that I'd prefer to spend the date doing something else, when his fingers wrap around mine, leading me to his car. It's black and sporty, the windows tinted so dark I can't see the interior. The inside of the car smells of his cologne—woodsy and fresh, the seats a soft, buttery leather. A maze of lights and buttons on the dash scream of wealth.

Nerves course through me the second he puts the car in gear and places his hand on my thigh, resting it there like this is comfortable and normal.

"Tell me about yourself." He glances at me, his eyes expressive and open—the opposite of Lincoln.

"There's not much to tell."

His smile hitches. "That lie again."

"I work at a coffee shop near my house. I volunteer at the aquarium because I want to be a cetologist when I graduate, and other than that..." I lift my shoulders. "I just like to spend time with my family and friends. What about you? I'm sure it's been quite a change to not have anyone you know here."

He nods slowly, like the realization is percolating through his thoughts and forming words. "I didn't think much of it at the time. I thought it would be fun and exciting to move so far away and be independent, and in some ways, it has. You know? Not having my parents there to fall back on has forced me to be a little smarter and more responsible, but I miss them, and I miss my friends like crazy. Football keeps me busy, though. I swear, I spend more time in the gym and on the field than I do in a classroom."

He doesn't mention a job, and I'm not surprised. Most college athletes don't have much time for work, at least not during their sport's season, and I can tell by Derek's clothes that always fit perfectly and are thicker and softer than the cotton tees most college students wear, his wide brushed nickel watch, and his car that is newer and nicer than what my parents drive, that he comes from money.

"Are you going home for the holidays?" It's not even Halloween yet, but I've been hearing this question a lot recently.

He flashes a quick smile when he turns to check his blind spot.

"Yeah. My mom's big on traditions. She's likely already planning the menu and all the details for both Thanksgiving and Christmas."

My smile is a shared awareness that he enjoys this fact. "Have you always loved football?"

Derek looks at me with those caramel brown eyes. "Since I could walk."

I want to tell him Paxton is the same way, how he's been obsessed with the game since Grandpa gave him a nerf football. How he and Grandpa have been dominating the TV and living room every weekend to watch college and pro games. How Grandpa used to come for Thursday and Monday night as well, but with getting remarried to Camilla, the visits became more intentional. But, bringing up my brother twice on a date seems like a bad omen, especially considering his and Derek's often arduous relationship.

"What started your love for the game?"

"Honestly?"

"No. Please lie to me. Tell me it was something you were cursed with. Tell me you're forced to do it to keep your family alive."

Shock hits his eyes. I see it, the question of whether I'm joking and if I'm always sarcastic and loud. I should likely assure him now that it's in my blood. "I'm kidding. Tell me."

"My dad used to play. He played in college until he tore his ACL sophomore year. He couldn't recover, unfortunately. I think it messed with his head. There's a cruel reality that occurs when you first get injured that suddenly makes you feel like glass."

"Does he worry about you getting hurt?"

He nearly touches his ear to his shoulder as he debates an answer. "Sometimes. Maybe. I think he lives vicariously through me at times, hoping I'll make it farther than he did."

I consider that kind of pressure as Derek parks in the back of the lot, away from the rest of the cars. I don't blame him. I'd be afraid to drive this car, let alone park somewhere frequented by high school and college students.

Inside is a maze of arcade games, dim lights, and a stench that is equal parts bleach and pizza. Derek leads us to the front counter, his pace a step faster than mine. I don't mind though, it prevents the silence from feeling awkward. The girl at the counter is young, her blue polo unbuttoned, revealing her cleavage. She leans forward on an elbow, her charcoal lined eyes wide and playful. If flirting were rated, she'd be the valedictorian, and stupidly, it makes me stumble and doubt everything from my ripped jeans to the barely-there lipstick I wore in an attempt to not look overdone.

Derek smiles. "Two for mini golf."

"Aren't you going to say please?" she asks, unwrapping a red sucker that she pops between her matching red lips.

He glances at me, a smile forming before he leans forward. "Pretty please?"

I consider how I'll be explaining this to Poppy later. Is he intentionally flirting with her? Did he look at me first as though to say he has plenty of options? Is he just a flirt?

I miss their next exchange until he starts laughing, but whatever was said has already ended, and Derek's lifting the two clubs off the counter.

"Do we need to get golf balls?" I ask.

He opens his opposite hand, revealing two balls, one light and the other dark blue, and I have a pretty good idea what she'd said.

I try to force the encounter out, erasing it from our short timeline, and cling to our easy conversation in the car and the warmth of his laugh, the caress of his gaze.

But, as hard as I try to focus on those easier moments, the mood of our date has changed. I'm grateful we left the coffee bar, though, because at least while playing mini golf, I have an excuse that allows the long absence of conversation.

"SHOULD WE TAKE A BREAK?" Derek asks as we wait again. It's a nice night, drawing a crowd to the small attraction. We've hit a log jam, two couples already waiting in front of us. "They have snow cones over there."

"I don't think I've had a snow cone since I was six," I tell him.

My fingers are already cold, relying heavily on me moving to remain warm, but I follow him toward the small stand, ready to relive how long my mouth will be dyed blue when I see Lincoln. He's sitting at a table, his legs kicked out, ankles crossed as he sits across from the same blonde from the party, the one who wanted to date him. She looks prettier than I'd remembered—likely for reasons filed under self-preservation and dignity. She's looking at him, laughing at something he's saying, her hand on his forearm. I can't stop memorizing each detail, the gray Henley that makes his skin look darker, the gleam in his brown eyes, the animated way he's talking that looks so easy—it feels intimate. I pull my attention away, ducking my face and speeding up, hoping there are tables on the other side so we don't have to sit near them.

"Derek." The voice makes my heart stutter and my steps stop.

Derek turns toward Lincoln, surprise lifting his brow. I assumed he'd seen him as well, but I forget that not everyone pays attention to details that rarely matter in life in the same way I spend too much time doing. "What's up?" he says, nodding.

Lincoln sits up, his attention remaining solely on Derek. "Small world."

"Sometimes too small."

My attention volleys between them, attempting to read each minute twitch and lift of the eyebrow, every spark that hits their eyes, and curves of their lips both north and southward.

"You guys want to join us?" Lincoln moves an empty tray off the table. "Come on. Take a seat."

Derek remains rooted for several seconds, making me wonder if he's waiting for me to reply, but then he moves forward, two steps ahead of me like he has been much of the night. It hasn't bothered me—until now—because now is, of course, when Lincoln turns his full attention to me, his expression a mask of indifference. He continues staring at me as I sit down, and I again spend too much time wondering where to place my arms—my sides, the table, or linked with Derek's like Lincoln's date does as she moves to sit beside him.

"Nikki, this is my teammate, Derek." Lincoln extends a hand toward Derek, and then waves toward me. "And my best friend's sister. Guys, this is Nikki."

Asshole.

My stomach feels tight, annoyance giving a roundhouse kick to what was left of my happy mood.

"Raegan," I say, reaching across the table to shake her hand.

Nikki's fingers are shockingly warm—hot even against my chilled skin, but she doesn't flinch or make a comment about my icy touch. Instead, she smiles. "It's so nice to meet you both." She looks at me, her smile widening. She has a great smile, one that reminds me of Julia Roberts. "Is it weird dating your brother's friend?"

Lincoln barks out a laugh. I cringe, regretting my suggestion to come here with each passing second. I want to tell her that seeing Lincoln with the same girl twice is stranger. That having my sister on the opposite side of the planet is strange. That it would take only an hour to reach space if we could drive vertically is strange, but I refuse to see my first date with Derek as even remotely strange. I shake my head. "Not really." I don't mean to glance at Lincoln, but my gaze skitters toward him, noting the way his eyebrows bob before he leans back in his seat. His gaze is steady and sharp, reading between the clouded lines.

"What are you guys up to this afternoon?" Derek asks, extending an arm across my shoulders, the weight so distracting I miss Lincoln's quip.

Nikki looks at Lincoln, flashing a wide smile, her side profile possibly prettier than the front. "We went to lunch at this fantastic Thai place over off of First. *So* good."

Lunch?

That's not just hanging out. That's a date. A bigger commitment than Derek and I made.

"Have you guys already played?" Derek asks, cocking his head toward the course.

"We were just waiting for it to slow down," Nikki explains, scooting closer to Lincoln when a breeze blows over us, tangling in my hair. I tuck it behind my ears.

"Yeah, we're taking a break because we got tired of waiting for people," Derek explains.

"Well, let's go together," Lincoln says.

It's a terrible idea. A guaranteed mistake.

"We were going to grab some snow cones," Derek says.

"We're not in a hurry." Lincoln leans back as though to prove his point.

Lincoln's too stubborn to accept any vague excuse, and Derek's too proud to say no.

"Why don't I get snow cones? You guys want anything?" I ask, looking at Lincoln and Nikki.

Lincoln slides out of his chair. "I'll help you." He brushes his hand against her arm. "I'll be right back."

Betrayal and anger meet, twisting painfully in my chest. I hold on to them, ignoring the less intense but more painful feeling lingering in my heart, taunting me. I nail Lincoln with a glare that demands he sit back down, but he continues toward me. I drop my attention to Derek. "Do you know what flavor you want?"

His eyes are narrowed, attempting to read the situation himself. But my clear abruptness toward Lincoln makes his lips curl and his shoulders relax. "Lime, please."

Lincoln steps beside me, his fingers brushing my lower back, adding to the reasons I wish I'd brought a jacket. I need more barriers. More space.

But there'd never be enough because he sucks up all the air and all the space.

21

My skin's memorizing the weight and warmth of his touch as we round a corner that's lined with thick shrubs that prevent me from being able to see Derek or Lincoln's date.

I tell myself it's a reflex and nothing more. That I'm not affected by him or his proximity. That it's first date jitters that have my heart racing and my thoughts colliding.

"Why do you seem so pissy? She's not a giggler. I thought you'd be impressed."

"*So* impressed," I deadpan.

"She's going to school to be a hospital manager."

"Good for her."

"She volunteers at a nursing home on the weekends."

"Last time I checked, I wasn't a checkpoint for who you date or sleep with."

"You aren't," he confirms.

His words are like a speed bump, slowing me to a stop. "Then why are you giving me her resume?" He stops as well, turning to face me before I continue. "I don't care. At all. I don't want to know how smart she is or how nice she is or anything else. I don't want to know."

"Yeah, wait until you're trying to sleep tonight. Or when you're trying to work or listen to a professor. Just wait."

I shake my head, dispelling his words and the thoughts they're orchestrating, the assumptions that will plague me for weeks and possibly months to come. "What is that supposed to mean?" My question is a demand, and when he starts to turn away from me, I grip his arm, refusing to let him ignore me.

He stops, his gaze on my fingers. I slowly release my grasp, losing the heat of his skin that radiates through each cell. "You know what it fucking means."

"You can't keep saying things like that when you act another way entirely."

He drops his head back, a sound too similar to a growl ripping through his chest.

I know him. Know that he doesn't date, that he isn't losing sleep over me—he's torturing himself because of Derek. Anyone else, and he wouldn't waste a second's thought.

It's an infuriating and hurtful realization, confirmed when his gaze flicks to the side in the direction of Derek and his own date.

I lower my shoulder and blow past him like I'm ten and on the field with Pax, my anger and determination making me feel twice my actual size. His fingers catch mine, tangling like a drift net that leaves me immobile for several seconds, my attention hooked on his, working to decipher the hard mask that is his constant. My lungs burn, filling with salt water, though I'm nowhere near the sea. It's another reminder of the dangers of being too near him.

He reaches forward, hooking his free hand around the back of my neck, each callused digit pressing tighter than the last, marring my skin with his touch in a way I know I'll be able to still see the mark in a decade, two—a lifetime.

The gap between us closes. It was his step that closed it, submerged me so deeply I can't tell the surface from the ground. Lincoln's eyes flare, and his fingers constrict further, then his eyes fall shut, and he shifts, his chest still firmly against mine. His kiss is as sure and hard as my feelings toward him, demanding and intense as our lips crush against each other, taking and giving until the lines between the two are so blurred I don't know if I'm trying to please him or myself.

"We can't," I say, dragging my lips away, though my hands dig into his biceps, contradicting my words.

He presses a hand against my lower back, grinding me closer. I feel his desire against me, stripping the boundaries and limits between us. I pull in a shaky breath, my lungs struggling to work as need builds and quickly overflows, consuming me. My body bows to meet his, desperate to feel his touch against each fraction of my body. A growl rips through his chest, vibrating against mine. I swallow it, licking each delicious groan from his lips that are still stained with the flavors of coffee. A sweet and bitter reminder of his date waiting mere feet from us.

I pull my chin back, the rough scratch of Lincoln's five o'clock shadow a tantalizing distraction, working to pull me back under.

He's a rip tide—a danger that would swallow me entirely. And I want him to. I want to dive right in and let him take all my thoughts away and bask in the delicious pain and bliss currently consuming me.

"Let's go," he orders, kissing that spot on my jaw that makes me dizzy.

I shake my head, the shore of reasoning still in view, albeit a far distance. "We can't."

"She means nothing." His hand slides over my backside. Each contour of my body works to memorize his touch as the harsh reality of his words brings a startling reminder of how bad this idea is. How I'm hurting Derek, who has been nothing but honest, and a stranger who I hate to admit seems like a nice person, and myself because I don't think I could weather the storm of Lincoln, and live to tell the story.

"I know. And neither would I after tonight."

His grip tightens, like he realizes I found a way to escape from his pull. "Don't think. Just..." his voice is husky, drunk on lust and the desire I still feel pressed against my belly. His lips fall against mine, a plea turned demand in the form of a bruising kiss. Hope tries to replace the lies in my head, but it's like waking up a few minutes before your alarm goes off in the morning—trying to buy more sleep, but the moments are already stolen by the reality you work to postpone, and therefore you remain in a restless state of torture until the beep finally starts.

I move my hands to his chest, pushing him back so I can breathe again. He obliges, but for the first time that mask he wears is gone, confusion marring his brow and lust dilating his eyes. "Don't go with him," he says.

His words wrap around my heart like a vise. A painful reality that has me crossing my arms over my chest in attempt to soothe the pain and raise some sort of defense against him. "Is that all this is? A competition from the damn field?"

"You don't know him," he says, clarifying it is exactly that.

"I hate you." I spin around, loathing my options to return to where Derek and Lincoln's date wait for us and the snack stand where the girl behind the counter is watching us with rapt attention. I place a cold hand to my cheek that's burning with anger and embarrassment.

"You just humped my leg. Clearly you don't hate me that much." His tone is filled with petulance and anger that makes me feel childish and rings on my innocence.

I stare at him, watching the mask slide back into place. "You're a coward."

He laughs. It's deep and bitter, a sound that makes me think of pain rather than joy. "You're naïve."

He's probably right. I want the good. I want the whole. I still expect the fairytale, though I learned a long time ago that glass slippers and talking mice were lies and that poisoned apples are readily available, spread by those who feel threatened by the glimmer of loss or defeat.

"I hope she gives you chlamydia."

I forget about the snacks, refusing to stay here any longer, and turn back toward Derek, wiping the back of my hand against my mouth, and when that doesn't remove the stain of his lips, I pull the neck of my shirt up and fiercely wipe the fabric against my lips until they feel raw.

Derek's sitting at the table, laughing at something Lincoln's date has said. I can't remember her name, anger blinding most of my coherent thoughts, and the guilt for that and wishing her an STD crashes into the realization I just made out with her date, building into a tidal wave that reaches my eyes.

"I'm sorry. I'm not feeling very well. I think I'm going to call a Lyft."

Derek stands, his smile slipping into a look of concern. "Are you okay? I'll drive you. Come on. Do you need anything?" His questions are like the lashes of a whip, punishing me. Lincoln appears then, rubbing salt into each freshly laid wound as his gaze travels to the spot where Derek's hand rests on my arm. I avoid his gaze, and his date, and mine, and focus on my gray Toms.

"I'm okay. I think I'm just tired."

Derek nods, his gaze traveling over my face and body as though attempting to read the lies Lincoln left across my skin. "Let's go." He sets a hand between my shoulders, his thumb sliding against me in a calming and rhythmic manner that is off beat to my heart, adding to the culmination of guilt and regret that is growing like an incoming tide. I step away from his touch, and though it makes my guilt increase, my sanity can't withstand another second of comparing his touch to Lincoln's.

"Maybe you should sit down? You look a little pale." Lincoln's date stands. Her concern and kindness creating a whole new level of self-loathing.

"I'm always pale." It's the first bit of truth I've shared with her.

"I'll take her home. She lives near me." Lincoln steps forward. I take two backward.

"I've got it taken care of." That edge has returned to Derek's voice—a sound of anger and resentment I've only heard him use with Lincoln and Pax.

"Pax would kill me if I didn't help out," Lincoln tells him.

My hate for Lincoln increases as I stare at him, willing him to acknowledge me though he hasn't since he came back. I'd know because I've always felt his attention—it's like he's the moon to my tide, pushing and pulling. Right now, the only thing I need and want is space from him, and he's trying to manipulate the situation to prevent exactly that.

"Nikki, I'll take you home first, and then I can drop her off." Lincoln returns to using pronouns to refer to me.

"I'll be fine." I take one more step back, and Lincoln jerks his head, his eyes hitting me like a force that nearly knocks me off my feet because that mask is slipping again, anger and fear making his brown eyes so dark it's difficult to see his pupils.

Fear?

Is he afraid to lose?

"Yeah. We're good." Derek's hand reconnects with my side, gently tugging me to follow him.

"I actually live over near campus. Are you heading that way?" Nikki steps forward, reading the situation and navigating it far better than I currently am. She smiles at Derek. When she smiles, she's at least an eleven.

Derek glances at me, trying to read my face and what I want him to say. Unfortunately, we don't know each other well enough for this. Only Poppy and I do, and Poppy would know that even if my eyes were pleading with her to do it, my heart is far too fragile to manage, and she'd take control. It's what she does. "You're okay with this?" he asks finally.

"Maybe we just stay. Maybe I just need some water?"

"I'll get her home and remind her to call you," Lincoln says. He steps closer to Nikki. I watch as the two embrace, noting his hands remain above her waist and are too limp and loose to consider the moment intimate, yet she's holding onto him like she's worried she's lost a piece of him. It's close enough to imprint the shadow of her perfect body to his.

I turn, denying myself the verification whether they kiss or not. "Thanks for tonight," I tell Derek. "I'm really sorry it's ending like this. I'd like to do it again. Well ... not this part. But, going out."

He smiles, his caramel eyes relaxed and kind. It's shocking how easily I can read him and understand so many of his motives when I've known Lincoln for three years and feel like it's a guessing game each time I look at him.

"I'm holding you to it," he says. His fingers tangle with mine, and he pulls me closer, wrapping his arms around my shoulders. I take a long breath of his cologne that reminds me of the forest—of earthiness and spice and regret for having suggested we come here tonight.

"Let's go, Lawson," Lincoln clips.

If I didn't already feel childish and immature, that comment would have done it.

Vindication burns in my veins, an impulse that often leads Maggie, and one that Pax seems to have missed, leaving me somewhere in the middle. I press my hands to either side of Derek's face and lean closer, kissing him on the mouth. His unshaven chin is rough and sharp, scratching my skin. It takes him less than a second to register I'm kissing him and even less to kiss me back, his lips closed in a polite and sweet first-date kiss that under normal circumstances would be sure to leave my mind wandering down paths wondering what kind of kisser he is.

I pull back, falling to my heels and turning to face Lincoln and Nikki, my smile as brazen as my kiss. "It was really nice meeting you, Nikki. Sorry for ruining your date."

Her smile is kind, but I can see the reservation in her eyes, the one that's not sure if she wants to trust me.

She shouldn't. Even I don't trust me.

"It was nice meeting you, too. I hope you feel better."

Lincoln's jaw looks like steel, clenched as he stares at me, his onyx eyes void of emotion and anything else I briefly search for. He steps forward, not addressing anyone as he places his hand at my hip, his thumb brushing my side as his fingers wrap around my back. If his grip were tight, it might seem possessive, but if I were to move too quickly or pause, I know his hand would easily fall. I test the theory after just a few seconds, slowing my steps to allow someone to pass. Lincoln's hand falls to his side. He tilts his head, glancing at me as he passes. I follow him through the arcade and out to the parking lot, where he leads us to his black truck, stopping at the passenger door which he opens, and turns to face me.

I think too hard about each of my movements, feeling like a newborn giraffe as I climb into the cold cab of the truck. Lincoln closes the door and walks around the hood, getting into the driver's side. Unease intensifies the cold seeping from the leather seats through my jeans and thin shirt.

Lincoln slams his driver's side door and starts the engine. He glances in his mirror and turns to look behind him before backing up. I've never been in his truck, never rode anywhere with him. My time alone with Lincoln has been minimal. But if this makes him uncomfortable, he doesn't say, and it certainly doesn't show as he keeps his right hand firmly on the steering wheel, his gaze on the windshield.

I try to pretend this is easy. A simple ride from a friend—my brother's friend, and that this isn't strange. That I didn't stick my tongue down his throat and feel his hard on. That I didn't just widen my chances of going to hell by cheating on my date and his.

We slow at a red light, and I think he's going to say something or maybe reach forward and turn on the radio—something to fill this silence that is eating at me and making me replay this evening and my mistakes on a constant loop. I wish he'd turn on the heat at the very least. It would provide only a small reprieve of sound, and more importantly, some warmth. It's so cold, my muscles are beginning to ache, yet I can't ask him if I can turn it on. I can't form words, though my thoughts are drowning with millions of words—questions and accusations.

Silence spreads.

My annoyance builds. I don't know why I kissed him. Why I paused, and why I reacted to him.

Finally, the light turns green, and my turmoil of thoughts slow as Lincoln slams his foot against the gas pedal.

We go three blocks, and then he jerks the wheel, turning down a side street, where he puts the truck into park and turns to face me, a scowl etched across his face. "You're infuriating."

I pull my head back with the extra shot of confusion he's just poured down my throat.

"*I'm* infuriating?"

"You're not going to make me jealous," he warns.

"I wasn't trying to." I wasn't. I was trying to tell him our kiss was a mistake and prove immunity toward him—something I've been trying to convince myself of for three years.

"Bullshit." He spits the word, his head snapping forward. There's so much intensity as he calls my bluff.

My heart rattles so loud in my chest that my ribs begin to ache. There are days and moments where my barometer of truth and fantasy become so blurred it's difficult to decipher the lies. "It was a mistake," I tell him. "I'm not this girl. I don't do this."

"It was a kiss. It's not like you were giving me head."

I cringe at his harsh crudeness. His views of sex and other intimate acts are so callous—detached.

"And you would have been fine if your date had been making out with Derek?"

"Why should I care?"

I nearly choke, my scoff and bitter laughter tripping as they race to get out first. "Because she was your *date*. There's an implied sense of commitment when one agrees to go out with another."

"Then what's your excuse?"

The rattling in my chest becomes a banging as three years of desire are met with the reality of tonight and the consequences that come with my actions.

"Stop it," he grinds out the words, his voice low and quiet.

My gaze flits up to meet his, the cab of the truck so dark with shadows, it's difficult to see if his mask is in place.

"You're filtering yourself," he says. "Stop it. Just be real with me."

"I don't know how to." My admission seems to float through the air, echoing in the small space so long I regret the words more than kissing him, and even more, I regret putting myself in this position again. I could have insisted I ride with Derek—I'm positive we're both aware of this fact, however, the realization that I'm here speaks louder.

Lincoln's shoulders rise, and he shifts, resuming to sit forward. He pulls out with a swift jerk that makes the tires screech with protest, leaving several shards of my heart freshly stained on the asphalt.

22

When Lincoln pulls up to the house, my relief dies a quick and painful death at the sight of Paxton's car in the driveway.

"Shit," I mutter, reaching for the door handle. The cold air instantly seeps through my tee, and as my feet meet the driveway, losing the small bit of warmth Lincoln's truck offered—after twenty minutes of painfully recalling each moment of the past hour—I realize that I left my car at the coffee and wine bar. I blame my idiocy on that kiss that clearly stole more than just my pride.

"Raegan!" My name is screamed from the front door where light spills out onto the darkened front yard, followed closely by a scream of excitement that has me forgetting my car and the mistakes I've made as I sprint toward the person I've missed the most over the past two years: Maggie.

We collide in a tangle of limbs and giggles. She's hopping up and down. Like me, sometimes her emotions are so elevated she can't keep them in—foot stomping and bouncing are two of the multiple ways it finds a release.

Her hair smells different, earthier and less sweet, and it's longer. She's also thinner, and as I pull back to look at her, I realize she's added a stud to her nose and upper lip, and a collage of tattoos to her right arm. Tears cloud my vision as I pull her close, hugging her again, regretting that I wasn't there for each of these moments and memories and that she hasn't been here for mine.

When we separate again, it's her pulling away, her eyes scanning over me several times, silently taking an inventory of the changes the past two years have brought me. She shakes her head slowly, releasing me only to wipe her wet eyes before hugging me again. "I've missed you so damn much," she says, stroking the back of my head. "So damn much."

"I didn't know you were coming home."

"Neither did I," she says, laughing. "They asked me to take a new assignment and allowed me to come home for the week."

"The week?" It's impossible to hide my disappointment. Though I wasn't expecting to see her for another year, the idea of her leaving in a matter of days feels more painful than waiting the expected duration.

"Mags, you remember Lincoln?" Pax asks from behind me.

Maggie wraps an arm securely around my waist, tethering me to her as we shift to face him. Lincoln's truck is parked, and he's standing next to Pax, his gaze a contradiction to his smile. "Hey," Maggie's voice sounds more like mom than I'd remembered as her arm slips from me and moves forward to hug him.

"You okay?" Pax asks, taking a step closer to me, toeing a loose piece of gravel on the driveway.

"Yeah." I cross my arms over my chest as a gust of wind delivers a chilling blast. "Today was just so busy. I didn't get a chance to eat. I started to feel kind of light-headed."

"Well, then you're going to be glad to hear that Dad made fried chicken."

"Tell me there's mashed potatoes."

Pax grins. "I think he gave up on trying alternative sides after you boycotted dinner last time."

"He served French fries and beans with fried chicken!"

Pax laughs. "And mom made the gravy."

"Sold!"

"You wanna stick around?" Pax turns back to Lincoln, who's invested in a conversation of surface topics with Maggie.

"Yes. You want to stay for this," Maggie tells him. "If it's meatloaf or any seafood dish, you always say no, but fried chicken is a definite yes."

Lincoln's eyes land on me, his reluctance clear even in the darkness.

"Come on," Pax says, hitting him with an elbow before moving toward the house. "I'm freezing my nuts off out here."

Lincoln's gait is steady and smooth, any uncertainty gone as he walks beside Maggie, both of them pausing when they near me. Maggie hooks her arm around my neck. "I want to hear everything. God, you look so old. It seems like I just left, and you were sixteen. You look like a woman now. A freaking hot ass woman." Her arm constricts, tugging me closer. "How are the whales?"

We hit the living room, and a shiver runs down my spine as the heat slowly runs over me. "It's been a tough year," I tell her. "The pods are barely coming into the Sound. We haven't seen them in several weeks."

"What's happening?" she asks.

"Pollution, over-fishing, tourism ... same stuff, new day."

Maggie frowns. "I'm sorry." Sincerity coats her voice, knowing how far my love for the animals stretches.

"Me too."

"Is there anything that can be done?"

"We're trying. You know how hard it is to enforce laws that get little attention. And when so few feel the impact of what's happening, it's hard for people to care or even consider how it's impacting a species they know little about."

"Isn't that the truth," she says.

"Speaking of which, I need to call Greta and see if she can get one of the other volunteers to go out. I'm scheduled to go out in the morning."

"You are?" Maggie's eyes shine with anticipation. "Do you think there's any chance I could come?"

I blink back my surprise. "Would you want to?"

"Hell yes. You wouldn't believe how much I've missed the ocean. I didn't realize how hard it would be to be landlocked. I would love to get out and see the ocean."

"It's going to be cold," I warn her.

She grins. "I could use a little of that, too."

"You're taking her whale watching?" Pax asks.

"Be jealous," Maggie teases.

"How come you never offer me to go out?"

"Well, you know, because it's my job, not a tourist attraction, and also the fact you pretty much live at the gym."

"What if we all went out? We can go after you get off. Rent a boat or something?" Pax suggests.

"Did you win the lottery while I was gone?" Maggie asks.

Pax ignores her, looking at me. He's listened just enough to watch the noose dangle in front of me. "Technically, I can probably swing it, but if I ask, you guys have to be committed. I don't want to ask for this favor, and then you guys don't show up."

Pax draws a large 'X' over his chest. "Swear."

"You guys are going to be so bored," I warn them as Mom comes in from the kitchen, wiping her hands on a dish towel.

"I thought I heard you guys." Her eyes stay on Maggie. I can't imagine how she's feeling right now. I was worried she was going to have a nervous breakdown in the weeks following Maggie leaving. The idea of going through that again makes my stomach churn.

"I invited Lincoln to join us," Pax says.

Mom finally shifts her gaze, taking in the rest of us, a permanent smile on her face. "Good. Good," she says, closing the gap between us and placing a hand in Maggie's. Come to the kitchen, guys. I'll pour some wine."

"I'm serious about the boat," he says to my back as I follow close behind Mom, wishing I could hide in the folds of her skirt like I would as a kid. "We have an early practice tomorrow. I can be ready by ten." He looks at Lincoln. "You should come, man."

My heart thumps, rattling the cage that works to keep it in place. The scents of thyme and fried chicken distract me from my thoughts for several seconds, my mouth watering, and my coldness a distant memory.

"Where are you going?" Mom asks.

"Rae's taking us out on a boat tomorrow," Maggie tells her. "Did you know she could do that?"

Dad flips a piece of chicken, grease popping like a firecracker that has him taking a step back. "She had to get her license to drive the boats," he says. "It's a nice perk since she volunteers so many hours there."

"But, it's about to all pay off," Mom practically sings the words.

"What? Are they going to hire you?" Maggie's eyes land on me, bright with enthusiasm.

"Hopefully in January," I tell her.

"That's awesome! You'll have your degree and the experience. You're going to be able to transfer anywhere," she says.

Pride spreads from one ear to the other as Mom smiles at me. "You should go." She looks at Lincoln. "Rae knows the Sound better than any guide."

I don't look at him. Doing so might be misconstrued that I care about his decision, and I don't care, unless his current decision includes leaving, breaking whatever is going on with Nikki off, and plans to steal a microphone and belt the lyrics to Frankie Valli's 'Can't Take My Eyes Off You' Heath Ledger style.

"Where have you been? I thought you had today off work?" Dad asks as I round the island and grab a glass to fill from the tap.

"I did." I take a drink, feeling the weight of Lincoln's gaze on my shoulders. He's listening. I know he is, and I hate him a little more for it. "I went and played miniature golf with Derek."

Paxton's attention snaps to me. "What?"

Maggie pulls her head back, a slow smile climbing as she grabs a filled glass of wine and takes a front row seat.

"You can't date my teammates," Pax says.

"It's not your decision," I tell him.

"Dad, tell her she can't date a football player." Paxton turns his attention to Dad, looking for a comrade.

"I have to side with Paxton on this one," Dad says.

"Why would you?" Mom asks.

"That's incredibly sexist of you, Dad," Maggie adds.

"No. It's reasonable. Dad *knows*." Paxton throws a hand out toward Dad.

"Knows what?" I cry.

"Yeah, Dad, what do you know that we don't?" Maggie takes a measured sip, her claws out, ready to battle. It brings me in a full circle, back to when she dated Jeff who performed at the coffee shop, and he tried to forbid her from dating him.

"He's older. More experienced. That's all I'm saying," Dad raises his hands, palms out.

"How would you know? Have you asked him how many sexual partners he's had?"

Dad winces at Maggie's directness.

"You guys are all overreacting," Mom chimes in. "It was one date, and they played mini golf. I don't think we need to get all excited just yet. Let her find out if she even likes the guy."

"Why would she go on a date with him if she didn't like him?" Dad asks, something far too similar to fear rounding his eyes as they flash my way, and I can read the silent dread on his expression, wondering if I'm having sex with Derek.

I glare at Pax, silently demanding he stop the conversation now.

"There's only one thing he wants from you, and you know it." Pax points a finger at me, escalating the already tense situation.

"Good conversation? Intellect? Humor?" I list off.

"What do we know about this guy?" Dad asks, looking at Mom.

I clamp a hand over my eyes and tip my head back, growling with frustration. "Conversation over."

"Yeah, this isn't going anywhere good," Maggie says. "At this point, Pax and Dad are going to have stockings filled with prunes because they're clearly full of shit."

Mom raises her glass in a toast. "Prunes!" Maggie giggles, raising her glass to the same toast.

Pax huffs out a sigh, retreat in his shoulders but missing from his eyes that remain on me. "Outside," he says.

Lincoln's eyebrows shoot high on his forehead, the surprise catching my attention.

Pax moves toward the back door a few feet behind him.

"You should let him just go out there and cool off," Maggie says. "He'll get over it. Besides, I want to hear who Derek is."

Three years ago, I likely would have done exactly as she's suggesting, but since Maggie left, my relationship with Pax has grown. We've relied on each other more and more in her absence. "I'll be right back." I flip on the outside lights and close the door behind me, regretting again that I don't have a sweatshirt.

"I know you don't want to hear this," Pax launches into it right away, fists stamped on his hips. "But you don't know this guy."

"Neither do you."

"Is that the excuse he gave you?"

"Pax," I draw out his name, my exhaustion with the conversation so far past overdone that I'm ready to scream. I rub my hands over my arms, trying to prevent myself from becoming a human popsicle. "You love half the guys on the team, and we both know you wouldn't want me dating any of them. This has nothing to do with knowing Derek or liking him, it has to do with me getting involved with your football family. And I respect that. I get that. Trust me. I don't want to step on your toes or get in the way, and I won't. Trust me."

He drops his head back. "If he hurts you, I won't be able to play with him anymore. I won't be able to keep my emotions off the field."

"Why are you assuming he'll hurt me?" The question is completely uncensored. A reaction caused by my decisions from tonight rather than a cognizant thought. "I told you, Pax. I just want to have some fun this year. I'm not looking for anything serious. He's not going to break my heart."

He scrubs his hand over his cropped hair. "This is a terrible idea."

"Probably."

He tips his head down, caught off guard by my words.

"Kidding," I say, smiling when he looks at me for clarification.

He stalks toward me, locking me in a headlock. "I'll break his legs if he dicks around with you."

"I'll let him know."

"Good. You should."

"I will." I push my elbow into his side. "But we need to go inside. It's freezing."

"You know you can call me anytime, anywhere."

"I could. But you'd ask questions."

He balks, and I laugh, reaching for the door.

"Why'd he take you out in the middle of the day?" Pax asks as we step into the warm kitchen, my muscles tightly bunched as I slowly thaw. "Who does that?"

My gaze swings to Lincoln, wondering what he told Pax. He stares back at me, and though I don't know him well enough to understand his motives, I'm positive his look screams of defiance.

"I suggested it," I tell Pax. "I thought it would make it easier to talk and get to know each other."

"See?" Mom says. "You guys have nothing to worry about. This is Raegan we're talking about here. She knows what she's doing." She sets a large bowl of gravy on the table with a ladle—my family has never bothered with a gravy boat because we each could eat the contents of one. The mashed potatoes are still in the pot the potatoes boiled in, and the crescent rolls from a package are cooling on a cookie tray in the center of the table.

Maggie pulls out the chair beside her—my chair. Though in the past three years, hers is periodically filled by Mom. "How was your date?" she asks. "He's cute."

"Who?" I ask, sliding my chair closer to the table.

"Derek. Mom told me his name, so I Googled him. He has a baby face," she continues as Dad passes her a plate stacked high with fried chicken, the scent making my stomach rumble so intensely I feel nauseated. "But his eyes look kind."

"We actually started at that coffee house we used to go to," I tell her, taking second helpings of chicken because I already know I'm going to be eating thirds tonight.

"Which coffee house?"

"The one Jeff performed at."

"Jeff?" Pax asks, barking out a laugh. "God, that guy was a joke."

"Careful," I warn him. "She hasn't met your girlfriend yet."

Maggie leans back. "But, I've heard stories."

Pax eyes me, and I raise both hands. "I only told her about last Christmas when she got drunk on Dad's eggnog and puked on the old recliner."

Mom covers her mouth, obviously reliving the moment. Maggie shakes her head, her lips pressed into a thin line. "You guys better be giving Pax all the dating advice you used to shovel out to me." She eyes Mom and Dad. "Because this girl sounds awful."

"That chair was so ugly. That was the only redeeming factor," I say.

"It was Rascal's chair," Mom says.

"Rascal passed away when I was thirteen," Maggie says.

"But he was such a great cat," Mom insists.

"We're going to have to sign you up for hoarders eventually, aren't we?" Pax asks.

I shake my head. "No. We just keep inviting your girlfriend over. She's gotten rid of that chair, the rug in the hallway, the vase you made in kindergarten—"

"We get it," Pax interrupts my half-completed list.

Lincoln laughs, the sound surprisingly easy and comfortable, fitting in almost too well. "Wait. How did I not hear about this? She got that wasted?"

"She claims she had the flu, but she couldn't even walk in a straight line," Dad says, adding a pile of corn to his plate. Maggie is too busy listening, not filling her plate and passing the food my way.

"We had no idea," Mom says. "She had disappeared, and Cal and I"—she glances at my dad as if clarifying the details—"we assumed she and Pax were fighting or something, and then suddenly she walked into the living room, holding an empty pitcher, and made it three steps before defiling Rascal's chair."

"You're selling her a little short. It was at least ten steps," Dad says.

I nod. "She spilled the remains of her eggnog on Poppy before she reached the chair."

Lincoln groans. "That's horrible, man." He looks at Pax. I already know Lincoln doesn't care for her. I overheard them discussing her this summer when Lincoln went camping with us: five days of me trying to avoid my reflection at all cost because I didn't want to have any memories of my messy buns, sports bras, and makeup-free appearance knowing Lincoln was seeing me.

"Okay, we will definitely come back to this topic, but for now, tell us about the date while it's still fresh." Maggie pauses, her hand gripping the large spoon in the mashed potatoes. "Why'd you want to go back to the coffee house? Has it changed? God, tell me it's gotten better, and that *he* wasn't there."

A grin pulls at my cheeks. "Derek actually suggested it, and I didn't remember the name of it until I got there. I was experiencing PTSD all the way to the front door until I could confirm Jeff wasn't there."

Maggie laughs. "I bet you were. He loved telling you his problems. 'She has an old soul. She understands me.'" Maggie does a terrible impression of Jeff, with a thick gypsy accent that he never spoke with. It doesn't matter, we're all laughing just the same.

"Do people still read poetry and sing?" she asks.

I nod, grabbing a crescent roll because she's taking too long with perfecting her little dome of potatoes, and I'm ready to start eating off her plate. I chew a large bite and take another.

"I bet that was weird. Derek doesn't perform though, does he?" Maggie lifts her brows.

I shake my head, swallowing the crumbs of my roll. "He said his roommate told him about it." I shrug. "It might be cool, I've just been scarred for life and couldn't stay there."

"Plus, you're a really bad liar," Maggie adds.

"Literally the worst," Pax says.

"Which is why you guys should be glad I like you."

Pax's laughter is instant and loud, a sound that pulls my lips northward.

"So, is he nice? Funny? Smart?"

Talking about him in front of Lincoln makes my stomach churn and temporarily feel full. "I don't really know him well enough to say," I tell her honestly. "He seems nice enough."

Maggie flinches. "Nice enough?"

"He's nice," I clarify. "And he's smart. He's majoring in business, so dad probably knows more than me at this point. But, yeah."

"So, how did you guys end up together if you were on a date with Derek?" Maggie asks, looking from me to Lincoln, her gaze remaining on him, directing the question thankfully away from me.

"I was actually there with a friend," he says.

"What a small world," Maggie says.

"Who were you with?" Pax asks.

"Nikki." Lincoln looks at his filled plate and lifts his fork.

Paxton's surprise is evident as he pulls his chin back, his eyes growing round. "Nikki?"

Lincoln chews the bite of mashed potatoes he'd forked up, lifting his gaze so slowly I forget that I'm starving. Coffee-colored eyes dance between mine, thoughts processing so fast I can't catch any one of them. "She called and asked to hang out."

Pax cuts a bite of fried chicken. "Yeah? You're going to start hanging out again?"

Lincoln tears his eyes from mine as he grips his glass of water, taking a long drink before he shrugs. "I don't know, yet."

23

With Maggie being home, I can't use a recycled excuse to leave the table early, but her two-year absence is becoming more strikingly obvious as she looks to each of us when someone laughs at an inside joke or gives an update on a situation. It makes the section of my heart sequestered to sisterhood and the knowledge Maggie will be my best friend for life to ache with guilt and a fresh realization about how much she's missed and how impossible it is to keep her apprised of so many things that don't seem like a big deal until I look back and realize they've been an integral part of our lives.

"Okay, Pax. Back to your girlfriend. Let's air this dirty laundry." Maggie flexes her fingers and leans back before pushing her emptied dinner plate away. Dinner came to an end slowly, everyone enjoying seconds and some of us thirds, sipping our drinks slowly, and joining in the conversation to stretch the meal. I was concerned Derek would be upset that I abruptly ended our date and left with Lincoln, and now, I can't even care about it.

Tiredness sits at the back of my thoughts, reminding me I've been up since before 6 a.m. every day this week and falling into bed after midnight. While Pax dodges questions about his failing love life, I consider what time I need to wake up to be at the docks on time and remember then that my car is still at the coffee house I met Derek at. I scrub a hand over my forehead, checking what time it is. I might be able to get Poppy to give me a ride so I don't interrupt my parents from getting their time with Maggie. I try to recall her schedule and if she told me she had plans tonight.

Eyes burn into me, breaking my thoughts and the dread of knowing Poppy is going to give me the third degree for not calling her as soon as my date ended, and will ask a million questions that will lead to my kiss with Lincoln, and that is going to be really difficult to dissect with her tonight when each of my emotions feels like it's been weathered between kissing Lincoln, kissing Derek, and Maggie's surprise visit home. Lincoln's staring at me, silent questions sitting heavy on his lowered brow. The brown of his eyes appears both lighter and grayer with the gray Henley he's wearing, a replica to the thick cloud cover that is constantly seen hanging low on Mt. Rainier, often blocking her from view entirely.

I look away.

"I need to call Poppy. I'm going to see if she can give me a ride to my car."

Dad leans back. "One of us can take you."

"No. You guys should visit. It won't take long."

"I can take you. I've already had this conversation a hundred times more than I wanted to." Lincoln pushes his chair back, not waiting for my answer.

Bossy, pain in my ass.

"That's okay," I start, searching for an excuse for him to stay behind as well that doesn't include the massive web of thoughts he's procured and tangled.

"We'll be back," he tells my family, and surprisingly, none of them say anything. Not even Paxton, who I thought would give at least a warning speech or inquiring stare.

"Thanks," I say quietly. "I need to grab a sweatshirt," I tell him. "I'll meet you in the living room."

He stares at me too long. I know he's thinking something, but I don't look close enough to try and decipher his thoughts. It's a risk I can't afford right now, my pride bruised, and my emotions battered as they pull in opposing directions.

I round the corner of my room, flip on the light, and pull open my closet.

"Pink. Interesting."

My heart launches into my throat at the sound of Lincoln's voice catching me off guard.

"What are you doing?"

"I didn't picture the pink bed. I imagined blue." He peers around at my light gray walls, his gaze leaping across each heart I cut from copies of my favorite novels and strung across my room.

I lift a brow. "You spend a lot of time picturing my bedroom?"

A slow grin reveals his straight, white teeth. The ones that bruised my collarbone and were erased by the gentle swipe of his tongue. I've thought of him doing the same dance of pain and pleasure to the rest of my body too many times. "You didn't pick it out," he says it like a fact. Like he knows me.

"I did," I lie.

His eyes cut to me, and then he sags against my wall. The gesture too easy and comfortable. He makes my entire room look drab in comparison. "Bullshit."

"How would you know?"

"Are you ready, yet?"

"Why do you do that?"

"Do what?"

His question makes my temper spike. He knows what, and his coy smirk confirms that he's baiting me. I grab a sweatshirt Maggie sent me from Prague. It's baggy and warm, dark green with the country's name printed across the front of the hoodie. I tug it over my head and discover Lincoln six steps closer to me—and only one away—as I pull the fabric clear of my face. My heart responds immediately, jumping around like a fish who's been pulled out of the comfort and security of the water.

With him standing so close, I search his face for clues—for understanding of what he's doing. I try to recall if it had been me who ended our kiss or him because although I remember it being me, the pangs in my chest make it feel like it was him. Why is that? Why does it feel like he rejected me?

"What?" he asks, his voice a quiet rumble as he searches my face in return.

"Nothing," I answer too fast, my voice too high, making it sound like a lie to even my own ears.

"Is this because of Pax or because of Derek?" he asks.

This.

The situation is so much more than a *this*.

"I don't know. Is this because of Pax or Derek?" I ask him, reversing the question, because he's never shown interest in me until now—until that first party when Derek and I were talking.

"You think I'm jealous?" He's so close, his breath skates across my face, warm on my cheeks and cool on my lips.

"I know you don't like him."

"The only way he fits into our situation is that I refuse to take his scraps."

"You keep saying it's not a competition, but all your words and actions say the opposite."

His jaw tics. I've exposed a nerve, or maybe I've struck it. It's wrong, but it makes me feel almost relieved that he's feeling conflicted, considering my heart is feeling so battered at the moment.

"It's your move," he tells me, then turns, retreating out of my room and taking every ounce of air with him.

I stand there, stunned, hating that he's already out of view. I've been obsessed with all things Lincoln for three years, and I have no idea how it's turned into this situation where I can't even trust myself.

I pull my hair from my sweatshirt and leave the confines of my room, searching for air again, and I find it in the living room. Lincoln's checking his phone, bringing out more of my insecurities with the realization there's a ninety percent chance that whatever message he's received is from a girl—*another* girl. He looks up as I approach, careful to leave a wide gap between us for my own sake and so I don't muddy the waters further. I need to analyze every second of the past few hours with Poppy to gain a little perspective.

I follow him outside where the cold air takes my breath away, a sharp wind cutting across my face and what's exposed of my neck. I shudder, passing the grass that's fading from green to tawny as the sun continues to sink into the Pacific a little earlier each day. Dad calls this false winter, a period of cold weather before it warms up again and then turns to fall. Being that our weather changes faster than Paxton's girlfriend's mood, he's right, but only because the weather is unpredictable at best.

Lincoln doesn't open my door. I should be relieved, but I'm not. It leaves a bitter taste where chivalry had been. If it weren't for the whole bit of not having rights, I think I'd prefer crawling back in time to 1810, back to the Early Romantic Period, when romance was popular and wide spread. When men aspired to sweep women off their feet with grand gestures and whispered nothings that meant everything.

Instead, I'm stuck between a brooding football player who wants to conditionally stick his tongue down my throat, and a football player who maybe wants to stick his tongue down my throat solely because my brother hates him.

Critics are right: romance is dead.

Lincoln starts the truck and turns the heat to auto, turning the temperature up to seventy-five before backing out of the driveway. I glance across at him, allowing the darkness to grant me some anonymity.

He doesn't turn to look at me.

"Are you mad at me?" I ask as we near campus.

His eyes cut to mine, shining off a set of headlights going the opposite direction. "I'm not mad at you. I'm pissed at the situation."

"What *is* the situation?"

He slows at a stop sign, his gaze finding mine again. "I don't fucking know."

That makes two of us.

"Did you kiss me today because I was with Derek?"

We've been paused for several seconds, and no cars are in sight, but Lincoln continues idling. "You're too young," he says. "You're not even nineteen."

"You're only twenty-one."

His jaw crooks open, but he doesn't say anything.

"Now who's censoring their words?"

"You're a young eighteen."

"Are you seriously calling me immature right now?" I fold my arms over my chest, anger pooling in my veins, making me feel too warm.

"No. You have more of your life figured out than most thirty-year-old's. But, how many guys have you dated? How many guys have you had *sex* with?"

"Why is that relevant?"

"Because I don't want to be the guy who breaks your heart."

This creates rule ten: never date someone who already sees the end. And, Lincoln Beckett already assumes we'll fail.

"Are you really that full of yourself? You're making massive assumptions right now. I told you, I want to date around this year. No commitments."

"Yet, you're here with me. Again."

"Because you made a scene and practically forced Derek to take your date home."

"It wasn't a date," he says.

"It looked like a date."

"You could have said no." He calls me out, avoiding the proverbial finger I've pointed squarely at him, knowing just as I had assumed that if I really hadn't wanted to go with him, I could have said as much.

"You weren't exactly making it easy." It's a weak excuse, but there's some truth behind it because I've seen Lincoln's stubbornness at work. Witnessed his dedication when the doctors told him his shoulder would take twelve weeks to heal, and he shaved it down to nine. Proof sits on our fridge under a penguin magnet I brought home from the aquarium that has his name on the Dean's List. Mom was so proud, she made him his favorite dinner and gave him three boxes of Cocoa Pebbles—his favorite cereal—and knitted him a blanket. It was a big deal because Mom doesn't knit. She learned how to when Paxton was little, saying she wanted to make him and Maggie blankets like her mom had done when she was little. Turned out, my mom doesn't have the patience to knit, which is why the blanket she eventually made me when I was ten was the size of a baby blanket. It was her way of adding him to the family.

He drops his chin back and releases a low, rumbling growl of frustration.

"What?" Attitude makes my question flippant. He knows damn well he didn't make things easy, regardless of how I could have drug on the scene and flipped him the bird and left with Derek.

Lincoln looks at me, his eyes looking black in the darkness of the cab. "All I can think about is kissing you again. I want to taste you and battle your fucking independence until you realize you want to kiss me, too. I want to drag my tongue across you until you can't remember your own name, let alone his." He stares at me, his lips parted as his breaths grow heavier. "I want to consume you."

24

My breath hitches as my heart goes three times faster than comfortable. Beating to a new rhythm, one he just promised.

Consume me.
Consume me.
Consume me.

"Don't look at me like that," he warns.

"Like what?" My words are hushed, my lungs forgetting how to breathe, while my heart hammers, pumping something foreign through my bloodstream that makes each of my limbs feel lighter and my head to swim with heat, desire, and a three-year longing to color in the remainder of the picture and find out where this may lead.

"Like you want me."

I grasp for reason, for sense, for anything that might make stopping myself seem reasonable or right.

"Raegan." My name's a whisper on his lips, one that seemingly grows wings and flies right into my heart where it flutters chaotically, breaking inhibitions and fears until I'm releasing my seat belt and leaning across the middle console, watching his seat belt retract as he reaches for me. His fingers are warm and rough as they slide across my cheek, tangling in my hair. His lips capture mine, his teeth grazing my bottom lip before his tongue swipes the same path. The knowledge that he wants me makes me feel brave, brazen as I clumsily shift to move closer to him, wanting to feel him against me, desperate to feel him *everywhere*.

Lincoln palms my ass with one hand, pulling me toward him, encouraging me. I straddle his waist, releasing a soft moan as the feeling of him settles against me, the hard planes of muscle and bone nearly indecipherable. He swallows the sound, his fingers flexing painfully into my flesh, demanding me to get closer until I feel him against each part of me—places I don't consider needing it like my thighs and calves, my shoulders, even the sides of my knees are rejoicing as his warmth soaks into me. He tips his head back, grinding his hips against my denim covered entrance, our lips parting a short space before his flutter back over mine, the pressure light and gentle—a contrast to his hard length. His fingers release my backside, clasping the other side of my face, pulling me closer to him as he devours my mouth. I part my lips and greedily run my tongue along his. We're both too high on each other to be gentle and slow, each kiss and swipe of our tongues a scorching translation of our desires. I shift my hips lower and tilt my head in an attempt to kiss every last crevice of his mouth. He groans, fisting my hair and tugging just enough to enunciate the sliver separating pain and pleasure. I'm drifting—lost in ecstasy and denial—and his teeth graze my bottom lip, sucking it into his mouth and making my body vibrate in ways I didn't know were possible. Every bit of me feels alive and hyperaware as I focus on the connection points between Lincoln and me: his palm pressed against my jaw, the other back firmly on my ass. The fast beat of his heart I feel through the hard planes of his chest, the width of his strong thighs beneath me. I feel him everywhere, and yet I yearn to feel more of him. To shed the layers between us and lose myself in him.

A fist rakes the driver's side window, making me jump. Lincoln pulls his face back, his hands gripping me tighter. The cab is highlighted—a fact it seems we both should have realized. We both turn to find an older man with graying hair and a blue and green Seattle Seahawks baseball cap, a red coat wrapped around his shoulders. "Everything okay?" he asks through the closed window. His smirk confirms that he knows what he just interrupted. "You kids should probably get out of the middle of the road." He makes a wide gesture to the four-way stop. "I watched three cars already pass you." He nods at us. "She's too pretty to be road-kill." He walks away without another word, the slam of his car door echoes softly through the silence of Lincoln's cab where suddenly everything seems more pronounced—every breath, every fall of our chests, every second that passes. Maybe it's because we both know we should be asking questions and clarifying intentions. Perhaps it's because the ugly and bitter side of my heart that always fears rejection is whispering all the reasons this won't ever last.

I pull back, and he doesn't stop me. Beneath his thin Henley, the stacks of muscles in his shoulders fall as he licks his lips that are still red and swollen from kissing me and making promises I wish I could forget.

I wonder if he can taste me like I still taste him? The lingering taste of thyme and rosemary and the sweetness of honey that he'd poured on his dinner roll. His fingers slip from my thigh. A minute ago, I could feel him everywhere, yet I didn't even realize his hand was still on me.

"This complicates things," I tell him, swinging a leg back over to the passenger side and trying with every last bit of my remaining dignity to not face-plant on him or the truck.

"Why?" His eyebrows quirk upward, like he's finding humor in the situation.

Why?

Why?

Why!

If I could stomp my foot right now, I would. Everything has just become more complicated from my date with Derek to the fact that Lincoln is my brother's best friend. My entire life, people have told me I'm expressive. I don't have resting bitch face because my expressions never turn off. Therefore, I have I'll-cut-you face, don't-talk-to-me face, tell-me-your-entire-life-story-because-I'm-smiling face, and a slew of others that even strangers are easily able to read. Apparently, Lincoln can read my I'm-ready-to-slap-you face because he sighs deeply, my heart plummeting before I can set up the emergency barricades. I steel my emotions, working to pick up the fallen pieces of my heart, myself, and my pride like discarded articles of clothing strewn across the cab. This wasn't sex. His fingers barely grazed my flesh.

"My entire life is a plan," he says, shocking me. I was expecting him to list one of a million excuses, but this was not one of them. "Can we just wait and see?"

"Wait and see?" The words sound bulky and awkward on my tongue and even more so to my heart.

Wait for what?

See what?

If you're still interested in me tomorrow?

If a more attractive girl hits on you this weekend?

"One day," he says. "I'm going to hear all your thoughts. Even the words you don't want to share with yourself." He puts the truck in gear, and before I can rebuff him and pretend I'm unfazed, that I can accept casual just as easily as he can, he's driving, leaving me with an unfamiliar and unwelcomed tune of, "Stop overthinking it."

There are literally a thousand "ifs" in my mind currently, and it's impossible to not overthink any one of them.

25

The Pacific Northwest is chock full of legends. Stories that tell the creation of both the continent and the entire world. One of them claims that Paul Bunyan, a lumberjack who was said to be seven feet tall, dug a giant hole along the Washington coast, creating the Puget Sound and with the rubble, Mount Rainier. With the Sound's unique shape between bodies of land, it's understandable why stories were created and shared. People like to have reasons and a clear understanding of how and why things work, and if they don't, it's easiest to simply ignore the unknown. Push it back out of one's mind and cares. Replace the thought with something more forgiving and straight forward.

Maybe that's why I'm reading through my chronicle of texts with Derek, dating back to the first invite he sent me to go to the fated party where a small intersection was built. I search for understanding, reading the growth of our relationship between lines that convey jokes and clear directness.

"Ready?" Maggie asks, stepping into the kitchen where I'm waiting with an untouched cup of coffee. Her blonde hair is still damp, sporting a pair of jeans that are now a size too big and one of the coats from her closet.

"You want to run by Beam Me Up and grab some breakfast?" I ask.

"Hells yes. I need sugar. *All* the sugar."

I grab my large sage green coat from the closet, the one that makes me look like a marshmallow because it's fluffy and wide, but it's waterproof and is the warmest coat I own, allowing me to focus on something aside from how cold it is while we're out on the water.

"Do you guys still have those strawberry muffins?" Maggie asks, following to the passenger side of my Civic.

"Yeah. There's a citrus one, too, I think you'll like."

"That sounds so good." She closes her eyes and tips her face skyward toward the gray skies, the dense fog still clinging to the ground, like it's trying to hide my indiscretions from last night.

I slide into the driver's seat, watching as Maggie reaches for something tucked into my windshield.

"What's this?" she asks as she gets buckled beside me.

I stare at the wilted paper crane, working to recall if it had been there last night when I'd picked up my car after silence chased Lincoln and me to the coffee and wine bar where I withdrew from the car and the uncomfortable situation. I don't remember seeing it, but even though Lincoln hadn't consumed my body, he certainly had my thoughts, and so I have no idea if it might have been there since school yesterday. "I don't know," I tell her.

"There's writing on it," she says, staring at the marks that the dampness reveals like a spell. She tries to pull it, but the wing rips instantly, the paper too soggy to withstand the pressure. "Is this another one?" She reaches toward the floorboard, a bent and squished crane in her hand. It has to be the one from the party. The one Poppy had found and likely forgot about as we headed into the lion's den.

"You know what the crane represents?" Maggie asks.

"Precision?" I joke.

She shakes her head. "Good fortune, I think." With nimble fingers, she untucks and unfolds several creases and folds until the crane is a mere sheet of paper, its beauty stripped, revealing messy letters set together in sequences of words all tilting toward the bottom right corner. I lean closer to her as Maggie reads it aloud: "You're so selfish. Why can't you just stop meddling—stop asking for so much. You are what's wrong in this world." Maggie jerks her head toward me, her eyebrows furrowed and her lips still parted. "What in the actual fuck? Who wrote this? Is it a joke?"

Chills have claimed real estate up my arms and down my neck, chilling me as I consider how many other cranes I've received and never read. "I don't know," I give the same lame excuse. "I had no idea they were letters."

"Rae, this is freaky."

I shake my head, running through everyone I know and have interacted with over the past several weeks. "Maybe it's a joke?" My voice wavers, waiting for my older sister to provide assurance and validity.

Maggie scans over the letter again. "I don't know. Can you think of anyone who would joke like this?"

"Pax?"

She shakes her head, disputing the idea I knew was wrong before I even voiced it. There's no way Paxton would leave fake letters for me.

"I'm sure it's nothing." I tuck my hair behind my ears, glancing around the neighborhood, taking in the manicured lawns, bare sidewalks, and the large houses that shadow both sides of the street. There's nothing but familiarity and comfort, making the idea of there being a threat associated with these letters seem like a nightmare you wake up from with a racing heart and cold sweat chilling you, only to realize it was all a figment of your imagination. A fear orchestrated by your thoughts, testing your ability to handle the impossible.

I grip the steering wheel, the chill of the leather biting into my palms, helping my thoughts settle further as I take a breath and put the car into drive.

"You should ask your friends. Maybe it's a joke, but if not, you need to let others know," Maggie says.

"I'm sure it's nothing." Conviction has returned to my voice, confidence radiating through each syllable as we pull into the drive thru of the coffee shop I work at. Shannon's at the window, her blonde hair tied into two pigtails, and her eyelids painted a shimmery purple.

"Hey!" Shannon calls, her voice chipper as she peers into my car. "Did you miss us so much you needed to see us today?"

I give a courtesy laugh. "Hey, Shannon. This is my older sister, Maggie. We're actually stopping for some breakfast and caffeine."

Shannon leans closer. "Nice to meet you!" She waves at Maggie. "What are you guys up to today?"

"We're going out onto the Sound. Go see if we can find any whales," Maggie answers.

"That's so cool." Shannon looks at me. "I saw you on the news! I had no idea you had a brother."

She barely knows me. Yet her inflection and long gaze make it clear she's looking for an invitation to know more about Paxton. "Really? He comes by at least a few times a week. I'll be sure to introduce you next time. We're actually about to meet up with him."

Her smile notches up into something salacious, her intentions clear. "What can I get you ladies?"

I glance at Maggie who's undeterred with the brief exchange. "You want your usual?"

She nods in response. "Please."

I place an order for us and for Pax, Arlo, Caleb, and Lincoln as well, though my doubt for Lincoln showing up has been growing since he dropped me off at my car without a word. I made it back to the house faster, expecting him to just go back home, but he surprised me by returning, his mask in place with a new set of barriers as he sat with Dad and made small talk about school and football, his gaze never steering in my direction.

When Shannon closes the window to gather our order, I roll my window up, rubbing my hands together before I turn the heat up.

"She was a little *obvious*," Maggie says.

A laugh surfaces from my chest. "Right?" I look at my sister again, still trying to rearrange the memory of her in my head to fit how she looks now. "What are you doing?"

Her eyes are intent as she looks at me, holding the soggy paper crane to the vent in front of her.

"I'm sure it's a joke," I tell her. "Think about it. No one writes letters like that. It's like words from an old cheesy movie or song lyrics or something. People don't actually talk like that."

"Someone left this on your car last night. They know where you live. This isn't a small thing."

"It might have been there before I got home. It was dark last night, and I wasn't looking for it. Besides, it has to be a joke."

Doubt weighs on her lips as she tries to smile, a teetering glimpse of hope that keeps succumbing to suspicion. "Let's just see what it says."

Unfortunately, time is on Maggie's side, our order taking far longer than it should due to the new girl Sabrina spilling a filled pot of coffee that requires everyone to pause while it's cleaned up.

Jake appears at the window, a crooked grin calling me to roll my window back down. "Shannon mentioned you ordered the entire store."

"I'd settle for half if I can get it in the next three minutes."

He barks out a laugh. "You've seen her work, right?"

I glance at the clock on the dash of my car, taunting me for being late after threatening Pax that I'd leave him if they were late.

"You in a hurry?" Jake asks, leaning forward, his fingers wrapping around the edge of the metal landing.

I shrug. "It's not a big deal. Has it been a busy morning?"

His blue eyes skate to mine like they do whenever I try for nonchalance. "Where you guys heading?"

I shuck a thumb toward Maggie. "This is my sister, Maggie. The one who's been living in Nepal. I'm taking her out to the Sound today."

Jake's smile grows. "I've heard a lot about you. It's nice to meet you."

"You too." Maggie says.

"Let me see if I can help Shannon."

"Thanks. I owe you."

"I'll remind you of that," he says, turning back into the coffee shop.

"He seems like your friendly next-door stalker," Maggie says.

I roll my eyes. "Not even close. I've worked with him for two years."

"So?"

"The letters just started."

She shakes her head. "That means next to nothing."

"He's cool," I tell her.

"That's what people said about Ted Bundy, too."

I maim her with another glare. "Not the same. Plus, we're friends. If those letters are real, the author clearly doesn't like me."

Shannon appears a few minutes later with two drink trays and three bags of food. "You seemed a little unsure about what your brother wanted, so I packed some extra stuff," she says as way of explanation as she passes the bags to me.

"Hold up," Jake says from behind her. Shannon's forced to shuffle back so he can move forward, handing me a large cup. "In case your order wasn't..." his words trail off as he glances toward Shannon still hovering nearby. "And I packed you guys some water and bagels in case you need something besides sugar."

"Does anyone really need anything besides sugar?" I ask, taking the contents from him.

He grins. "Don't fall off the boat."

"Sound advice. Don't let Shannon take orders from any college football players."

His eyes crinkle with silent laughter. "See you tomorrow. Nice to meet you, Maggie."

Maggie sits forward, flashing the paper crane. "Hey, have you ever seen these?"

Jake's eyebrows lift marginally. "Sure. They're origami or something, right?"

"You know how to make them?" she asks.

He chuckles softly before shaking his head. "You guys making them?"

"No," I interject. "She's just caffeine deprived. Jet lag and all that." I glare in her direction, silencing her. "I'll see you later, Jake."

Jake lifts a hand to wave as I drive forward.

"You need to remove detective off your list of possible careers, because that was so bad, Captain Obvious."

"I wasn't trying to be discreet. I wanted to let him know that I was onto him."

"It wasn't Jake. Trust me."

"I got it," she says, carefully unfolding the last corner to reveal a series of words that look like they were trying to cleanse themselves from the soggy page.

"What does it say?" I ask when she remains silent too long.

"This is creepy shit," she says.

"You're probably reading it with the wrong tone. If you change it and think of it as a joke, it won't be creepy."

"Your smiles feel like lies. I thought we understood each other, and now nothing makes sense. We can get past this. Overcome the deceit you bury around yourself like a moat. I'll do it. I'll do it for you. I'll do it for him. I'd do anything for him."

I want to assure her it's a joke, remind her again that it's her serious tone that make the words sound so cryptic, but the words to refute the point dive into the deep end of reasoning. Maggie reads it again before lifting the other letter, reading them both silently while I pull into the marina, spotting Pax's car.

"Who's him? Derek?"

"I have no idea. Like, two people knew we were going out."

"Maybe he told someone?"

"Can we not tell Pax?"

"We need to tell the police," Maggie says.

I quickly shake my head. "What if it really is a prank?"

"What if it's not? Stalkers are real, Rae. And they get obsessive and crazy. What if he's following you?"

A loud knock on my window makes both of us jump.

"Wow. Jumpy much?" Pax asks, bending at the waist to look in my window.

I pull in a deep breath, trying to even my erratic heartbeat as Pax chuckles. "You guys jumped like a mile."

Maggie swings her door open before I can plead my case again. "We have a problem," she says.

26

"If you're going to try and convince me to stop eating beef again, I have to cut you off now, because it's not going to happen."

I climb out of the car, watching as Caleb appears from the passenger side of Paxton's car. I wait with bated breath for one of the back doors to open, for Lincoln to appear.

He doesn't.

I knew he wouldn't. I expected him not to come.

Yet, him meeting that expectation hurts nearly as much as holding it.

My gaze skitters to Maggie, catching her reaction to Paxton's joke. Her lips are turned down as she shakes her head once. My thoughts scatter, trying to recall when my sister transformed into an adult. Being seven years older than me, she's always looked mature in my eyes, but that childish glow that always sparked humor in her eyes is absent, replaced with an intensity the past two years of living in a third-world country and fighting a political and moral war like it's hers to win has transformed her into an adult.

An engine rumbles, stealing my attention. A black truck slides into the spot next to me. Excitement climbs in my chest, my breath catching as my heart beats too fast and hard like I'm on a roller coaster and have just lost sight of the tracks, knowing I'm about to plummet. The engine cuts and Lincoln appears from the driver's seat, a backward hat concealing his dark hair and a pair of aviator sunglasses providing another layer of protection from his emotions.

"What's up!" Arlo calls, exiting from the passenger side, ambling over to us like a puppy, excited to greet us.

Maggie extends the letters to Pax. "It's serious," she says, before turning and introducing herself to Arlo.

Pax's brow furrows, looking to me for direction before glancing at the letters.

"I think it's a joke," I explain. "Some stupid prank."

I can't tell if he hears me, though, because he's reading the letters, his attention shifting between the pages before snapping to me. "What are these? Where did you get them?"

Maggie exchanges a silent look that rings an 'I told you so.'

"They were left on my car."

"When?" His voice is verging on abrupt.

"This was from last night," Maggie says, pointing at the soggy letter, the page folding in on itself like a limp spaghetti noodle. "While she was at *home*."

Pax blows out a long breath as Caleb leans over his shoulder, reading the letters before looking at me with raised brows.

"What's going on?" Lincoln appears beside Pax, pushing his sunglasses atop his head, his presence calling me like the pull of the sun. The desire to soak in each detail of him has me looking from the thick fringe of sooty lashes shielding his dark eyes to the gentle dip above his perfectly shaped lips which bring on an entire onslaught of thoughts and memories that twist and tangle until I'm caught swimming upstream as I try to focus on the conversation while taking in the wide expanse of his chest.

Pax's eyes cut to me. "You don't know who they're from?"

Lincoln plucks the letters from Pax, reading them too quickly before his intense gaze is on me. A warning bell erupts in my head, recognizing the doubt in his gaze that makes me feel even more inferior for having to discuss this new foreign situation that I don't want to stick a toe inside, let alone open the doors for everyone else to peer around. "Where did you find them?"

"My windshield."

"They were folded as paper cranes," Maggie adds.

Lincoln pulls his chin back. "Like the one you guys found a few weeks ago at that house party?"

I nod, pointing the letter with brown frayed edges from having been stepped on. "Maggie found it on the floorboard. I'd forgotten all about it," I add, feeling it necessary to explain why I still had it.

"Are there more?" Lincoln asks.

"A few."

"How many?" Pax asks.

A section of my thoughts has been sequestered to this question upon Maggie discovering the contents were far less innocent than I'd ever suspected. "I don't know? Maybe three? Four? I don't remember."

"How do you not remember?" Pax asks, anger stripping his calm demeanor.

"I didn't realize they were letters. I thought they were just... I didn't know what they were." Reflection has me realizing I was naïve to not have considered they meant something. I think I knew, understood it that afternoon Poppy came over and discovered one on our front porch. I just didn't want to, or maybe I'd hoped it meant something good rather than a potential threat.

"Are they always on your car?" Caleb asks, his voice the opposite of Paxton's, composed and clear. He's studying to work in criminal forensics and has been obsessed with everything dealing with the inner workings of people's minds and intentions.

"One was on the front doorstep and one was on the counter at the coffee shop last week."

"Okay." Caleb's voice is still level, but my answer has him lifting a shoulder and taking a fleeting glance around the parking lot. "Has anyone asked you out recently? Someone you turned down?"

I shake my head. "No."

"It could have been anything," Caleb continues. "Maybe coffee? A study group? Anything?"

"I've been so busy..." I shake my head, trying to recall all the conversations I've held in the past several weeks that have resulted in me declining an offer.

"What are you thinking?" Pax asks, looking at Caleb, who's scanning over the letters once more.

"It's a stalker," Maggie answers, stepping forward so she's at my side. "She's being stalked."

The word sits in my thoughts, refusing to fit into any of the patterns or scenarios I've constructed.

"What?" Pax swings his head from Lincoln to Caleb, looking at his long-time friend to dispute the idea, just as I am.

"It's not a stalker," I say.

Caleb rubs his lips together, taking too long to meet our inquiring stares. "It may not be a big deal. Not all stalkers are dangerous."

Pax blinks hard and fast, like the sequence of words doesn't fit together, and he's working to find a proper arrangement for them. "Stalkers aren't all dangerous?" His tone turns belligerent.

"How do we know if he's dangerous?" Maggie asks.

"He?" I ask. "This is definitely a she."

Caleb scrunches his nose, like he knows we won't like his answer. "It could be a male or a female. Typically, men tend to be stalkers, but the author talks about a guy. It could be Paxton? At this point though, there's not much we can do but wait."

"What?" Lincoln snaps. "You're telling me we just have to wait and see?"

Caleb lifts a shoulder. "They may expose themselves—they might have already, and Rae just wasn't paying attention. We have to wait and see. The person might get bored or lose interest. They might try talking to you. They could try calling. It's tough to say. We don't have much to go on to classify their behavioral traits. Regardless, you need to let everyone know. It might spook them and show you're not interested."

"You want me to tell everyone that I'm being stalked?" I ask, considering this to be like telling everyone I might win the lottery one day—hypothetical and crazy.

"You have to," Maggie insists. "People need to be paying attention and watching out for you and whoever this is."

"They're contacting you, which is good," Caleb adds. "Predatory stalkers are technically the greatest threat, and they don't generally reach out to their victims."

"You're telling us there are safe stalkers?" Pax's voice drips with sarcasm and accusation, anger bristling from his bunched shoulders and balled fists.

"I'm saying not all stalkers pose a physical threat," Caleb clarifies.

"Could it be a joke?" I interject. "A prank from someone?"

"It could, but..." Caleb starts.

"But what?" Lincoln asks.

"Obviously, I'm not a qualified expert," Caleb says. "But, I'd consider this second letter as a threat. They mention lies and deceit, which means they're feeling betrayed by you."

"Your date yesterday," Maggie says.

Caleb's eyes flash to hers. "In my unqualified opinion, I'd wager they know about it."

"What do we do?" Pax asks.

"Tell everyone," Caleb repeats. "We should file a police report, tell her professors, people she works with, friends, family, everyone who can help keep an eye on things."

"What if we just ignore whoever it is? If they don't have the satisfaction of a reaction, maybe they'll just move on," I suggest.

"It doesn't work like that," Maggie says.

"What if we leave a note for whoever it is?" Arlo asks. "We tell him or her to move on, or they'll regret it."

Caleb quickly shakes his head. "You don't want to respond. That gives them power. It's better to pretend you don't even know the cranes are letters. Don't give a reaction. And, if you have the other letters, we should look at them. You need to keep them. The police will want to see them."

"Profile him," Lincoln says, looking at Caleb.

Caleb shakes his head again. "I can't."

"Try. Just give us some basics. Is it someone she knows? Are they old? Young? An ex-boyfriend?"

My thoughts race, cycling through the descriptions Lincoln fires one after the other.

"Men tend to stalk more than women, generally speaking, they're in their thirties. He might be socially awkward."

"That's it?" Lincoln asks.

Caleb shrugs. "This isn't enough to construct a profile."

Lincoln works his jaw, his gaze crossing over the parking lot, tripping over me before stopping at me, an unreadable expression darkening his features.

Pax blows out a long breath. "Mother fucker." He twists his neck, seeking a release from the obvious tension. "I'm going to fuck this asshole up."

"This is why you had to tell him," Maggie says.

Pax rocks back on his heels. "You weren't going to tell me?" His accusation lands on me, full force.

"I don't want this to interfere with everyone's lives. We don't even know what it means. No one's bothered me. It's just these stupid cranes that show up. I'm still not fully convinced it's not a prank."

"We should go. We should go to the police," Pax says.

Seagulls cry overhead, their wings outstretched as they watch us, waiting to see if we have any food. "What about the boat?"

"You have a stalker. Who cares about the fucking boat!" Pax's reaction is fast and loud, emotions and fear making his blue eyes unfamiliar as I maim an accusing glare at him.

Maggie steps forward. "We should still go out. No one knew we were going out, and we can't let this control her life. We just have to set up precautions. There's six of us. Safety in numbers."

Pax glances at Caleb. "This is a terrible idea."

Caleb shrugs in response. "Not really."

"Pax is right. We need to get the police involved," Lincoln says.

"We will," Maggie says. "When we get back." She looks at me, her eyes unwavering as she places a hand on my arm. "Let's grab the food, and we'll get out there."

Pax breathes out another deep swoosh of air that mixes with the wind and my reluctance to accept this new chapter of my life.

27

"Muffins!" Arlo cries, opening one of the bags. "Speaking of stalkers, a girl I work with might be a bit obsessed with you. She packed all that food for us when I told her we were going to see you." I hand Paxton the drinks.

"And, she works with a guy who was quick to help with anything she might need," Maggie adds.

"He's harmless."

"Jake?" Pax asks.

Maggie nods. "Yup."

"He hooks me up. Gives me those really good cookies with the toffee bits on top." Pax looks at Arlo for confirmation.

"Yeah. I don't like him," Maggie says.

I hand the last two bags of food to Caleb and lock my doors. "Before we start condemning people for offenses they're not responsible for, can we just take a moment to discuss the likelihood of this situation being a prank?" I lead them across the parking lot, our feet crunching loudly on the pea gravel while the seagulls return, their numbers doubled, realizing we had food all along. "I mean, nothing has happened. No one's approached me, no one's called me, nothing except these strange letters, and there's not even a pattern for them. They just appear once in a while. Not daily, not even weekly." I glance at Caleb to ensure he's listening because it's his psych major that I'm posing this alternate reality to.

"It could be," Caleb says. "Generally, if a person were stalking someone, they'd make themselves clear. They'd be calling a ton, trying to hack your email, sending gifts..." his words cut off as we approach the cement dock. "Do you know anyone who would pull a prank like this though?"

I eye Arlo.

Arlo quickly shakes his head, pulling his hood up as his nose turns a darker shade of red. "It wasn't me. Paxton would put my nuts in a vise."

Pax nods. "Damn straight I would."

"I don't know. I'm sure I know someone who would do this. I went to school with a bunch of spoiled rich kids who spent their high school careers thinking up ways to torment each other."

"You said Poppy found the first letter," Maggie says. "Do you think she'd play a prank like this?"

"No," Pax says automatically, shaking his head.

"I don't think so either, plus, after her breakup with Mike, she's had a tough time. I don't see her making jokes about something like this. But, that still leaves ninety-nine percent of the kids I went to school with, and a bunch more who I now have classes with. People I work with..."

"Did you piss anyone off recently?" Pax asks. "That weirdo who kept calling after you stopped going out with the Whale Watchers."

I inwardly cringe, hating the way Pax refers to the group who stood up for the ocean and all of its inhabitants when no one else would, risking their safety and time. "They're trying to stop illegal poachers, not creep around."

We stop at the stark white Sedan Trawler the aquarium uses for outings. "You have to wear a life jacket to be on board, and I don't even want to hear any excuses. Joe was an Olympic swimmer, and he still has to wear one." I grip the side rail and extend a hand for Maggie to take. "Be careful. The deck might be slick this morning since it's so cold."

A smile runs from ear to ear as Maggie steps forward, climbing aboard the small passenger boat that is made for speed and to hold a large quantity of tools and supplies. The others follow, but Pax sags back with me, following me to where I work on releasing the rear knot, bending so his face is so close his breath tickles my cheek.

"If you're not telling me something, I'm going to—"

"What? Punch someone in the face and lose your spot on the team? Get arrested?"

His jaw clenches, an indention forming on the hard plane of his cheek. "This isn't funny, Rae."

"I know. If you missed it, I'm not laughing, either. But, I don't think this person is an actual threat. If I did, I'd tell you. I think someone is trying to make a bad joke."

He expels a deep breath. "You're sure about that?"

"What's that supposed to mean?"

"You went out with Derek after I asked you to stay away from the team."

I glance at the boat where Lincoln is watching us. The memory of his heat, the promise of his words to consume me, the way my body still feels deprived with his absence all at the forefront of my mind. If my dating Derek makes my brother feel betrayed, he'd hate me for Lincoln. "Does it bother you because you don't like Derek, or because he's your teammate?" I grasp at straws.

"Both," his response is immediate, proving he's either spent a lot of time thinking about this or none at all. I'm hoping it's the latter. "Grandpa always teased about my friends wanting to date you one day, but now that it's becoming a reality, it's ... really weird."

I laugh in spite of myself. "Welcome to my world. I can't remember having a friend who wasn't interested in you at one point or another. Even now. Did you see how many muffins and cookies and doughnuts were packed into those bags? I'm not sure she left any food for paying customers."

Pax flashes a knowing grin. He's been aware of this for years and has always enjoyed pushing the boundaries of flirting, making a handful of friends believe he was reciprocating interest. "You're a masochist," I tell him.

The air is punctured by his laughter. "I can't help it if they all want me."

Shaking my head, I point at the boat. "Get on board, or I'm leaving you here to the birds."

I hate untying boats. It's a task I had to learn to be certified and licensed, but one I've strayed from since. I pray I don't look like an injured gazelle as I take a quick leap into the boat.

"What are you guys talking about?" Maggie asks, her head turning between Pax's strained smile and my determined grin.

"Pax was reveling in the knowledge of my friends having crushes on him."

Maggie grins.

"And grieving over the fact guys I know are starting to notice Rae," Pax says, a mournful frown becomes deeper as he looks at Maggie. "I thought I was past all that after you moved out."

Maggie laughs. "The difference is they have a chance with Rae."

"You remember that time Saltzman climbed into your bed?" Caleb asks, choking on laughter.

Maggie rolls her eyes. "How could I forget?"

"Saltzman?" I say, trying to draw a face to the name.

"Bobby," Pax says. "You probably don't remember him. He hung out with us a ton freshman year of high school, but it turned out he just wanted to see Mags."

"I woke up to him trying to spoon me," Maggie says. "At like three in the morning. And I'm like ninety percent sure he'd stuffed a sock in his pants because there was a lot going on down there, but everything seemed a bit off."

"I don't want to hear about him getting a hard on for you." Pax shakes his head. "Even if it was a cotton one."

"Kaden used to be obsessed with Rae, he just never had the balls to tell you," Caleb says. "Hell, do you remember junior year? Joey stopped talking to you for like a month when you told him he couldn't ask her out."

My eyes swing to Pax, accusation burning through the exterior he tries to assemble with a quick smile. "Joey was a dick," he says, switching gears.

I take a drink of my mocha, considering what high school might have been like if my brother wasn't the prom king and football captain. If my mom hadn't been the principal. If I were brave enough to cross outside of the barriers of comfort and security I constructed like they were mandatory and necessary. Alternate realities, ones that have appeared in my thoughts over the years from teen movies and shows that always made it look like high school students had endless time, friends, and sex trickles through my mind hitting pegs in my mind like a pinball machine, recalling the endless hours I spent studying and doing homework, volunteering to set myself apart for colleges, volunteering at the aquarium. Even if I didn't have the same parents, would I have changed? Would I have been more interested in smoking pot and sneaking shots? Would I have left my innocence at the hands of a guy whose cost was a simple smile?

Doubtful.

I've wanted the white knight since I was little, and though I've always wished to slay my own dragons, I wanted the knowledge he'd be there at my side.

Lincoln's stare draws me out of my thoughts, his gaze heavy and intrusive like he knows exactly what I'm thinking. His brown eyes pierce mine the moment I look at him, recognition making his jaw grow tight, though I have no idea what he sees because my thoughts are consumed with wondering what he sees—what he *thinks* he sees.

"Ready to get this show on the road?" Maggie asks. "What do we need to do?"

I maintain Lincoln's stare for another second, trying my hardest not to look affected though I feel stripped. I pull in a breath of sea air, shifting my attention to the cloudless sky and then to Maggie. "Life jackets," I say, pointing to the large cabinet they're kept in.

Maggie nods, leading the way, joking with Paxton about another high school memory that was before my time.

Arlo hangs back with me. Lincoln doesn't give a parting glance, disappearing with the others.

"You worried?" Arlo asks.

I shake my head, my thoughts too preoccupied to form a response.

"I know you don't want Pax to get crazier, but maybe we should make sure you're with us if you want to go out or whatever."

"I really think it's a prank," I tell him. "It just doesn't make sense to be anything else."

Maggie appears, clipping her lifejacket into place over her bulky coat. "I can't breathe," she says.

I laugh, moving forward to help loosen the straps, forgetting about brooding stares and cryptic letters, focusing on the sea and my sister as I lead her into the cabin and straight for the helm. "You can drive the boat once we get out."

Maggie's eyes shine. "I don't even get to drive a car anymore."

I grin. "You can drive my car home if you want."

She shrugs. "I don't miss it that much. Just the convenience, you know? And knowing I could leave if I wanted to."

I nod, considering the life she's tried painting for me on numerous occasions, one that includes sleeping on a small cot with two roommates and eating the same foods several days in a row. "Do you miss being home?"

She nods. "I miss you guys, but I like what I'm doing. It sounds insane, but I like not having tech everywhere. My days feel longer and fuller, like I'm accomplishing something."

"You are. You're helping so many."

She grins. "Only about twenty-six people, actually."

I shake my head. "What you're doing is going to leave an echo. It will reach their families and their children one day, and so on and so forth."

The spark of hope shines in her twisted lips, like she wants to believe my words but has seen too many realities that contradict the chance.

"Want to tell them to either hang on or get inside the cabin?" I ask, starting the engine.

A new smile replaces her conflicted grin, and she ducks her head out, yelling to Pax.

ARLO IS MY GREATEST SURPRISE. Standing at the bow, his attention is glued to the water, a wide smile gracing his entire face. Caleb remains in the cabin, drinking his coffee and swearing off Northwest winters, though the sun is surprisingly warm when I catch its direct path.

"What are you doing?" Maggie asks, watching as I reach for the gear to lower into the water that will record any calls.

"Making sure you get to see an animal today."

Her blue eyes grow wide. "What? What are you doing?"

"We have a family of dolphins here, and we've been working with a team who's been studying their communication. It sounds crazy, but dolphins talk like humans. They have whistles and clicks and squeaks and they use a unique one for each member of their pod. They use at least sixty-thousand different calls, and researchers have been able to translate a few, like shark and something that roughly translates to a warning."

"You're telling me dolphins talk?" Arlo asks.

I nod. "They're crazy smart. The Navy and NASA both use them and invest a ton of money into studying more."

"Use them?" Maggie asks.

I nod. "It's fairly controversial for marine biologists because they've trained dolphins to guard certain areas and to locate threats."

"I had no idea they could do that," Maggie says.

"Yeah. They're pretty amazing, and I've kind of made friends with one. He must be napping because he usually shows up by now." I glance back out, waiting to see his dorsal fin break through the surface.

Maggie steps up beside me, shielding her eyes with a hand as the water reflects bright in our eyes. "Will he be alone?"

"No. There's eight of them—a small pod. But, they stick together. Blue will come closer than the rest, though."

Seconds later, the surface breaks, a dolphin gliding through the air before splashing back into the water.

"What!" Arlo cries out, his eyes stretched as he looks at us to see if we saw the same phenomenon. Maggie laughs, her hand gripping her chest.

"That was insane!" she says, laughing again. "Pax!" She turns around, but he's already there, Lincoln and Caleb close behind.

"Did you see that?" She asks, spinning to face the water again, as Blue swims the length of the boat. "Are you seeing this?"

"I see it. I see it," he says.

"There's a dolphin swimming like five feet away from us!" Maggie continues.

Bending the Rules

"I know. I'm standing right beside you," Pax says.

"This is insane," she continues, her eyes locked on Blue as he tosses a chunk of seaweed into the air and then chases it.

"Is he eating the seaweed?" Caleb asks.

I shake my head. "No, they're carnivores. He's just playing. Showing off a little."

"What if you jumped in? What would he do?" Pax asks.

It's a question we've discussed at great lengths, but have yet to test, fearing the relationship we've built with Blue is already verging on dangerous because it's created a trust with humans, one we have no way of ensuring. "I don't know. Likely, he'd try to play with us. Dolphins are very friendly and social and have been known to swim with people and other animals, but we try not to encourage him to even come near us. Technically, we're not funded to research the pod. We're supposed to be tracking and counting the animals, not focusing on any of them specifically. Plus, if they assume all people are friendly, it puts them in danger. It's complicated."

"Everything gets more complicated as you get closer to it," Lincoln says, taking a final look at Blue before walking to the far side, watching as the other members of the pod surface, keeping a safe distance from us, just like he does from me so much of the time.

"I just want to go swimming in there," Arlo says.

"It's fifty degrees. You wouldn't enjoy it very long."

"You get used to it. You just have to dive in," he says coyly.

I shake my head. "Only if you can do it in fifteen seconds."

"Fifteen seconds?"

"Water this cold lowers the time you can hold your breath."

"Fifteen seconds?" Pax asks.

"Twenty-five tops, but he's from a warmer climate. He might not make fifteen."

"If you hadn't shown me pictures of Great Whites, I'd be proving you wrong right now." Arlo tips his head at the darkened waters.

I chuckle. "There are no sharks out here. Blue wouldn't come around if there was. And Great Whites aren't going to come into the Sound. That's an anomaly that happens once in a blue moon."

Arlo glances at the sky. "Looks pretty fucking blue right now."

28

"You totally downplay how awesome this is," Maggie says as I tie the final rope, docking us back at the marina. "I had no idea you could do half of everything you showed us today. That you have a freaking dolphin BFF."

I scoff. "Hardly."

"How do you get the chance to study them closer?" she asks.

"Get accepted to be a volunteer or intern for one of the organizations that study them."

Maggie scrunches her nose, like she knows the answer before asking, "Is it really hard to get accepted?"

I pull in a deep breath, sanding my hands together to regain feeling in them. "Super hard. I've been applying for two years to the groups here in Washington, and I haven't even heard back from them. And unfortunately, my volunteering at the aquarium actually hurts my chances, because they don't see aquariums or zoos as anything positive."

"But you guys release animals back into the wild," Maggie says.

"We do, but we also have some that will never be released because we study them."

"More complications?" she asks.

I nod. "More complications."

"You've just got to impress them," Pax says. "Wine and dine them. Send whoever leads it some tickets to the next Brighton home game. Dad can get you boxed seats."

"Yeah, I'll get right on that. I'll send Doctor Alexander Swanson a gift basket and wait for his acceptance letter."

Pax grins. "Problem solved."

"Doctor Alexander Swanson?" Lincoln turns, his eyebrows dropped as he looks at me for confirmation, his gaze pressing like a bruise onto my skin, leaving another mark that will take days to heal and far longer to forget.

I nod, too invested in his expression and the way his mask has slipped as the day has worn on to gain sense and look away.

"Why? You know him?" Pax asks.

"Not directly. But my dad's his lawyer. They golf together. I think he's attending his wedding next week."

Hope blooms in my chest before I can stop it.

Maggie turns her bright gaze from me to Lincoln. "That would be perfect. You could introduce them."

"You were bitching about finding a date. Rae could go with you. Lower the pressure," Pax says, making my heart wince.

Lincoln's gaze darts to mine, straying before I can even attempt to recognize his thoughts. "Yeah, we'll see."

It's the most non-committal answer I could imagine—equivalent to the 'maybe' response Mom is infamous for that always translates to a 'no' once we're out of the public eye.

"Man, I'm going to need a nap before dinner," Pax says, rolling his shoulders. "Practice blowed this morning."

"Mom said something about dinner with the team tonight?" Maggie asks, making my heart break into a sprint. I spent much of last night struggling to understand the game board between Lincoln and me and had hoped today would shine some clarity on the situation, but instead, everything just feels more confusing. The last thing I want to do is find myself in a room with Lincoln and Derek again.

"We can go out?" I suggest.

"No way. I want to meet Coach Evans." Maggie waggles her eyebrows, making Pax groan. "Plus, Mom said it's a catered event. Mexican food."

"Catered?" I ask.

Maggie nods. "Mom and Dad are so much cooler with money."

Having terms like catered dinners and vacations abroad are still unfamiliar. It wasn't that long ago that we cut coupons and stopped at five different stores to pick up all the sales.

"Plus, Coach Craig wants to talk to you. I was showing him that defense you pointed out, and he wants to pick your brain." Pax ruffles my hair, then sets off, his feet crunching against the gravel as he looks back to see if I'm chasing him.

I'm already closing the gap, making him laugh as he pivots and veers to the right, a move I read before he zagged, allowing me to close the space and grip his shoulders. Pax slows, taking my weight easily before coming to a stop and dipping so far forward I have to bite my laughter to keep from squealing with fear as I close my eyes.

He slowly rights us, releasing the hold on my legs as he squats to bring me back to Earth. "You closed your eyes. That didn't count."

"Don't be a sore loser."

His laughter elicits a smile as he wraps an arm around my shoulder, walking hip to hip with me to our cars.

"Who the hell is Coach Craig?" I ask, debating my evening plans. "And does he really want to talk football with me? I mean, I'm not even a part of the program."

Pax shrugs. "He asked me to introduce him to you. Said he wanted to hear your thoughts on a couple of things."

"I can't believe you guys still do that," Maggie says, catching up to us with Lincoln, Caleb, and Arlo at her sides.

Pax rubs his hand over my head again, knocking strands loose from my ponytail and deserving the shove from my elbow.

"We'll smell you later," Pax says, reaching to push me in retaliation, but I move away from him before he can, finding sanctuary in the frigidness of my car.

Maggie continues talking to them for a few minutes while I start the car and turn the heat up, the fan blowing so loud I can't make out their words as I check my phone, finding a text from Poppy.

Poppy: Party tomorrow. Where are we going?

I think about the letters and Arlo's invitation to go out with them, hating that I'm invested in accepting beyond the knowledge Lincoln will be there, but also because it removes the tiny threat that hangs in the recess of my thoughts like gallows—silent and intimidating.

Me: ???

Poppy: Have you heard from Derek today?

Me: Maggie actually got home last night. A complete surprise. She's only here for a few days. We hung out with Pax this morning.

I don't know why I don't tell her the others were with us. Maybe because I feel guilty for not having invited her? It wasn't intentional. I just wanted to spend some time with Maggie without trying to juggle my attention. I also fear she'll be able to recognize my indiscretions like a bad rash.

Poppy: What? She's home? That's great! What are you guys doing tonight?

Me: Pax is having a team dinner. You can come over if you're interested or we can go out.

Poppy: You really want to go out if Derek isn't going?

The second mention of his name has me cringing as I replay last night. The text I sent him, assuring him I was home safe and apologizing again for cutting the date short, though my unspoken apology was far greater, expanding to an uncertainty of both my actions and my feelings.
'You're worth the wait.' Was his almost immediate response.
Sweet?
Seemingly.
Contrived?
Possibly.
Genuine?

My uncertainty is growing, resentment darkening a part of my heart, the one reserved for the fables I've loved and harbored.

Poppy: You said your date went well.

Me: I lied.

Poppy: ???

Poppy: What does that mean?

Me: It was weird. Awkward. A little forced. I don't know if he actually likes me or just pretends to because he knows it bugs Paxton.

Poppy: He likes you. It's totally obvs.

I take a deep breath, playing out how my best friend will react to my telling her about Lincoln. The ways I tell her and how they might impact her reaction.

Poppy: Does this have something to do with Lincoln?

Poppy: Liking Derek doesn't mean you aren't allowed to still have feelings for Lincoln.

Me: I don't know.

The passenger door opens, startling me as my eyes jump to see Maggie slide into the seat beside me.
"Ready?" she asks.

Me: I'm driving home. I'll call you later.

"Yeah."

. . .

Our drive home is spent with Maggie sharing stories about her two roommates who I feel like I know through the numerous times I've heard about them layered into her life abroad. It makes that small nagging part in the back of my thoughts take shape as I listen closely to the details and missing words that make up my sister's life. The one that doesn't include us and won't for another year at least.

"I'm beat," Maggie says as I pull into the driveway. "Do you know what time the team is supposed to show up?"

"Five, I'm guessing."

"I think I'm going to go soak in the tub and take a nap. Enjoy my last few days of indoor plumbing." She unlatches her seat belt and reaches across the console, catching my hand as I turn off the engine. "Thanks for taking us out today. That was beyond awesome."

I smile, though it feels fragile as I stare at Maggie, memorizing her here and now, engraving each new detail of her to the front pages of my memory so I don't have to work as hard to recall my sister's laugh or smile, the way her blue eyes are edged by green and how she tips her chin back when she laughs. "I'm really glad you're home."

Her smile turns brittle. "Me too." Neither of us acknowledges the tremble of her voice or gloss of tears that she blinks away. We don't have time to, and while it doesn't feel like we have time to nap either, I follow her inside and upstairs where I trade my jeans and shirt for a pair of sweats and a thermal top. I consider the piles of homework and laundry I need to do, how I need to call Poppy and face several truths, but then a knock on my door has me turning, and I see Maggie in a pair of flannel pajamas, an eye mask around her forehead.

"Indoor plumbing's kind of overrated." She crosses to my bed, flipping the blankets down. She pats the bed beside her, and though it's on the opposite side of where I normally sleep, I don't say anything as I cross the space, climbing in next to her and absorbing Maggie's warmth and new scent as tears make silent tracks down my cheeks, knowing I'm going to forget too much of this day, regardless of how hard I try to hold onto the seconds.

. . .

It feels like I've only just closed my eyes when the bedroom lights start flickering off and on in quick succession. Then, Mom starts belting Heart of Glass by Blondie, but she sounds more like Steven Tyler after sucking on a helium balloon. Dad's at the doorway, providing the terrible light effects.

"I thought you loved us?" Maggie cries, pulling the comforter over her face.

Mom climbs on the end of the bed, her hand raised as a pretend microphone as she continues her song.

"We're up," I tell them, clapping a hand over my eyes.

The lights stop flashing, remaining in the on position, but Mom continues butchering the lyrics, missing every other word and adding several made up ones.

"This is brutal," Maggie grumbles, reaching for a pillow.

"Pax should be here shortly," Dad says. "We just wanted to make sure you guys didn't miss the party."

"So thoughtful," I murmur.

"Sorry, was that you asking for an encore?" Dad asks.

"No. No. We're good. We're up." Maggie shoves the blankets off and sits up. "I need a shower. You want to go out tonight?" She looks at me, my heart leaping at the possibility of not only spending time with Maggie but avoiding the football team.

I nod. "Yes."

Her smile is automatic. "Let's get ready. We'll eat and then we'll go out while the team finishes their football whatever."

Dad's phone beeps in quick succession with multiple messages. He glances at the screen, his head tilting back several notches in attempt to read his phone. He started to need reading glasses a decade ago, and only recently started to rebel. "Since my job is done here, I'm going to go deal with this. School issue."

"Don't forget. Dinner. Forty-five minutes!" Mom calls after him.

Maggie starts singing Heart of Glass lyrics on point as she sashays out my room and down the hall.

Mom climbs into bed beside me, taking Maggie's spot. "It's nice having her home, isn't it?"

I roll toward her, placing my head on her shoulder. "It's going to be hard to see her leave again," I whisper the words, knowing I won't be able to say them without my voice breaking.

Mom pulls me closer, her hand twining around my waist. "I know." She kisses my head. "I know," she repeats, running her free hand over my hair.

A throat clears from the doorway, and the unwelcome sight of Lincoln makes my heart stutter, caught in a compromising position that exposes too many of my vulnerabilities and familiar undertones of my adolescence. "I'm sorry," he says, his voice a deep velvet, soothing the storm starting to wreak havoc in my thoughts. "Pax asked me to find you. The restaurant is here, and he didn't know where to direct them."

Mom presses another kiss to the top of my head, then slides out from under me and sits up. "Don't be sorry. I appreciate you coming up here. They're early." She rotates her wrist, looking at her watch to verify the fact. "I hope it stays warm. Thanks, Lincoln." She disappears, but he remains at my opened door, his brown eyes seeing too much.

I sit up, the blankets near my feet, and my hair windblown and messy down my back. "What?" I ask, my voice bordering on abrupt.

He swallows, then slowly takes two steps into my room, stopping several feet from my bed. "What's wrong? Why are you upset?"

I want to laugh. Ask him why he cares. Remind him he's a contributor to this massive imbalance in my life.

I want to cry because he doesn't even realize this.

I shake my head instead. "I just woke up."

Two more paces and he's close enough I could likely touch him if I were to reach out. "Having something you want on borrowed time is almost more painful than not having it at all."

The multiple interpretations of his words cross and tangle, wondering if he's talking about Maggie or a personal confession. If I'm the borrowed time or he is.

"I'd hate whoever you dated. Whether it was Derek or some other asshat," he tells me like it's a confession, his gaze holding mine.

I swallow, waiting for his expression to give away his thoughts that are carefully concealed behind his flat eyes and stoic countenance.

"Why?" I finally ask.

He shakes his head once. "You know why."

"Why won't you just say the words? Why can't you tell me you like me?"

Lincoln's jaw flexes, and he looks away. "What would that do? Would it change anything?"

"Change what?"

He moves, pacing three steps forward and then back, running a hand over his dark hair, making it stand in perfect disarray. "I don't do this bullshit. I don't get involved because I know where it leads. I can't make promises and pretend to be something that I'm not. I've seen the outcome of that situation."

My heart stalls, wondering who he allowed in.

"Trust me, I don't want to like you either."

His right brow rises with surprise or maybe a question. "Because of Paxton." I can't tell if his words are a clarification or a question because he continues looking at me as though he's waiting for a response, but there's no inflection.

"Because I don't want to be someone's conquest."

His gaze drops. Shame or maybe guilt allowing me a brief reprieve from his trail of inquisition before he's staring at me again, his eyes nearly black, an abyss that seems both endless and daunting. He nods. "That's all it would be."

I swallow back the emotions and words that want to refute his admission, a fraction of my heart knows he's lying. Knows that the words he carefully omits are proof he has feelings for me. However, he's vocalized the opposition on more than one account, making that proof feel like a bandage that's falling off, losing all semblance of protection.

"Glad we're on the same page." I stand, coldness shooting up from the light hardwoods through my bare feet, nearly as unwelcoming as his clarity. We stand nearly toe to toe, his jaw ticking as his eyes graze over my face.

My pride wars with uncertainty, wanting to prove he watches me too closely—and desperate to get away from his prying eyes that likely sense the fresh wound he just plowed into my heart without the slightest spec of regret or remorse. I'm in so far over my head the world seems black and impossible to navigate.

I step around him, reaching my closet where I grab a clean pair of jeans and a top I'd bought with Poppy before school started. I yank open my dresser drawer, trying to ignore the knowledge Lincoln is behind me, possibly watching me as I fish for a clean pair of underwear.

When I turn around, Lincoln's back is to the door as he faces me. "Don't hate me. It's better this way."

"Because caring for someone other than yourself would be so difficult?"

"Because every day it gets harder to keep my distance. I shouldn't be here. I shouldn't have gone this morning. I shouldn't have turned my car into the parking lot when I saw you with Derek…" He remains rooted in place as my thoughts spin endlessly.

"You don't know what you want," I accuse him. "You push and then you pull, and neither result makes you happy." I grip the clothes tight against my chest. "And I can't catch my breath. Getting involved with you would drown me."

Lincoln runs a hand through his dark hair, his eyes sweeping over me, exposing a hint of pain and something that looks like desire or maybe hope. He crosses the room, stopping when he's only a breath away from me.

29

"I'm not a villain. I just know where this would lead: a long road to a longer recovery." Lincoln's breath coats my skin.

"That's where you're wrong. I'd rather take everything I can from the borrowed time than never get the chance. Saying good-bye to Maggie is going to be impossible, but I'd take that pain a thousand times over not seeing her."

"But, you'll still be able to get up in the morning."

"And so would you." There's conviction in my words, knowing how quickly I'd be replaced by a thousand other women who'd be willing to morph into the perfect reality for him. "That's why I'm the one drowning, and you're still debating the conditions."

I stride past him, knowing I've said too much—revealed he impacts me far more than a physical level and that he has the upper hand.

He doesn't move to stop me or silence the confirmation. His silence echoes across the space with each passing second.

I don't breathe until the bathroom door is locked, my back against the white paneled wood, keeping me up as my knees and shoulders sag. His words play in my head like a soundtrack on repeat, drilling doubt and questions into my convictions and sanity.

Once showered, I stretch my time alone, curling my hair into long waves and applying my makeup, adding thick lines across my lash lines and shadowing my lids before swiping a gloss across my lips. It feels like my own version of a mask, a middle finger directed toward Lincoln to prove I not only will escape his tides, but I'll come out on the other side.

Black ankle boots complete my outfit before I head downstairs, steeling myself with each step as I focus on surviving the next hour before Maggie and I leave.

Mom's at the bottom of the stairs, and she does a double take before smiling at me. "You look nice."

"Mags and I are going out."

Her smile wanes, that edge of sadness reappearing.

"Raegan," Pax says. "Coach Craig, this is my sister, Raegan." He turns his attention to me. "He wants to go over the tape of Texas with you. See if you can catch anything we're missing."

Coach Craig smiles. He can't be much older than Maggie. Likely, he's a football player who never made it to the draft, and this is his way of continuing his dream, living vicariously through dozens of others who he can attribute their success to his knowledge. I've met too many like him before. He steps forward, a pressed, powder blue dress shirt under a navy sports jacket that enunciates his wide shoulders. His hair is a dark mahogany, the light revealing hints of red. I'd bet a burrito he spends more time on his hair each morning than I do based on the sleek pompadour it's combed back into, the edges perfection.

"It's nice to officially meet you," he says, extending a hand, his blue eyes shining with a smile that touches his lips, a heavy dose of a five o'clock shadow that I'm sure is intentional makes looking at him feel nearly sinful. He's beautiful in the way models on the pages of magazines are. His hand is warm, shaking mine fully, not just taking my fingers like so many do.

"It's nice to meet you, as well," I say, debating my next words.

"Paxton, is there somewhere I can plug this in? Maybe somewhere quieter where the team isn't going to keep walking in front of the screen?" Coach Craig asks, lifting an iPad.

He nods, glancing at Mom. "You mind if I set them up in Dad's office?"

"No. That's perfect. Go ahead."

Pax leads us toward the kitchen, but Coach Craig waits for me to follow before falling in behind me. I pass by several of their teammates, spotting Maggie with a plate of chips as she talks to Coach Harris. Derek is by the fridge, a drink in his hand, his eyes on me, drinking in each inch of me with appreciation shining in his caramel eyes.

I feel Lincoln watching me before I notice him, tucked back, talking with Arlo and Quinton, their starting defensive linebacker and Ian, the defensive linebacker who never remembers me. I turn my attention back to Derek, the easy smile on his lips that tells me all I need to know. I pause for a moment, turning to Coach Craig. "I'll be right there."

Coach Craig blinks, working to read the situation. His eyes cross to Derek and me, then he flashes a quick smile. "Of course." He continues toward Pax.

"Could we talk later? I agreed to watch some tape with Pax, but if you have a few moments, I'd really like to talk to you for a few minutes tonight."

Doubt crosses his features. "Is everything okay?"

"Yeah. I just…" I blow out a short breath. "I just want to make sure we're on the same page."

"I'll be here. Anytime you're ready."

I try offering a hopeful smile, but with my feelings so frayed, I'm not certain it's convincing.

Coach Craig and Pax are in Dad's office, a space I rarely venture into because it's filled with old books and a giant desk that's always littered with a thousand papers. An overstuffed brown leather couch sits across from a large flat screen that's usually dictating news stories. Pax is connecting a cord to the TV. He stands back, changing the input until a football field covers the screen.

Pax backs up like he's going to leave, and I attempt to lasso him with my gaze. He pauses, setting the remote on the small end table where a Tiffany stained glass lamp sits—a gift from Mom when Dad got his position as Dean of Business.

"Paxton shared with me some of the patterns you caught with Colorado, and I was hoping you might look at Texas with us because they've been slaughtering teams, and everyone's attributing it to their offense, but anyone who knows sports, knows an offense is nothing without their defense."

"Coach Craig, I'm flattered—"

He gives a gentle laugh. "Craig. Just Craig. They have to call me Coach because the school insists, but it's really weird to have others call me coach. It makes me feel old." He brandishes a wince that makes him look almost boyish, making me second-guess his age.

"Craig," I start again. "I don't know that I'm qualified to give you much advice. I'm sure you guys would have seen the same plays. I just got lucky."

Coach Craig glances at Pax. "He warned me that you'd say that." He smiles again, his stare deliberate, like he has a confidence that quells my own. "If you don't find anything, that's fine. You're kind of my last hope, though."

"Coach already has it dialed to the part we need help with," Pax says.

I glance at the screen again. "Okay. Sure."

Pax grins. "I have to get back out there. Last time I stepped out while the team was here, Mom put on that old Derek and the Dominos music."

I want to object to him leaving, but I worry it will come across as an insult, so I keep my mouth shut and move to the couch, sitting at the far end while Craig hits play. He backs up, hitching his jeans slightly before allowing a fair gap as he sits beside me.

"You can see they usually always set up in a three-four," he says as the defense lines up behind the line of scrimmage. "They have a really strong defensive end. He likes to force people left, which might be our greatest advantage."

Few quarterbacks are lefties like Pax, and though it's something teams study closely and are aware of, they often slip up because they're used to pushing quarterbacks to the left, exploiting their weak hands.

He lets the game play for several minutes, not interrupting it with any more commentary or pauses, allowing me to watch. The problem is, to truly understand a team, it's necessary to watch numerous games in order to truly decipher patterns and strengths, and all I have are a few clips and a short window with an impending conversation on the other end.

"Do you mind?" I ask, reaching for the remote he placed between us.

"No. No, go ahead," he says.

I fast forward to watch them line up again, skipping to see their formations on numerous plays before I rewind to compare their first downs, and then second downs, and so forth.

"They're fast," I say. "Their nickelback is who I'd watch. They know Pax is a south paw, and they won't be able to compensate very well, and I'd bet they already know that. If I were them, I'd have my nickelback rush the quarterback to gain a false sense of superiority for the team, and as soon as they made the snap, I'd have the safety, the nickelback, and the cornerbacks rushing to cover the weak side."

"Lay a trap?"

I nod. "Not that they will. I'm just saying that's what I'd do. They might not. They're fast enough they wouldn't have to." I fast forward to the one play that stood out the most to me in the quick flash of plays. "Their defensive end is also a lefty. I'd make sure to warn the blind side because he's a bulldozer, and he's going to be stronger playing a game against Pax."

Craig watches the play with rapt attention, only pulling his gaze from the screen when I hit pause.

"I'm sure you already know all this, though."

Craig shakes his head, a smile toying his lips. "When Paxton told me his little sister was good at reading plays, I expected…" he closes his eyes and shakes his head, a dry laugh blowing between his parted lips before he opens his eyes. "I don't know what I was expecting, but it wasn't this. You read the field better than most players I've ever met."

I shrug off the compliment. He has no idea how many hours of football I've played and watched.

"You have an eye for the game."

"Thanks," I tell him, standing as I flip off the TV. It's been over thirty minutes, and I'm hoping the heavy dose of testosterone filling the house has Maggie nearly ready to leave.

"Pax said you used to play as a kid." His smile is friendly, inviting me to pour out the story of my youth.

"Briefly." It's the best summary I can give without getting into the dicey details. "What about you?"

He wets his lips before his smile grows broader. "Briefly."

Laughter bubbles from me before I can stop it, the sound too flirty and friendly, and as his dilated eyes flash to my mouth, I know he hears it as well.

"So, you're a freshman this year?" he asks.

I nod. "Did you attend Brighton?"

He licks his lips again, calling my attention to watch. "I graduated three years ago."

The year before Paxton started, a year after Maggie, making him six years my senior. That familiar feeling of drowning settles over me, the lapping of water at my ears, the stinging sensation against my lungs trying to refuse the sloshing of each wave I keep venturing toward. "Do you know my sister Maggie?" I ask, chucking my thumb toward the door as I take a measured step back.

Craig shakes his head. "I had no idea Pax had sisters until the first dinner here. I meant to introduce myself, but I haven't seen you around. I figured these dinners weren't really your thing." He shoves his hands into his jean pockets.

"It's been a busy fall. Work and school, plus, I feel a little outnumbered and out of place with thirty something people here."

He laughs, confidence radiating as he stares at me, like he knows I'm already dealing with too much and can't begin to consider his intentions.

"We should probably get back," I say, glancing at the TV where the iPad is connected and hating that it forces me to put the door at my back when all I want to do is escape.

I step too close to Dad's desk, allowing a wide berth between us as I disconnect the cord and quickly roll it up before grabbing his iPad. As I turn, a paper on Dad's desk catches my attention, unfamiliar script that seems out of place among all the sheets with words printed in the same Times New Roman script from his computer.

"Thanks again for looking at this with me," Craig says, stepping forward to take his piece of tech. "If you're up for it, I would love to sit and diagnose some more strategies with you. The district is tough this year. These guys are swimming with the sharks, and your insight really helps."

"Yeah. Maybe. My schedule's kind of crazy right now, but let me know, and I'm sure I can work something out."

He flashes another smile. "Great. I will."

"Rae Rae." Arlo appears in the doorway with a filled cup that I'm betting he's wishing was something besides water. "Pax said you were back here watching tape. Did I miss the party?"

I nod. "Unfortunately, you did. We were just heading to grab some food."

"You guys should. The enchiladas are money."

I use his interruption as an easy out, leading them back to the kitchen where many of the team members are still eating as they laugh about something that was said.

Maggie spots me, standing from her seat next to Pax.

"I'll trade you Coach Harris for Coach Craig," she whispers, fanning her face. "He was hot. Where'd you leave him?" She clamps her lips closed as he appears from the hall behind me, smiling like he might have heard her words.

Maggie's eyes grow round with embarrassment, but then she laughs. "Eat. I'm taking you out tonight." Her words are too loud, drawing attention from several people, including Craig and Derek.

"Sounds like trouble," Craig says, hope evident in his blue eyes.

"Where are you guys going?" Pax asks, standing and collecting his empty plate.

"A piano bar downtown called Iron and Oak. Blythe and Patrick opened it a couple of years ago, and I want to stop in and see them." Maggie pushes a clean plate into my hands. "Plus, I'm going to miss her birthday in a couple of weeks, so I need to get all the celebrating in now."

Pax grins. "I'm in on this tomorrow. If you guys need a ride tonight, though, call me."

"Twenty-four hours without Candace?" Maggie asks.

He pulls his head to the side. "We're taking a break."

"A break or a break*up*?" Maggie asks.

I know it's a break. They've done this a hundred times already, but I allow Pax to admit his chosen fate. "We'll see," is his vague response.

Maggie glances at me for clarification, but hounding Pax about this in front of his coaches and teammates seems almost cruel, so I move toward the food, my stomach grumbling at the sight of real food, realizing I haven't had anything but coffee and sugary sweets this morning.

"Were you guys able to catch anything?" Pax asks, refilling his water.

Craig grabs a plate, falling in line behind me. He nods, glancing at Coach Harris. "You should sit down with her. Let her watch your defense and read them so you can mix it up. She reads the field like it's a guidebook."

My cheeks grow warm, feeling the attention of too many on my back.

"Don't be embarrassed," he says, his voice quiet, meant only for me. He places his hand on my back, my hair the only veil between his skin and mine, my sweater a dual V neck with a minor drop in the front and a heavily pronounced drop down my back, falling below my shoulder blades.

The enchiladas are my scapegoat, allowing me an easy exit as I scoop two onto my plate, skipping over the condiments and backtracking to the other side of him in order to get taco chips. "I hate the limelight," I tell him in way of explanation.

His smile appears, like he finds this charming, even intriguing as his eyes follow me too long.

Maggie appears, a full glass of red wine clutched in her hand. "If you're free, you're welcome to come out with us."

Craig looks from me to Maggie, the boyish appeal I'd seen earlier vanishing. "It's a game night, so I can't stay out too late, but yeah. Sure. Why not?"

"Raegan, why don't you take my seat," Derek calls from the table, scooting his chair back and standing.

The table is filled, though half the team is a short distance away in the living room, including Lincoln, who's standing near the front door, speaking with their head Coach. His eyes flash to me like he feels my stare. He maintains our connection, crossing his arms over his chest when Craig asks Quinton for his seat beside me.

The seat on my other side vacates long enough for Derek to take it, pulling my attention back to the dining room.

"You know, I was thinking of doing some tourist things next weekend for our bye week. I've been told it doesn't get more Seattle than the Space

Needle, and I saw they have a restaurant at the top. We could go get some dinner and then tour the city."

"She can't." I turn at the decline, finding Lincoln, a hand on the back of my chair. "She's my date to a wedding next weekend."

If looks could kill, Lincoln Beckett would die right now as I glare at him.

30

I glance in my rearview mirror, waiting to see headlights, though I know they won't be Craig's because he told us he was going to stick around at the house for at least another hour. Still, the idea of him coming out with us is nearly as unwanted as the explanation I need to provide Derek, considering he left before I finished eating.

"What's going on?" Maggie asks, watching me from my passenger seat.

"Have you ever liked someone you know you shouldn't?"

"Are we talking about the hot coach? Because he's not that old. It wouldn't be a big deal. I'm sure Mom and Dad would get over it pretty fast. I mean, he's a year younger than me." She shrugs like the idea is simple.

"I'm not talking about him."

Maggie leans closer. "I'm listening."

"I just mean the question as a hypothetical."

"Is it for self-preservation or because you're worried you'll hurt someone?"

"Either."

"Well, it depends. If it's self-preservation, you should listen to that voice carefully. In my experience, it talks the loudest when you're around someone you know is going to hurt you deeply or those you know have the *capability* of hurting you most. It takes sense to avoid the first and a lot of strength for the second."

"What about in the case of fearing you'll hurt someone?"

Maggie shakes her head. "Life is too short to make sure you're pleasing everyone. When it comes to matters of the heart, you have to care less about what others think and more about what you need."

I think about her words and debate if they'd change if she knew Pax was the one I'd be hurting.

"You sure there's nothing you want to talk about?"

I glance at her again, wishing our time didn't have a definitive ending. "I'm sure."

"What are you going to do when Coach Craig tries kissing you tonight? Cause he's totally going to put the moves on you, just to give you a heads up."

My gaze jumps to her, fear rounding my eyes. I've kissed two boys in a little more than twenty-four hours. Adding a third name to my list makes my stomach roll with unease. "No. Definitely not."

Maggie's laughter fills the space of my car, a warm and welcoming sound compared to the dread she's just evoked. "He might be a gentleman and ask you on a date first?"

"I can't date him. He's Paxton's coach, and he doesn't seem like one to understand boundaries."

"Did he make a move on you?"

I shake my head. "No, he just … stares a lot."

Laughter echoes, making my lips involuntarily tip northward. "He was hot. You want guys like him staring at you," she assures me. "Unless, there's someone else…"

My GPS interrupts her, advising us to take a left.

"I've barely made friends since starting college. I don't think I'm ready to start a relationship with someone who will bring me farther outside of that world."

"I support that, though, you could entertain the idea of putting him on the back burner and dating him in a year. He's hot, and he has a confidence that makes me guarantee he'd be a really great lay."

"I'll keep that in mind."

Maggie points to an empty parking spot that I glide my car into as I consider her words. I know exactly what she's referring to because being on the receiving end of Craig's stare made me feel like he was imagining me with my hips propped on the desk and my legs spread. It's shockingly similar to the look I've caught from Lincoln, though with Lincoln there's an edge to it that seems significant, a quiet and refined authority that has me positive he can read more than just my thoughts but my body.

"Derek seemed a bit intimidated by Craig," Maggie adds. "Jealous and extremely driven." She winces. "I'd be careful. Guys who are overly ambitious seem to forget about their partners and are rarely present. They're always working toward the next goal. The next achievement." Maggie pushes her door open, leaving me to follow after her advice I'm memorizing like a prophecy.

"Granted, he's young. It might just be that he hasn't found the right balance." She links her arm with mine. "He's still cute. Your options are flush." I'm grateful she didn't overhear the invisible claim Lincoln declared because I have no doubt she'd be sharing an opinion on that as well, and I'm torn debating if I wish it were positive or not.

We pay for our clear day out on the Sound as we face a cold wind, unblocked by any cloud coverage. Our conversation coming to a halt as we quickly navigate our way to the bar.

The sign for Iron and Oak is a giant lit keyboard, only a short distance. "Is there going to be a problem with my ID?"

Maggie pauses, pulling me to a stop. "You don't have a fake ID?"

"Technically, yes. But it sucks."

She holds out a hand, waiting for me to show it to her.

I dig around in my purse, catching the card I conceal in a narrow pocket.

"It says you're thirty-five and Hispanic."

"Poppy got them."

Maggie tilts her head back, laughing so hard she grips my arm to maintain her balance. "Mom and Dad got so lucky with you." She rights herself, digging through her purse. "I think I might still have my old one in here." She cries out victoriously, spearing the air with a small rectangular ID. I examine the picture first, noting the blonde hair and wide smile, then glance at the age and name. "Anna?"

She nods, excitement ratcheting her grin into a contagious smile. "Come on, Anna." She threads my arm through hers, hauling me to the front door.

I never hung out with Maggie's friends. Our seven-year age gap practically guaranteed we'd have little in common, and Maggie's friends only regarded me on the few occasions they were around when she was stuck babysitting me on days Grandpa had an appointment or couldn't make it for whatever reason. I'm reminded of this as three ladies greet Maggie, sharing shrieks and giggles between unintelligible words, their gazes crossing over me fleetingly, trying to recognize me.

"Guys, this is my sister, Raegan."

"I didn't remember you had a sister," a brunette says, holding a near empty martini. "Your brother, him I remember. He made me consider an early career as a cougar."

The table erupts with laughter, too many of them nodding in agreeance.

"You guys would probably pounce on him if you saw him now," Maggie admits, sliding her jacket off and directing me to the end of the table.

"He played football, right?" A girl with long brown hair asks.

"Still does," Maggie says, reaching for two menus. "He's the starting quarterback at Brighton."

"You should have brought him along," another woman cries out, laughter chasing so fast I don't know which one spoke.

Maggie takes it in stride, laughing off the comment. "I'll message him, but they have a game tomorrow, so I doubt they'll come. But, you can all thank me with a drink when your eye candy shows up. I invited one of his coaches to come out with us, and you guys are not going to be disappointed."

Cheers erupt as they lift their glasses with a toast. I think Maggie is lying, but she lifts her phone, shooting Pax a quick text before setting her phone down and answering a series of rapid-fire questions about her time abroad.

My phone buzzes, showing a text from Pax.

Pax: You guys okay?

Me: Yeah. Maggie was offering you up to her friends. Sacrificial lamb style.

Pax: Are any of them hot?

Me: There's lots of brunettes.

It's gross that I know he prefers brunettes, but it's a wide known fact.

Pax: Brunette doesn't equal hot.

Me: None of them are your style.

Pax: We'll go out tomorrow. Stay away from Craig. I had no idea he was going to perv out on you. Fucking D-bag.

Me: Maggie likes him. I might be able to flip him.

Pax: Shake him off on one of the brunettes there.

Me: Going to socialize. Byeeeeeee.

"What do you want to drink?" Maggie whispers. "You can get whatever you want, I'll drive home."

"I'm not getting wasted."

"I didn't say get wasted, I said order a drink. It will relax you. I can see you over there overthinking everything." She flips the menu over, running a finger down the list of cocktails, pausing when she hits a drink. "If you don't drink much, this is good. It goes down easy and tastes like juice."

Before I can read it, a waitress appears, placing drink napkins in front of us. "Can I get you guys anything?"

"Sex on the beach and a lemon drop," Maggie says.

The waitress nods, shifting farther down the table.

"Let me guess, yours is the lemon drop?"

Maggie grins. "Good guess."

"My parents are totally pressuring me to get married," a blonde explains from the opposite side of the table.

"What did you say to them?" A redhead asks, her gaze drifting to me again. Her complexion is flawless, and when she smiles, you see both rows of her perfect white teeth, a seamlessly rehearsed expression that makes me uneasy. I remember her from years ago, recall how unfriendly she'd been then.

"I tell them to introduce me to more trust fund babies," the blonde says, sparking laughter.

Maggie's knee bumps against mine. "Look who just showed up," she whispers.

Our waitress blocks my view as she sets our drinks down, but the moment she moves Pax and Lincoln come into view. My heart thumps, feeling so large I feel it beating on both sides of my chest. Pax is smiling, taking inventory of the table, but Lincoln's eyes are on me, reminding me of that distilled confidence that makes me lose my footing.

Maggie stands, hugging them both before completing a round of introductions that I miss most of because my attention is pulled between Lincoln and trying to not look at him, though he's paying attention to everyone except me.

"You guys can sit right here, next to me." The blonde who was talking about her search for trust fund husbands pats the seat next to her.

"You can only have them until I finish my drink. My time here is short," Maggie says.

"Why is that?" I jump, surprised by the unexpected appearance of Craig. He grins, catching my reaction. "Sorry, I didn't mean to surprise you." He shucks his jacket off, hanging it on the back of the chair on my other side.

On the other side of the table, Lincoln's gaze flicks toward me, irritation marring his brow, interrupting the Hollywood-worthy smile he was bestowing on the brunette I remember, like he knows she's the most likely offender of having a bitch switch.

"I'm currently enlisted in the Peace Corps," Maggie explains. "I was sent home temporarily because we had some disgruntled locals making threats, but I'll be sent on a new assignment soon."

Craig leans back. "No kidding?"

Maggie nods, launching into a brief summary of her job and the past couple of years in Nepal.

"Excuse me," I say when she pauses. "I'm going to find the ladies room."

"You want me to come?" Maggie asks.

I shake my head. "No. I'll be right back."

Maggie hesitates, but then sits back in her chair.

I weave around tables and those standing, making my way to the back of the bar, the sound of a new song playing on one of the two large grand pianos sitting center stage.

A bald guy with a beard smiles, taking a step closer to me, and then a hand falls on my lower back, and Lincoln steps beside me, freezing the guy in his tracks.

"What are you doing?" I ask, turning to gain a bit of space from him. But he moves with me, his hand going around my waist.

"We need to talk."

"We already did. Remember? It ended with you suggesting I wasn't worth the effort."

"That's not what I said." He shakes his head, his jaw flexing as he looks at me, his eyes shockingly clear from the mask that usually makes him appear so impartial.

"What do you want to talk about?" I demand.

He leans closer as my words are drowned out by the music, his cologne a clean and fresh scent that paints an image of the ocean in my head.

"Why are you here?" I ask.

He twists so his lips are at my ear. "You know why I'm here."

"You can't do this."

He shakes his head. "What?"

I sigh, pulling him in the direction of the restrooms. We step into an alcove near a table of women who crane their necks to catch sight of Lincoln.

"You can't..." I start, but Lincoln pushes the men's bathroom door open, pulling me inside before I can object. He locks the door of the two-stall bathroom before turning his attention to me. "What are you telling me I can't do?"

"This," I say, waving a hand between us. "You don't get to play the role of jealous boyfriend when you don't want to stick around past the sex."

His eyes blaze, knocking the next line of defense from my thoughts.

"We haven't had sex, and I'm still here."

"Only because someone else is interested in me. If he wasn't here, you wouldn't be." His gaze travels to the sink, and I turn to glance at the door, debating if this conversation should even be had right now and if we're dooming a decision that shouldn't be made with anger and jealousy still hot in our veins.

Lincoln moves, his palms falling against the tiled wall on either side of me, caging me in like I might flee. "You don't understand."

"Then enlighten me."

"My dad is about to marry his sixth wife." He pauses, his brown eyes reading my surprise as I try to read the intention behind him telling me this.

"You're worried you're going to be like him?"

"My mom destroyed him," he explains. "I've had five stepmothers since turning ten. You know what that average is." The corners of his eyes pinch, exposing a vulnerability that makes my heart feel like it's outside of my body.

I don't know how to respond. Each question seems more callous than the last, as I try to remove myself from the equation in an attempt to not be selfish with this moment. "But aren't you doing the same by never investing in someone else?"

His jaw flexes as a silent war takes place in his thoughts: the urge to tell me and the desire to not, which apparently wins out as his hands slide down the wall. "I know I'm being a selfish bastard. I'm trying not to, but you make me feel undone, and I don't know how to deal with it."

"You make a decision," I tell him, my voice a contradiction to my terrified and desperate feelings.

His gaze stops on my lips, focusing there so long I'm convinced he's going to claim my mouth with his.

"What happens with Paxton?" he asks.

It's not fair how he's still able to think and make coherent sentences when I can hardly breathe due to his proximity. "I don't know?"

"What about your parents? The possibility of me transferring?"

I shake my head. "Why are you focusing on obstacles that don't even exist?"

He spins, hitting the wall beside the large paneled mirror, making it shake. "They do exist."

"You're transferring?"

"My options are law school or the NFL, and since the NFL isn't guaranteed, my chances of law school increase daily."

"Is this really about these perceived obstacles, or is this because you want to remain single?"

His gaze shifts too fast, hiding the truth before he moves back to me, invading every inch of my skin before he spins away from me, dropping his head back.

"Consume me. That's all you want to do, right? A conquest. Sex. You already have your answer."

I don't look back as I unlock the door, knowing that if the room really showed the results of this conversation, there would be angry red streaks spread across each inch of the space.

Lincoln catches my hand, tugging me back to him with a quick jerk that has me stumbling into him. He steadies me, his touch and gaze confident as he captures far more than just my coordination. He runs his hands higher, my sweater bunching as his hands burn hot paths along my flesh. He looks down at me, an intensity shining in his eyes that makes me ready to pledge myself to him. It's terrifying and freeing, overwhelming and consuming. I cling to him, anchoring myself to him by holding his shoulders.

"You scare the hell out of me," his voice is a soft blanket, nestling around me on a cold day, soothing me. He dips his head, his lips connecting with my exposed collarbone. I practically moan with ecstasy. I've worked so hard to forget and ignore the way he makes me feel, and yet with a single touch, every cell in my body remembers, desperate and frantic for more.

His fingers press into my skin like he's trying to meld our bodies, his lips trailing up to my ear where his teeth graze my skin, making me shiver. Goose bumps reign across my flesh as each of my muscles fall slack, melting into him like a dependency. He takes my weight, a quiet growl ripping through his chest. I drop my head back, allowing him access to the part of me that seems to keep him coming back, but he threads his fingers into my hair, tipping my head up to meet his mouth. His lips brush against mine, painfully controlled when I want to go to war with his tongue, prove that we both want this.

He shifts, his hand, tangling in my hair as our breaths mix. I open my eyes, catching him watching me through lids heavy with lust. I close my eyes and push up on my toes, pressing my mouth to his and kissing him without abandon, translating a million thoughts and feelings and unspoken words. I twine my arms around his neck, bringing our bodies closer, my nipples painfully aware of his hard chest. I swipe my tongue along his, an electric pulse of desperation and need that makes me moan with the contact and taste of him. I swipe my tongue along his again, slower, firmer, with a determination that makes me forget the reasons and rules I shouldn't be in here with him and the aftermath that may result after I give him yet another piece of my heart. Lincoln's grip tightens, moving us backward several steps, and then the coldness of the tile is at my back, a stark contrast to the heat emanating from every part of my body as I crave Lincoln in a way I've never imagined. His hand falls from my hair, and he takes a step back. I want to argue—to protest the absence of him when my body is demanding he invade my space. Then his hand travels over my breast, his thumb skimming my nipple through the layers of my sweater and bra. My breath releases in a burst, my back arching as the contact stirs, building an anticipation and throb between my legs.

He presses his forehead to mine, his lips so close I can taste his breath. "I can't tell you the things you want to hear," he says, sending my heart colliding into a wreckage that leaves me feeling stranded and cold.

His fingers stop, reading my body and the way my breaths change from labored and needy to labored with anger. He brushes a thumb across the span of my cheek. "You make me want to," he tells me. "So badly."

I'm not even certain what words he's referring to. If they're ones of affirmation or love. Promises or a devotion that would ensure I was the only one he was pressing against dirty bathroom walls.

I don't ask.

I can't.

I shove against his chest, not wanting to touch him or even look at him. He doesn't move, keeping me caged to the wall while he stares at me. I refuse to look at him, refuse to give him the benefit of reading my thoughts.

"Move," I demand, refusing to touch him again.

He releases a slow breath and drops his head as he steps back, freeing me in all the ways I never wanted to be.

31

"Did you get lost?" Maggie asks, smiling at me as I resume my seat.

I had bought myself some much-needed time after parting ways with Lincoln, catching my breath and what was left of my dignity in the ladies' bathroom where I wished I wasn't wearing makeup because I wanted to wash my face. Instead, I gargled cold water, squirting soap on my fingers and rubbing it furiously against my lips, though I knew in the back of my head that it was both futile and childish. Soap had no chance of erasing the marks Lincoln left on my skin.

I smile politely. "Sorry. I just needed to make a phone call," I lie, hoping she forgot watching me put my phone into my purse.

"I was just telling Craig about you taking us out on the Puget Sound." Maggie stirs a fresh drink. I wonder if she forgot her offer to be the designated driver? Right now, I want to take advantage of my fake ID and see if alcohol has the chance to erase the last thirty minutes.

"It sounds fascinating," Craig says, leaning closer as a new song starts, the speakers too loud. His proximity feels invasive as I start comparing his hands gripping a tumbler with an amber liquid to Lincoln's. His fingers are shorter, almost stubby, his nails chewed severely, his cuticles red and sore on several digits. "I was at the beach cleanup," he continues. "I saw you there. You were one of the leaders."

"Organizers," I clarify.

He grins. "Your modesty is refreshing. These days, it seems everyone wants to take credit for every minute thing they do, and you refuse to take any." I move my gaze to his face, trying to decipher his reverent tone and semi-hating that he finds this attractive when I wish to be a confident and assertive person, rather than a doormat. He meets my eyes, humor and emotions I can't bear to see much less acknowledge shining at me.

"I'm going to order a drink," I say. "Want anything?" I turn from Craig to Maggie.

"Yeah... Yeah, let's get you something." She places a hand on my back as she rises from her seat. At the end of the table, Pax belts out a laugh while one of Maggie's friends strokes his flexed bicep. Beside him, Lincoln sips on a drink, his dark eyes tracking me like he has the right to.

"Let's go this way," I say, turning around though the most direct route is behind us, leading us directly by Lincoln.

"I need to make sure they don't think this is a full touch and feel bar," Maggie says, grabbing my hand and tugging me to turn back, a smile on her face that slips when my expression registers, making her delicate brows bunch.

I quickly paste a smile on my face. "Sure. Sorry. I thought it was this way," I lie.

Her forehead relaxes, and she reciprocates my smile before turning and leading us to Pax. I want to cower and hide, but my pride refuses to allow me the comfort. I lift my chin, standing beside Maggie with a manufactured smile while my heart batters wildly at the walls of its cage, loathing the way Lincoln keeps his gaze on everyone seated around the table instead of on me.

Maggie clears her throat, and Lincoln finally turns his attention toward us, but it never makes it past my sister. He exudes confidence and nonchalance, like he didn't just leave the bloodied remains of my heart in the bathroom. My heart beats an angry rhythm, demanding retribution, or at least a sign of compassion.

"Okay, time to establish a few ground rules." Maggie pulls Pax's arms, silently instructing him to stand. "Ladies, let me draw you a quick diagram." She turns toward Paxton, drawing a wide rectangle around his groin that expands past his hips. "No one is allowed in this region," she says. "You can fondle the biceps, he might even let you feel the abs, but remember he has a girlfriend, and he's still in college."

There's a mixture of responses ranging from cheers to groans.

"And," she says, turning her attention to Pax. "You have a game tomorrow. Don't let these wenches make you forget that."

Maggie drops his arm and turns back to me, resuming our path to the bar.

"Where are you guys going?" Pax yells.

"We need drinks and maybe some eye candy." Her grip tightens on my arm.

The bar is a long, shining counter painted as a giant keyboard that distracts me from the faces of the dozens of strangers. I take in the sleek beauty of the bar and the many details I haven't seen all night, the little bits of elegance like the large chandeliers dripping in glass cut like diamonds, and the lights bringing a classy and gentle glow at every turn.

"No! No! Stop!" A woman with dark hair stained with several strands of purple stares at Maggie and me. She's dressed entirely in black, her eyes heavily shaded in black eye shadow.

Maggie laughs, her grip on me releasing as she shadows the woman to the end of the bar where the two embrace in a fit of giggles. As the stranger smiles, a spark of resemblance blooms, and I recognize her as Blythe, Maggie's close friend from childhood, back when her hair was a light shade of brown that she often wore in a single braid and dressed in light pastels.

"I can't believe you're here," Blythe says, looking over Maggie, likely tracking the same differences that have been tripping me up over the past twenty-four hours. "Patrick!" Blythe yells over one shoulder.

A stocky guy with a headful of short, spiky blond hair and a black tee appears, his eyes warm and soft as they meet hers. "Babe?"

"Do you remember Maggie?" Blythe's eyes flash to me, and she smiles. "This is her sister, Raegan. Gosh. You grew up."

"Right?" Maggie cries.

Patrick lifts three shot glasses to the bar and reaches for a clear bottle, filling each of the glasses. "Reunions call for celebrations," he says.

We each reach for a glass. My experience drinking is about as long as my sex life, but rejection fuels my confidence, and I throw the liquid back in one drink. Tears burn my eyes as the alcohol scorches my mouth, throat, and stomach. I want to sputter and wipe my tongue on my sweater, but hide it all with a wince.

Maggie laughs. "Let's dance."

I shake my head. "I'm not in the mood to dance."

"Did you hear that, Patrick?" Blythe asks.

A crooked smile graces his lips, and he pours another round of shots. "Then you need another drink," he says.

I know it hasn't been long enough for the first drink to register, and a second is a bad idea, but I take it as well, the burn slighter and more bearable, unlike the rejections from Lincoln that seem to burn deeper with each experience.

Maggie watches me, laughing as I release a deep breath. "Now are you ready to dance?"

The three of us forget about the others we left behind, making our way toward an open space. Few are dancing, but Maggie and Blythe don't seem to notice—or maybe they just don't care. Maggie's boldness has always been something I've envied. The tempo picks up as a new song begins, and the alcohol helps numb all the fears and feelings that have been sitting in my head like a tide pool, forgotten by the ocean, leaving a slickened path that leads to jagged rocks. The past is heavy with questions and doubts, and the future exhausts me, but this, the now, Maggie's cheerful smile and warm grip, ground me to the present that feels bearable as I lose myself in the music and nameless faces.

WE DANCE until our feet hurt, until the crowd has grown around us, until I feel *him* watching me.

"I'll be back. I need to check in with Patrick and be sure everything's good," Blythe says, making a quick exit that has Maggie slowing.

"I'm so tired," she admits. "That fourteen-hour time difference is kicking me in the ass right now. With pointy shoes." She runs a hand through her hair, a thin coating of sweat making the back of her neck and brow glow. "You ready to call it a night?"

"I'm your ride or die. If you're ready, I'm ready."

A loud laugh bursts through her lips as she wraps her arm around my shoulders, tucking her face close to mine. "I'm going to miss you so damn much."

I want to tell her I know, that her impending exit is already looming like winter, cold and unforgiving. "Should we call for a ride?"

"Probably. I failed you."

I shake my head. "It doesn't matter. We had a good time." I'm sure I'm sober enough to drive. It's been well over an hour since we shared another shot, but among the many lessons drilled into me since my tween years was to never take the chance of driving under the influence, knowing the risk never outweighs the consequences.

"The best."

"We should see if the others are still here," I tell her.

"Oh, shit." She straightens, her jaw falling with a full second of silence before she quietly laughs. "Let's make sure Pax doesn't need saving. Knowing those women, he's going to need our help."

I finally look up, trying to find Lincoln to see if he's in the compromising position I've already suspected a half dozen times in the past minute. He's at the bar, one elbow on a painted piano key with a drink in his hand as he watches us.

Maggie follows my gaze. "You gonna tell me what's going on?"

"Nothing's going on."

Doubt has her dropping her chin, but I shrug in reply, refusing to dive into the story—not tonight, not now when I want to revel in my time with her as I fight to remain present.

When I glance back at the bar, Lincoln's gone. A tease to my brain that questions if I really saw him. Then he's in front of us with two glasses that he offers Maggie and me. "It's water," he says.

Maggie accepts one of the cups without hesitation, downing half the glass in one gulp. I eye his hand, refusal on my lips. "Are the others still here?" Maggie asks.

Lincoln glances in the direction of the table we'd shared. "A few. Craig and Pax left a while ago. He got a call from Candace."

Maggie's attention snaps to me. "Already?"

"This is typical."

She sighs loudly. "Damn. Maybe tomorrow, we hide his phone."

"Good luck," I tell her.

"I'm going to go do a quick good-bye. I'll be right back." She squeezes my shoulder before slipping away.

"Why are you here?" My question is as brash and accusing as a thunderstorm, brandishing the promise of regret and annoyance.

"I stayed so I could give you guys a ride home." He tucks his free hand into his pocket, still holding the glass of water intended for me.

"You can't do this," I tell him. "You can't care when it's convenient. Like me only because someone else is paying attention to me."

He gives a small, nearly imperceptible shake of his head. "I don't give a shit about Craig."

My glare is as sharp and bright as lightening. "Bullshit. You wouldn't be here if it he didn't come out with us." My words are a torrent of rain, revealing the truth.

Lincoln stares at me, his face frustratingly void of emotion.

"You have to stay away from me," I tell him.

"Is that what you really want?"

"Yes." My answer is a burst of lightening, the positive and negative particles that have built too great, combusting with a startling and shocking intensity. One I regret the second the word leaves my mouth. I can't take it back though, because I know his presence only makes it more impossible for me to recover from him.

He flexes his jaw and then nods. "Okay."

Panic send my heart falling, tugging my heart into a direct plummet.

He gave up that easily.

That quickly.

THE HOUSE IS dark when Maggie and I climb out of the Lyft, my heart still miles behind us as I struggle to pull in a steady breath.

My phone buzzes with a text, and I pray it's Lincoln telling me I'm wrong, and that anger fueled my response. Defeat fills me as I see it's from Pax.

Pax: Craig texted me. Said he forgot the charging cord for his iPad in Dad's office. Can you please bring it to the game tomorrow?

Me: Yeah.

Knowing I'll forget by morning, I break stride from Maggie. "I'll be right up. I just need to grab something."

The house is dark, allowing fears to trickle into my thoughts at every squeak. Maggie nor Pax has mentioned the cranes that carried letters of fear into our minds earlier today. I'm grateful, hoping they're convinced it's nothing but a hack like I'm striving to do. Unfortunately, the darkness has my mind wandering into a labyrinth of scary 'what ifs' that don't seem to vanish even with the lights switched on.

I stop at Dad's office door, phone in my hand though I doubt it would be a successful weapon or a means to call for help because chances are I'd drop it at the mere sight of a threat.

I push the door open wide and flip on the overhead light before stepping inside.

"Rae?"

I jump, my heart launching itself on a catapult to the other side of the house as I turn and face my dad sitting at his desk. "You scared me," I admit.

He blinks several times then shifts his chair, rolling closer to his desk. He's wearing another Brighton sweatshirt, his hair mussed. "You startled me, kiddo. What are you doing?" He looks uneasy, almost nervous.

"Pax messaged me. His coach left a cord that he needs." I move toward the TV, grabbing the cord I'd winded but left behind. "Are you okay? Something going on with work?"

"There's always something going on with work," he says, making a face that I suspect is meant to look goofy, but fails. "Did you guys have a good time? It's late. Lie to me and tell me there was no drinking, loud music, or guys involved."

I shake my head. "Only for a second. But we robbed the bar and were out in like two minutes flat."

He drops his chin, fighting a smile as he attempts disapproval.

"What did you do tonight? I heard the team left early."

Dad nods. "I went to an open gym and am just trying to catch up with work." Dad started playing basketball for the first time in his life a couple of months ago. He said it was to get fit. Pax claims it's because he's worried about getting older. I'm still undecided.

"It's late." I glance at the large clock that hangs across from him, telling us both it's past our bedtimes. "You should go to bed. Don't you and Mom have something in the morning? She mentioned you guys would be home a little after noon."

He scrubs his face with the heels of his hands. "I forgot." A long sigh has him draping back into his chair. "You're right. I'll go shortly. I just need to finish this up." He grabs a pen, and slowly twists back to his laptop.

"Night," I say, returning toward the hallway.

"Night, kiddo."

32

Thump.

A pillow hits me, then falls to the floor. I slowly open my eyes, straining to focus on my bedroom.

"Are you hungover?" Maggie asks.

"Maybe." My eyes fall shut.

"I was kidding. You're not hungover. You didn't drink enough for that." She launches herself onto my bed, her elbow falling on my bicep sharply. I swallow the pain, appreciating that something can hurt more than my thoughts for a second. "Why are you being a bum? It's Saturday. Breakfast." She leans so close to my face, we both go cross-eyed. "Feed me!"

She rolls off the bed, taking my covers with her.

"Why do you hate me?" I groan.

"Three words. Biscuits and gravy."

"I'm not hungry."

"Well, you better get hungry because Pax is at Frank's Diner as we speak, waiting for a table."

"On a game day?"

She nods. "Said he wanted to carb up for the game." A grin crests her face. "Come on. Mom and Dad went out—something about a conference or something. I don't remember. All I know is Frank's has huckleberry pancakes, and I will literally fight you if I have to."

"I don't have my car," I tell her, rolling to my back.

She nods. "Actually, you do. Lincoln drove it back last night. Left your keys in the mailbox."

My brow furrows. "What?"

She hitches a shoulder. "Are you out of excuses, yet?"

"How do you know he drove my car back?"

"He asked for your keys last night."

"And you gave them to him?"

"He was sober. I figured we'd ride home in the Lyft so we could chat about boys without a spy, but apparently, I was more tired than I realized," Maggie says, referring to her sleeping during our ride home. She swats my backside. "Up. Shower. Dress. Let's go."

She leaves my room before I can digest that Lincoln drove my car home. Thoughts pull at my brain in endless directions, making everything feel too heavy as I trudge to my closet and pull out a pair of jeans, avoiding all my shirts and sweatshirts I've collected over the years that have Brighton's name across them.

I hurry through my shower, not wanting to be alone where my thoughts feel like ammunition that will maim me. My makeup is an afterthought, fast and light before I pull on a pair of sneakers and take the stairs to find Maggie.

"Ready?" she asks from her seat on the couch where she's watching the news, her makeup perfect, her lips a light shade of red that enunciates her sweetheart's bow and flawless skin.

"Yeah."

"Do you mind if I drive?" Maggie grabs her purse. Her smile is quick, but her gaze is slow, sweeping over my face. "You okay?"

"Yeah. Yeah," I repeat the word, striving to sound more convincing.

Her smile grows, following me to the door. Sure enough, my car is parked in the driveway.

The air is cutting and brisk, but warmer than last night. Clouds have returned, making summer feel like a distant memory as the damp air swirls into a cloud with each of our breaths. Water is pooled in the driveway and clings to our skin as I make it to the mailbox and discover my keys.

I toss them to Maggie, who beams as she moves to the driver's side and climbs into the chilled cab. She starts the car, her fingers anxiously curling around the wheel. She checks her mirrors, then shifts the car into reverse and hits the clutch and the gas. My Civic lurches, sending us both forward and then backward into the seats. I brace myself, both hands on the dash seconds before she slams on the brakes, jerking us forward against our seat belts.

She cackles, throwing her head back. "Sorry."

"You good?"

She nods. "It's just been a while. I've got this."

She punches the gas again, and though it's still too hard, it's softer than the first round, and slowly, she eases to a level speed. Maybe she senses my mood or attributes my silence to my being tired, but she fills the silence on our way to Frank's by recounting the night, never requiring a response from me. Her driving is improving except for times when she had to come to a complete stop, the same whiplash occurring with each stoplight.

Relief kisses my skin in the fashion of a breeze as I get out of the car, my muscles strained from Maggie's attempt to parallel park that had me digging through my glove box because I was certain she was going to hit both cars at one point.

"I told you I had it."

I don't point out that while the paint jobs of both cars survived, my nerves didn't come out nearly as untarnished.

"Finally," Pax says, standing as we enter the filled lobby, a small Styrofoam cup in his hands. "I had to let five families go. What took you so long? I called you an hour ago."

"Traffic," Maggie lies.

Pax scoffs, but drops it. "Don't look at me like that," he says, turning his attention on me.

"Like what?" I ask.

"You're judging me. I needed coffee. I was desperate."

"In a non-recyclable, non-biodegradable cup that will be here when your great, great, great, great grandkids are born *or* be the cause of them not being born." I nod. "Yeah, I see that."

He glowers at me, but turns, making a sweeping gesture with one arm with a silent offer of his seat.

Maggie looks at me, but I shake my head, too antsy to sit. She beams. "One day, your future wifey is going to thank us for all your good manners."

"I have a feeling your future husband won't be giving us the same appreciation speech," he quips.

Maggie scowls. Pax finally softens, offering a weak grin.

I will miss this. Poking and prodding at one another. The silent bonds that band us together and keep us coming back. The next time we meet like this, more than just time will have passed. Memories and experiences will have changed each of us.

Maggie starts to make a wisecrack, but I miss it, going to help hold the door open as a large family makes it toward the door, the mom carrying a toddler and the dad carrying a car seat with an infant. While I'm holding the door open, an elderly couple passes through, and then a man in a motorized scooter who stops briefly to thank me.

I start to move away but stop as I catch sight of someone else making their way toward the entrance, my gaze back on Maggie and Pax, who are clearly bantering as they exchange words and laughter.

"Found your keys?"

My heart aches as it speeds up, going from a resting rate to completing a marathon in one second flat. The spice of his cologne wraps around me, drugging me into a haze that has flashes of last night blinding me. His hands on my skin, my breast. His mouth hot and greedy, taking more than it gave. I swallow the mean words that surface with the memories. "Yeah. Thanks for driving it back. You didn't have to."

Lincoln's brown eyes rake across my face, reading each of my features like a diagram. "I know you're upset with me," his voice is husky, his eyes remorseful. I don't want to listen to him, but I also can't seem to move, my feet rooted in place, waiting to hear everything he has to say. "I don't mean to keep hurting you. I hate that I hurt you."

His words tangle with memories from last night: the way he let me go so easily, his rapt attention on others at the table, the way he only came back once they were mostly gone. "You're making this sound complicated, and it's not. You're not interested." I shrug. "It's that simple."

"If it was simple, I wouldn't be here. I'd be able to sleep at night. I'd forget the way you feel and bury myself into someone with less baggage, who I wouldn't care half as much if they came out on the other side hating me. Nothing about this is simple." His chest heaves as he expels a deep breath that clouds. I want to capture the tiny molecules in my mouth like one catches snowflakes, but instead, I watch as they quickly vanish.

"I can't be this girl who you come running to when you're bored." I meet his large browns, wishing I knew how to break the code that keeps the mask he wears locked in place.

He scoffs. "You really think that's how I see you?" His eyes narrow at the corners as he looks at me so intently it feels almost intrusive.

"I don't know how you see me. Sometimes, I think your attraction to me is only because you know I should be off limits. Sometimes, I think it's because you only want what Derek might want." Other times, in the recesses of my mind, I think of the way I sometimes catch him staring at me with a tenderness and longing that makes my knees feel weak and think he has a genuine interest in me—something deeper than lust that makes him listen close enough he can recall my words.

Anger flashes in his eyes, making them several shades darker. "And what am I to you? A trophy? A puppet?"

I rear my head back, confused about how the conversation took such a severe turn. "How did you go from apologizing to accusing me of seeing you as a trophy, when I've never said or done anything to objectify you?"

He drops his gaze to the sidewalk for several seconds. My thoughts scramble in an attempt to figure out his next words—his next accusation. Slowly, he looks back at me. "You deserve so much better than me." He grabs the door I'm still leaning against to hold it open and gently pushes me inside.

I don't want to go inside. I want to talk about things. Our exchanges are always so brief and compromised with outside influences. I just want to stand out here and hash things out once and for all, but before I can protest, Paxton pulls open the adjoining door. "I can't believe my sisters beat you here."

"Lawson, party of four," a host calls. She's around my age, but she's better at applying makeup, which makes it tough for me to tell for sure. Her gaze skates over us, doing a double then triple check of Paxton and Lincoln. Internally, I'm rolling my eyes, but externally I link arms with my sister, reminding myself this day has nothing to do with jealousy or boys and everything to do with her. Maggie smiles, then leans her head on mine for the short walk to our booth. My eyes feel misty again with the simple gesture.

"This morning our specials are crab eggs benedict and huckleberry pancakes. Both go great with our signature Bloody Mary." She flashes a smile that has more hidden insinuations than a lacy thong. "Your server is Ben, and he'll be right over."

"I wonder if Ben is going to stare at us like he wants to have a three-way right here, right now." Maggie looks at me, feigning hope with raised eyebrows as the girl disappears.

"Stop putting images in my head I can't erase." Pax rubs the heels of his hands against his eyes.

Maggie chuckles with satisfaction. "I waitressed for five years, and I always wondered why so many women hated female servers. Girls like our hostess is why."

"I'm your *brother*," Pax says. "Who cares if she's flirting with us?"

"She doesn't *know* you're our brother," Maggie quips.

"Rae…" Pax turns in his seat diagonal from me, across from Maggie, a pleading expression matching his tone.

"She's kind of right. That girl was a bit too obvious about her intentions."

"Thank you," Maggie says, sitting straighter in her seat.

"Well, if she returns, I'll be sure to hold your hand so she knows I'm taken by my *older sister*."

Maggie smiles, her shoulders and chin dropping with affection. "Being here probably makes you grateful you're an only child, huh?" she asks Lincoln.

He shakes his head twice. "No, the opposite actually."

Pax nods. "It would have served him well. He needed someone to keep that ego in check. Maybe it wouldn't be so inflated."

Lincoln tips his head back and chuckles. The gesture is easy and instant, as well as mesmerizing. "Your family sets the bar pretty high. I don't think most brothers and sisters would get along as well as you guys."

"Which is tragic. We all need a sibling who'll bail us out of jail, right, Mags?" Pax winks.

"Good morning!" Our server says before Maggie can reply. "My name's Ben. How are we all this morning?"

"Hungry," Pax answers. "How are you?"

The server has a friendly and wide smile. "I'm great thanks. Have you dined with us before?"

"We have," Maggie says.

Our server looks at me as if waiting for my validation, and I realize how little I've said since Lincoln arrived. "Can I get you all something to drink? We have freshly squeezed orange juice, coffee, hot chocolate…"

"Coffee for me," Pax says.

"Yeah, coffee would be great," Lincoln adds.

"Me too," Maggie says.

"Can I have hot chocolate and orange juice?" I flip over my menu, glancing at all the pictures of the drinks. "And a coffee?"

Our server's eyebrows jump high on his forehead. "Hot chocolate, coffee, and orange juice?"

I nod, and he stares at me a beat. "And are you guys ready to order or do you need another moment?"

"Pax?" Maggie asks, looking to him.

"Um…" He searches the menu for a few seconds before looking at the waiter. "If we could get a couple of minutes, that would be great." Pax leans back.

Our server flashes another quick smile. "No problem. I'll be right back with your drinks."

"And we don't want any straws!" Maggie calls after him. "They kill turtles!"

"Three drinks?" Lincoln asks.

Maggie laughs. "Have you been in her car? She never leaves work without at least two."

"I use reusable cups," I add. "But, the hot chocolate here is homemade. Real chocolate and sugar and milk and goodness, topped with whipped cream. You guys don't know what you're missing out on."

"What she means is, she has a hard time committing to one choice," Maggie says. "Which is why I get the biscuits and gravy, and she orders something sweet, and we share."

"Right now, you're *oversharing*." I slump back in my seat casually—attempting to look unaffected.

"Oversharing? That word doesn't compute. What is that foreign term?" Maggie uses a strong mesh of accents.

"Are you guys ready for the game?" I ask, glancing at Paxton before I steal a look at Lincoln.

Pax runs a hand through his light hair, making several strands stand up. "You know it's going to suck."

"Arlo will have to help block. You should have Hoyt do the same, and then have them run out to be receivers."

He nods, finishing the coffee in the Styrofoam cup he brought to the table. "This game is going to make me look bad. It's going to help Grant's chances of getting field time."

Another junior has been working hard to get field time, and even with my biased opinions of Pax, I know Grant is a credible threat. He's good, and if he were on any other team, he'd likely be a starter.

"You're going to have to change things up constantly." I don't want Pax worrying about those who want his starting position, because doubt has always been my brother's greatest enemy. "Pump fakes, trick throws, reformations ... you have to keep them guessing."

"What she said," Maggie says, pointing a thumb at me and lightening the mood.

"Four seconds," Lincoln says. "They just have to buy you four seconds, and if they can only do two, we'll start a rotation, left, right, middle. I'll be there. Chuck that ball as hard as you can, and I'll get it."

Pax breathes in deeply through his nose. "If our defense can hold them, we might have a chance."

He's never been boastful. It's one of the things I love most about my brother.

"They will," Lincoln assures him. "Our defense has been training for weeks for this game."

If I was the defensive coordinator, I'd be training specifically for this game as well. They're an even match and will make for a tough game.

"What are you guys doing until game time?" Pax asks.

I glance at Maggie, my plans completely reliant on her.

"Testing the bounds of gluttony," she says. "Eat all the food, watch all the crap shows, and drink all the coffee."

"And maybe take a walk," I add, knowing we'll both feel too sluggish to have fun at the game if we become permanent fixtures on the couch.

Maggie shakes her head. "Grandpa and Camilla are coming over this afternoon, if you have time to stop by."

"I can't. But I'll see them Monday. Did you hear back on when you're going to have to leave?" Pax asks.

Before Maggie can answer, our waiter returns with our drinks, setting my three options in front of me. "Need another minute?"

"No. I think we're good," Lincoln says, glancing at the rest of us for verification.

The waiter nods, turning his attention to Maggie and me for our orders before moving to the guys where Pax orders both specials, and Lincoln orders eggs benedict with extra hollandaise sauce and a side of bacon. I've been out to breakfast a handful of times with Lincoln, and he's always ordered the same thing.

"After the game, I plan to sleep in my bed and not move until noon tomorrow," Maggie says. "I've missed my bed."

"What about you?" Lincoln asks, his attention on me as I swat Maggie's hand away from my hot chocolate.

"I don't know. Something with Poppy."

"How's she doing?" Maggie asks.

"She's bummed she couldn't come out with us last night. She was stuck watching her brother, but she's excited to see you tonight," I say, adding cream and sugar to my coffee.

"Her breakup with Mike was pretty ugly?"

I nod. "Yeah, I think she's hoping dating someone else will help."

Maggie shrugs. "That line is a bunch of horseshit. Falling into bed with someone else when your heart is with another person only hurts more people."

"I don't think she still loves Mike." I shake my head, tapping my spoon on the rim of my coffee cup.

"Then what is dating someone else going to do?" Maggie asks.

"I think she's afraid to trust someone again." It's a guess, one I really shouldn't be publicizing with our current company, but Pax was genuinely angry when Poppy went camping with us this summer and fell asleep crying into her pillow each night.

"That guy was a twat," Pax says.

He wasn't. Mike was a good guy—a nice guy. And I know he loved Poppy because he'd call and text me following the breakup to ensure she was all right. The breakup wasn't because he didn't care, it was because he wasn't in love with her, and though I've never asked Poppy to confirm, I'm positive she wasn't in love with him, either, though I know she wanted to be.

"You guys should come out with us," Lincoln says. "I know you think those notes are a joke, but having people around who you know seems like a good idea until you know for sure."

Thoughts of Lincoln trapping me in the corner, his hands hot on my waist—kneading into my flesh, his breath hotter as it falls against my skin, tickling away my inhibitions.

Oh god. I have to say no.

"The notes." Maggie swings her head to me. "We need to do something about that."

I shake my head. "I thought we agreed it might be a stupid prank?"

Maggie looks at Pax, who shrugs, turning his attention to fixing his coffee.

"If anything else happens, we can discuss it. But, for now, safety in numbers and all that."

Maggie's hesitance to agree is etched in her narrowed eyes.

"And," I say turning my attention to Pax and Lincoln. "I don't think so."

"What? What happened to safety in numbers?" Maggie asks.

I puff out my cheeks with a weighted breath, opting for honesty rather than another lie I'll have to remember. "I feel so out of place at parties." I avoid looking at either Pax or Lincoln, fearful of the judgement I know I'd face.

Maggie grins. "Good. It makes me like you more."

I snort. Pax chuckles.

"I'm serious," she says. "If you loved college parties, I'd disown you. Underage drinking, sexual assault, people parading around like their bodies are all they have to offer. They're completely sexist, contemptuous, and have more superiority complexes than our living room on Christmas morning. They're gross."

"I love a good party," Pax says.

"That's why I call Rae more than I call you."

Pax slams an open palm against his chest. "Ouch." He extends the same hand, pointing at Maggie. "But you went to college parties all the time."

She nods. "And so should both of you."

I shake my head, working to catch up with her opposing words. "What?"

"You need to get out there, Rae. You need to drink too much, fall in love and get your heart broken, and then pick it up and do it all over again. You need to meet people because these are the friends you're going to have for the rest of your life, and you need to do stupid things because, after college, society isn't nearly as kind or accepting of you getting drunk and stripping to a really bad pop song."

"Tell me there's video," I say.

Maggie smirks. "You should go. And Lincoln's right, you should go with them. Safety in numbers and all of that."

I cringe, imagining myself getting drunk and stripping in front of Lincoln.

"I might need a designated driver if tonight's game is half as bad as everyone's assuming," Pax adds.

"Will the rugby team be there?" I ask.

"Rugby team?" Maggie looks at me with raised eyebrows.

I shake my head with a quick reply. "Poppy likes a guy named Chase who's on the team."

Lincoln presses his lips together, garnering my full attention. "I can guarantee it."

33

"How many layers are you going to wear?" Maggie asks.

"It's freezing," I remind her, getting into the driver's seat of my car before she can suggest driving again, my neck and nerves still weary after our outing for breakfast.

"Why do you look like someone just told you your favorite show is going to be canceled?"

With raised eyebrows, I glance at Maggie.

"You've been distracted all day. This doesn't have to do with the fact you're crushing on Lincoln, does it?"

My eyes round with shock and alarm. "What are you talking about?"

"I'll admit, you concealed it well."

I lean back in my seat, my shoulders falling with defeat. "I don't want to like him. I didn't mean to like him."

Maggie laughs. "Rae, you're eighteen. No one can tell you what to do or think, including yourself, so if you like Lincoln, go for it."

"Yeah, it's not that simple."

"It is. It really is. We overcomplicate everything, but it's that simple."

I shake my head. "No. My plan is to get over him, date around, have fun, and enjoy college."

Maggie nods. "That sounds like a great idea. If only you were the date around type."

I pull my chin back, offense still stinging my skin and constricting my throat. "You were just telling me at breakfast to date around."

She shakes her head. "I told you to date and get your heart broken."

"I can totally be the dating around type."

"Yeah. Totally. You shop around for guys by their front lumps. I know."

A bitter laugh breaks the sudden silence. "I'm serious. I'm going to meet someone tonight, and I'm going to make out with him and shove my hands down his pants. I'll report back."

"Better yet, keep a journal."

"A journal?"

"My roommate and I did this in college. We rated dicks."

I stare at my sister, shock rounding my eyes.

"What?" she asks.

"I don't know... That just seems ... incredibly ... *incredibly* ... sexist."

Maggie laughs. "It is. It *was*." She moves closer to me. "But, you don't have to pretend to be someone else. Just be you."

"I don't know who I am. I've dated five guys in my life." The recycled words almost sound truthful.

Almost.

"What happened last night? I realized you guys had something going on when you were both gone forever."

I want to pretend like I don't know what she's referring to, but tears are threatening to slip from my eyes. "He likes me, just not enough to date me."

"He said that?" Rage coats her question.

"In the shape of a million excuses."

She twists to fully face me, making me want to give her a safety speech about her seat belt. "Screw that. Have fun and shove your hands down all the guys' pants tonight. Hell, consider it science. Be like Paxton and his friends."

I roll my eyes. "I'm not breaking down penis sizes by hair color."

My sister laughs so hard, she leans forward, resting her weight against the belt barely holding her upright. "Go out tonight. Spend some time with Poppy and forget about everything."

Her words replay through my mind like a mantra as we park and head for the stands. We find Poppy, a mess of snacks in her lap and a welcoming smile on her face. Sometimes, I wonder if we have multiple soul mates, ones who serve different purposes, because there's something about Poppy that has always brought a calmness to me like a balm, easing the discomfort from all situations.

"Hey," she says, shifting the bag of snacks to the ground so she can reach forward and hug Maggie and then me. "It's so great seeing you." Her tone is sincere.

"You, too. Gosh, I thought Rae looked old, but it's really weird to see you both grown up." Maggie looks between us. "You look fantastic."

Poppy's cheeks turn a deeper shade of red that she can't blame on the bleak temperatures. "I can't believe you guys don't take advantage of the boxed seats. Dad's a dean. Use the perks!" Maggie says, sitting closer to me.

"The only people who sit in there are adults and guests. It's boring and stuffy."

"But warm," Maggie says.

"They have better snacks, too," Poppy adds, rustling through her bag until she pulls out a bag of peanut M&M's that she hands to Maggie.

"You remembered!" The astonishment in her voice is clear though uncalled for because Poppy remembers details about people like moms remember their children's first word and step at the call of a dime. Poppy smiles in response, plunging her hand back into her bag of treats until she finds Skittles and passes them to me.

"Is this team good?" Poppy asks.

I nod, ripping open the bag. "This is going to be a tough game for Pax."

"What does that mean?"

I sniff, my nose so cold it and my fingers are already starting to lose feeling. "They're going to be trying to sack him."

"Didn't they say he has one of the fastest releases in the league?"

"Yeah, but they'll still go for knockdowns."

Her brow furrows as she reaches for the green and yellow Skittles I save for her. "Why?"

"Get in his head. If he knows someone's going to be tackling him, chances are he's going to start looking for where the threat will be coming from or make a mistake in an attempt to prevent it."

"So, they're just going to keep coming at him?"

I shift my attention from the field to Poppy, hearing the concern in her voice that is etched across her face. "It'll be a tough game," I admit. "They're all going to get banged up and frustrated. This is going to be a game of patience and wills."

Poppy and Maggie get up to get new snacks twice with the excuse to move around for warmth and hot snacks. I don't go with them, my attention glued to the field where Paxton's patience is slimming by the second. He's been hit with nearly each set, his white jersey stained with mud and grass. Arlo is pacing, and Derek is yelling again. The game isn't bringing out anyone's best qualities. Lincoln is rigid, and I'm sure his shoulders are as tight as his covered jaw as he points a gloved finger at Arlo and makes a demand before turning his attention to Pax. I hope he's telling them to just work toward four seconds—a flash of time that will open windows for them.

Maggie grips my arm. "They have to win."

I don't agree with her or voice my concerns, focusing on the new lineup, noting there's a change that I can't decipher. "What are they doing?" I whisper. My attention is glued to the field, watching everyone scramble. I look at Pax, waiting for the reception, but then the ball flies into the air, and I realize Arlo just passed it downfield. The ball soars surprisingly far, and though it's not as straight as Pax usually delivers, right now, all we need is distance from their defense. My breath catches in my chest, watching as Lincoln dives for the ball. He catches it in one of the most epic plays of the night.

That play seems to alter the remainder of the game, renewing Brighton's intensity and confidence, and sending them into another victory that has the stadium erupting with raucous cheers.

Maggie's beside me, screaming with both arms in the air, and I realize in that moment, watching as the team overcomes their fears and shaken disposition, how full my heart feels, bringing forth a determination to corner Lincoln tonight and tell him exactly how I feel. How I'm willing to risk my heart being broken even if it's on borrowed time. Even if we'll be breaking a dozen rules. Even if he rejects me.

34

My body is consumed with equal parts nerves and excitement as I follow Poppy into the house at the address Pax texted to me. I allow the butterflies to take flight, not working to temper them like I have previously when I know I'm about to see Lincoln.

"Oh, he's cute," Poppy whispers, sagging back as a guy with curly brown hair and a straight nose approaches us.

The team isn't here yet. I can tell because the hordes of girls are milling around rather than focusing on anyone in particular. The acknowledgment has me missing the introductions, but I smile, following Poppy's lead and giggling when the guy we've been talking to tells us he's on the basketball team.

My laugh is too high, and I attribute it to the water bottle filled with orange juice and vodka Poppy and I finished before we came inside. She said it was to loosen up, and loosen her up it did. I've never seen my best friend so fearless and bold. I'm hoping it helps give me the courage I need to approach Lincoln.

The guy whose name I can't recall, nods.

"My best friend played basketball." Poppy places her hands on either of my shoulders. "Raegan was so good, she even got one of those little basketball things for her letterman's jacket."

The guy turns to me. "Oh, so you're...?" he points between Poppy and me, his words trailing off.

I wait for him to continue, my brows furrowed. "We're what?"

"Taco party fans."

I glance at Poppy, hoping for a translation. Her eyes are impossibly round, and then she belts out a laugh that hurts my ears. "Yup. We are. You're so smart!" She reaches forward and pats his cheek.

Realization dawns on me. My jaw drops. "Why would you assume that because I played sports, I'm a lesbian?" Offense coats each of my words.

The guy shrugs, like the answer is apparent.

Before I can say anything else, Poppy whirls us around, her arm tightly entwined with mine, and she hauls me deeper into the bowels of the party.

"Can we tell Paxton that guy tried to put his hands on your cooch?"

Poppy laughs. "Who cares if that asshole assumes we're lesbians? That might be the best excuse if someone we aren't interested in tries flirting with us."

"Don't you think that would be offensive and insensitive to people who are gay?"

"Probably…"

"I'd rather just punch whomever in the nose … or have Paxton do it." I release a deep breath, considering pulling out the second water bottle she'd made for me that's buried in my purse. "Do guys really think it's butch for a girl to have played sports? What if I tell him I drive a manual? Or that I like beer?"

Poppy giggles again. Holding a conversation with her started to get more difficult when she cleared the first half of her drink, it's now nearing impossible. "Don't worry about it. Don't even think about him. Let's go find some hot guys and make out." She shoves her hand in my purse and procures the water bottle. "Drink. Just a little. It will help. I swear."

I accept it with another sigh and take a long drink. The juice is warm, but it still goes down easy, the hint of alcohol heating my throat.

Poppy smiles. "Okay. Now. Who do you want?"

"What?"

"Let's make a top five list. That way we know to avoid each other's top picks."

"I..."

She spins me to face the opposite direction and raises an arm, pointing at a guy with long blond hair that's in a knot on his head. "He's on my list. Keep away from him, ho."

I slap a hand over my eyes.

"Oh, and him," Poppy continues, peeling my hand from my face and pointing to another blond. This one has shorter hair and is missing his shirt. His torso and biceps are corded with muscles that girls are petting like a damn puppy as he flexes.

"You're going to have a hard time competing with his ego. I'm pretty sure he already thinks he's the prettiest person here." I turn, taking in more of the people here. "What's with the ratios of girls to dudes?" I ask. "Who throws these parties?"

"You need to drink some more. You're still caring too much about inconsequential things."

"I'm impressed. You just used inconsequential in a sentence while drunk."

"I'm impressive, what can I say?" She curtsies.

"Dang, girl! Don't let Gore see you, because you might be the reason for global warming." A guy with short, spiky hair places his hands on Poppy's waist.

His pickup line has me rolling my eyes as I watch too carefully where he moves his hands.

She giggles in reply. "He's on my list, too."

"I'm on your list?" he asks. "What kind of list?"

"Guys she's not allowed to flirt with." Poppy points at me.

He turns his head toward me, a quick smile gracing his lips, but his eyes never rise higher than my chest.

What a winner.

"I think I saw a friend from class, so I'm going to..." I lie, pointing in the opposite direction. "If you need *anything*..." But Poppy seals her mouth over his before I can finish.

"And this is what a third wheel feels like," I mutter, taking several steps back so I can keep her in view.

"Hey."

My heart spins like it's on the teacup ride at Disney World as Lincoln steps in front of me, stopping me.

"Hey, President," a girl says his nickname like Marilyn Monroe sang the lyrics "Happy Birthday, Mr. President." Innuendos are practically being screamed by her eyes that are undressing him and her fingers that trail slowly across his torso.

My thoughts fall like a game of fifty-two card pickup. Do I say something? Do I try to up this game of flirting that everyone else seems so adept at? Do I focus his attention back on me and the fact he just admitted his attraction to me?

She leans closer.

My thoughts fall faster.

"Hey," he says, smiling at her.

"Want to go see the rest of the house?" Her words cause a twisting sensation in my heart.

"I'm busy," he says, slipping a hand around my waist.

The girl looks at me for the first time before flicking her attention back to Lincoln with raised brows like she can't understand his decision.

I'm not sure I do either.

"I like your shirt," he says, leaning forward, the scents of his cologne drowning me.

"You had a really good game," I counter.

His smile is almost shy, a contradiction to the flashy smile I often see him grace others with who compliment his playing. "Tonight was brutal."

"It was, but you guys did it. I didn't even know what you were doing in that formation before everything turned. I was so confused, and I could tell the defense was, too."

He grins. "That's a high compliment, coming from you."

I smile as my heart thunders, trying to piece together the right words to ask him to risk his friendship with Paxton and his free time for me.

"God, you're fucking kerosene," he mumbles.

I pull away, the word plaguing me with a million unwanted thoughts.

"I know being with you is going to get me burned, but I don't care. I can't stay away from you anymore."

My heart leaps as I shake my head, a million stories of my fears playing, all of them involve me being the one who gets burned, while he moves on to success and stardom.

"I can't breathe when you're not near me." His words trigger something in my heart that makes me reach for him, endless promises tangling into a jumble of words I don't quite know how to express.

"What about Paxton?" I ask.

"We'll figure it out."

"What about—"

His lips crush mine, ceasing my words that are reaching for reasons to keep us apart. He steals more than my words and thoughts in that moment, as I grip his shoulders, pulling him closer to me.

He pulls away too fast, his eyes heavy with lust. "If we go upstairs, people will assume the worst. Go to the bathroom. It's at the end of the hall on your left. I'll knock three times." He brushes his thumb across my bottom lip before he twists and disappears.

I feel my heartbeat pounding in my head and my neck, even in my fingertips as I glance around, wondering who might have seen us—waiting to see their shocked expressions to confirm it was real.

But everyone is preoccupied with their own agendas and crushes, leaving us in a bubble of anonymity that likely would have been abruptly popped had we pushed the limits. I pull in a deep breath, trying to calm my heart as I follow his instructions to the bathroom. I expect a line. Movies always portray long lines at bathrooms, and in my short college career, I've managed to avoid them, my aversion to public restrooms strong. Instead, the hall and bathroom are both empty as I close the door and debate locking it as I flip on the lights, blinking when the harsh fluorescent bulbs buzz and flicker.

A knuckle scrapes the door in three quick bursts, and my heart somehow beats faster, threatening to break my ribs that have worked for so long to cage in my feelings.

I open the door and come face-to-face with Lincoln, who flashes a pirate smile before slipping inside and locking the door behind him.

My tongue feels swollen and my head slightly faint as his fingers brush against my sides. I don't know if I should explain I'm a virgin or that I don't want my first time to be in the bathroom of a house I don't even know.

His smile grows like he can read my thoughts, making me wonder if it's actually possible for him get inside of my head. "I just need to be near you. I need to feel you."

I swallow. "I don't think I understand everything you're saying."

He shakes his head, his grin turning into a smirk. "I'm not sure I do, either. Just tell me all the noise that's guaranteed to come from everyone when they find out about us isn't going to scare you. Tell me this is more than just my name and your love for the game."

It's the first time he's ever exposed an iota of vulnerability, and it's like a sucker punch to the gut, making me drunk on him in a split-second. I slide my hands around his neck, careful to avoid his shoulder that I know is going to be sore after tonight's game. "I've tried telling myself I don't like you for three years. Trust me, this has nothing to do with the game, and sense left me a long time ago."

"Three years?" His breath fans across my lips as he steps closer, a victorious light shining in his eyes, making me regret the admission and for my cheeks to stain with embarrassment. "You've just made my fucking night." He leans closer, brushing my lips with his in a kiss that makes me forget secrets and rejections as I memorize his taste with each lick of his tongue, his hands gripping me tighter, pulling me into the current I've striven to avoid for so long. His kisses become deeper—urgent, and though my breath is growing faster, it finally feels like I can breathe, like he's breathing life into me as my remaining excuses tumble and fall away.

His fingers tangle in my hair, and his kisses turn languid, slowing as his tongue turns purposeful, leaving lingering paths of heat and promises of the many things he could do to my body, making my stomach and areas farther south clench with anticipation. A contradiction of emotions has me feeling both empowered and weak as I wrap my arms tighter around his shoulders, my chest flush against his, feeling the warmth of his skin through his long-sleeved tee and my top that I'm ready to beg him to remove. I want to feel his flesh against mine, memorize the heat and pressure of his body like I have his expressions.

"I want to feel you," I whisper, pulling only my lips away. "I want to feel you touching me."

His nose grazes my neck, nuzzling my flesh and sending a current of goose bumps down my back and arms, and then, like he senses my reaction to him, he flicks his tongue against my neck, sending a shockwave to my aching core.

I slide my hands down his shoulders, moving another step back so I can pull my shirt free, dropping it to the floor with a nearly silent kiss of air. It's the only sound as Lincoln's eyes drink me in, staring at my body like art enthusiasts stare at the Statue of David, making me feel reveled and beautiful, strong and desired.

"God, you're beautiful." His voice is husky with lust as his eyes move across the span of my torso, meeting my gaze as though imparting an honesty that makes my heart swell. "Do you have any idea what you do to me? How hard you make me?" He takes my hand, pressing it against the front of his pants, which are tented from his arousal. He groans, his head falling back and to one side.

I press harder against him as I lean closer, snaking my hand across his chest and up to the back of his neck, coaxing him to tip his head forward so I can kiss him again, desperate for the air he fills me with.

His lips are insufferably soft and patient, allowing me to take the reigns as I drop my hands to the space between us and run my fingers across the warm, hard planes of his abs. I slide my tongue against his, swallowing his groan as his hands fist at my sides, kneading into my flesh. His skin is hot against the pads of my fingers as I follow the dusting of his hair to the button of his fly, where I work to release another layer between us.

Lincoln's lips consume me, the featherlight kiss becoming an invasion as he marches me blindly backward until the counter bites into my hip bone. "I won't be able to stop," he says, his eyes finding mine.

"Then don't."

He huffs out a grin. "This is about you. I want to make you feel how badly I want you. How much I need you."

His words are trying to fit into the right shapes and sizes of the puzzle in my head, and then his hand is at my pants, his fingers toying with the button and then retrieving the zipper as his eyes remain steady and focused on mine, likely seeing my chest rising and falling with need and fear and desire all building until it feels like my body's about to combust.

"I want to taste you," he says, sliding a finger down the short path my gaped pants allow, bunching the lilac lace of my underwear. My cheeks burn with my innocence. My third boyfriend had finger banged me, but it was in the dark and under the privacy of his bedspread, so he never saw even my underwear, let alone *everything*. He slides the index finger of his free hand into the cup of my matching bra, following the line of my breast and nipple, making my next breath come out in a hiss. His fingers at my underwear bunch the lace, skating across my skin so soft and teasing. I'm desperate for him to move lower, trace my entrance where the pressure is the greatest.

He breathes out deeply. "You're so responsive," he says, his eyes still watching each of my reactions. His finger tugs at my nipple again, and then he gently pulls the lace covered cup down, freeing much of my breast and nipple. His eyes become hooded, still maintaining eye contact with me as his fingers brush the sensitive skin that feels heavy and hot against the pressure of his fingers.

"Do you have any idea how much you fuck with my head? I need you, Rae. I need all of you."

I'm not sure if I'm more afraid of the past or the future as I stare at him, recognizing the same vulnerability I see in my reflection when thinking of him.

"You already have all of me," I whisper.

His eyes close, his hand at my underwear stilling as his fingers trace over my nipple again. When his eyes open, it's as though the mask he's worn has been shredded, and I see the desire and severity of this moment. His lips tip into a gentle smile, and then he leans forward, his lips brushing mine, tasting like hope and strength. Then he presses a kiss to my lips, and lowers his face to my breast, taking my nipple into his mouth. The heat of his tongue and sharp grate of his teeth make me moan, and then his hands shove my pants lower. Anticipation nearly blinds me, making the entire room fade as he pulls on my nipple with his teeth. Finally, his fingers run across my entrance, a gentle soothe to the pressure still building inside, hungry for everything he's willing to give me.

He traces across my entrance, his hand still over my underwear, tonguing my nipple, intensifying each touch. His fingers slide into my underwear, and I shift my hips to meet his fingers, moaning before his fingers slide over my folds. "You're so wet," he groans, rubbing his fingers across me, easing me apart. He grazes a finger over my opening, making my hips shift with need, but instead of burying inside of me, he moves back across my folds, running his fingers across my clit and making me gasp. His mouth pulls my nipple farther into his mouth, and his fingers deliciously swirl around my clit, somehow easing and torturing me at the same time.

"Lincoln," My voice is a foreign and desperate plea.

My nipple's still in his mouth as he looks up at me, his fingers buried between my legs. It's the most erotic thing I've ever seen and makes me want to get on all fours and beg him to bury himself into me.

"Have you ever?" he asks, freeing my other breast and licking my already pebbled nipple.

I shake my head, and though I have no idea what exactly he's asking, I know the answer is no because my sexual experience can fit on one of those tiny Post-it notes you only use to mark the pages in a book.

"Tell me if anything hurts, okay?"

My heartrate increases, and my hips relax as I glance at the bulge in his pants, hoping that once he's inside of me this pressure will stop threatening to burn me up.

He stands straight, kissing my mouth again. Completely. Fully. "This isn't about sex," he tells me. "This is about you and me." Before the disappointment of his rejection can sink in, his finger slides into me, making my chest constrict and my breath hitch. "That's right," he says. His finger farther inside of me, my walls clenching around him while his thumb works over my clit, making my breaths come out faster and ragged until I can't decide if the pressure is subsiding or continuing to build, and then, Lincoln drops to his knees. He slides my pants and underwear lower, making my nerves pitch to an all-time high. The ghost of a smile is imprinted to the back of my eyelids before his tongue slides over me, and I can't keep my eyes open for another second, drowning in the pleasure. His fingers pull me open, exposing my clit as he licks the bundle of nerves with long, slow licks that turn faster and faster in pace with his finger sliding in and out of my entrance until the world turns white, and I shudder through my orgasm.

35

Lincoln leans his forehead against mine as I try to catch my breath, my heart still exploding in my chest as my breath comes out in heaves that he swallows, his tongue darting out to trace my lips, my musky taste staining my mouth.

My phone vibrates against the counter. I'm not even sure how it got there. I reach to silence it, refusing to allow anything or anyone to interrupt this moment I've waited three years for.

A second later, it vibrates again, rattling against the Formica to an unforgiving rhythm.

"You should make sure it's not Poppy," he says, running his fingers lightly over my sides.

I want to argue, but the double ring has me curious, turning my phone over to see Lois's name.

"Hello?"

"Raegan?" Her voice is rushed, urgent. "There's a situation at the marina. Some students from Brighton are on a boat, and they're harassing the pod of dolphins. They're drunk, and Greta wants to call the police. She's worried they're going to hurt themselves or the dolphins. I'm wondering if you might want to try and get there first. Save them from an arrest. I recognize one of them as your friend from the beach cleanup."

The heat that had been flowing through me seizes as I consider the outcomes. "Okay. Thanks for the call. I'll be there as soon as I can."

Lincoln's eyes shift between mine. "What's wrong."

I bend to pull my underwear and pants back into place. "Part of the football team decided to rent a boat and celebrate tonight's victory out on the Puget Sound. They're about to call the cops on them, but gave me a courtesy heads-up to see if I can make them stop."

He scrubs a hand across his face, his jaw growing rigid. "Fucking bastards. Forget them."

I know his response is solely fueled by anger as he bends to retrieve my shirt because in the next breath, he's calling Paxton.

I point toward the door, indicating my escape, but Lincoln grabs my hand, his touch gentle as he threads our fingers, recapping the situation to Pax. To ensure my brother doesn't hear me, I shoot Poppy a text, letting her know we have to go.

Lincoln murmurs a train of curse words, his gaze on me. "Okay. Yeah. I know." He sighs deeply before hanging up.

"You guys don't have to go," I tell him.

"There's no way you're going out there to meet a bunch of stupid fucking drunks without me."

"Pax coming?"

He nods once. "We should talk to him soon. It's better if he finds out from us rather than rumors." He brushes his eyes with his thumb and forefinger, releasing another sigh. "You aren't doing this just to help him, are you?"

"Derek?"

"Who else?"

"Are you really asking me that?"

He rolls his shoulder and then his neck. "He's not right for you."

"Rather than tell me all the reasons another guy isn't the one for me, I'd rather you tell me all the reasons you are the right one. Remove the politics and just be honest with me."

His gaze shifts between mine again, but his mask remains at bay. "I want to be with you," he says. "I told you before I want to consume you, I just neglected to mention the entirety of that desire." He steps closer, his fingers sliding across my jaw until his fingertips are in my hair. "I want your body and your mind. I want your heart."

My heart gallops out of my chest, seeking sanctuary in the safeness of Lincoln's broad chest. "I already told you, it's yours. It's all yours."

His lips seal over mine, his fingers burying deeper into my hair. Our moment ends before it barely begins, my phone buzzing chaotically with multiple messages from Poppy and Paxton.

"They're ready," I tell him.

Lincoln brushes his lips against my temple, his hand tracing down my back as I pull open the door, the noise and commotion of the party an unwanted contrast to the refuge we created.

We separate, knowing it will look suspicious if we appear together. Pax is at my car with Poppy. "Are they sure it's them?" Pax asks.

I show him my phone, the picture Lois sent for me to confirm it was Derek. It was.

"Shit," he breathes. "Coach is going to lose his fucking mind if they get arrested."

Lincoln appears, crossing the street to where I'm parked. "You want to take my truck?" he asks.

"I drive faster," I tell him.

He grins. "My truck it is."

I scowl.

Pax laughs. "I told you, I can't sit in your back seat. We have to ride in his truck or go separately."

Lincoln gives me a leveling look that makes my urge to argue only stronger, but my desire to get to the marina is stronger than my will, and so begrudgingly, I follow them.

Lincoln blasts the heater as we clamber into his truck, Poppy sitting beside me with a glassy expression that has me examining her more closely.

"You okay?" I ask her.

She grins. "Fuck Chase," she says, brushing her hair over one shoulder and fumbling with her seat belt. "I don't need him."

Clearly, she's anything but okay. "I take it you found the keg?"

"Oh, they didn't just have a keg. They had punch. Really good punch."

Guilt kicks me squarely in the ass, regretting that I wasn't there to watch out for her. "How are you feeling?"

"Amazing," she says. "I'm ready to go kick these guy's asses for making us leave. I, for one, was having the time of my life."

"I'm surprised you could reply to my text."

She giggles, shaking her head. "I didn't. Paxton did." She points at his seat in front of her.

I swallow, glancing up in the darkened cab at my brother.

"Where were you?" he asks. "Some dumbass was feeding her that shit like it was water."

Before I can reply, Lincoln shoves an unopened bottle of water toward us. "Time to drink up," he says.

I twist off the cap, handing it to her as Lincoln rolls her window down to allow the cold air to help sober her up.

"What are we doing?" Lincoln asks. "What's the plan? Are we going out onto the water? Do we just call them?"

"Jamal hung up on me, and Derek won't answer. Rae, you should try calling him," Pax says, twisting to face me again.

I glance at Lincoln, finding his gaze in the rearview mirror. "That's a good idea. He might answer for you."

Calling Derek is a terrible idea that is guaranteed to burn at least one bridge tonight, but I still scroll to his name and hit the call button. It rings twice before he answers.

"Raegan!" His voice sounds relieved.

"Hey. I got a call from someone I work with. They said you and some others were out on a boat at the Sound."

He laughs, yelling at someone. "Sorry," he says through laughter. "Yeah, we're out here shark fishing. Show these fucking monsters who is strongest." He whoops.

"You can't be out there and drunk," I tell him, trying to remain calm and my voice relaxed. "It's like driving a car while drinking. You'll get arrested."

He scoffs. "No one's out here. And if they do come, I'll sign an autograph for them." He laughs.

"Trust me. It won't work like that."

"Who do you like? I know you want me, but there's someone else, isn't there? Girls line up at my door, and yet something has you constantly distracted. Is it Arlo?"

I close my eyes, struggling to remain calm. "Derek, if you guys fall into the water, you'll drown. It's cold, and there are dozens of strong currents because the tide is high."

He laughs, fearlessly. "These sharks are who you need to be worried for. You want to come out here? I'll take you. I'll hire a fucking helicopter and give you a tour. Show you everything you've ever imagined."

"Please," I say. "You need to return to the marina."

"God, you're begging sounds so fucking good."

Tears prickle at my eyes as I pull in a deep breath. Before I can steady my emotions and voice, Poppy pulls the phone out of my grip and hangs up.

"Done," she says. "Let your team call the fucking cops. He deserves it."

"What did he say?" Paxton asks.

"You couldn't hear that? The son of a bitch was practically yelling." Poppy is in full ranting mode, her eyes wide with offense.

"If they're arrested, they destroy our chances of having an undefeated season. They'll be benched for the year," Pax explains as Lincoln pulls into the marina.

I've only driven the boat at night a few times, preferring the water when I can see Mt. Rainier and the shore rather than relying entirely on the tools of the boat.

Lincoln's hand strokes along my back as he passes me, going to where the boat is tied to the dock while Pax and Poppy board with the light of Paxton's phone's flashlight. "Can you hold this?" Lincoln asks, flipping on the flashlight on his phone as well. "Are you comfortable driving tonight? I can help."

"I didn't know you knew how to drive a boat. Do you have your license?"

His smile is shy. Of course, he does. Lincoln's lived a privileged life, attending a high school that is among the most prestigious and expensive schools in the state. "My dad and I spent a summer at sea when I was fifteen. It was hell."

I nod. "That would be really helpful. I've only driven at night a couple of times."

"See if you can learn their quadrants, and I'll get us there."

I stare at his confident hands, the width of his shoulders, and the stacks of muscles as he moves, then he stands, and his cologne mixes with the sea, and I've never wanted to kiss him as much as I do right now, now that I possess that right and confidence. I hand him his phone and start to turn, but he reaches for me, his fingers wrapping around my wrist.

"You're so fucking beautiful."

I hear my heart beating from the confines of his chest, happily thrumming as his fingers sweep gently over my skin before falling away as he moves to the next rope.

I board the boat, watching Pax help Poppy into a life jacket. "You should probably stay in the cabin," I tell her. "I don't want you falling out of the boat."

She hits me with a glare. "My happy buzz is quickly wearing off thanks to the frigid temperatures and this situation, thank you."

I nod. "The cabin has a heater."

"Sold," she says, following me to the cabin where I turn the key, the engine roaring to life.

"Raegan!" I recognize Lois's voice from the dock and quickly head out, leaving Poppy and Pax in the cabin. She pushes away loose strands of her hair being blown across her face by a stinging wind. "I'm sorry I called you. I just didn't want their futures to be ruined by a poor decision."

I nod. "No. I appreciate you calling me. I'm sorry about this, and I appreciate your help."

"Do you want me to come? I can help with the boat or maybe talk with the authorities if they beat you there. I have their last location."

"Are you sure?" She nods, coming aboard before I can ask her again.

Lincoln quickly follows her. "I'm Lois," she says, extending her hand to him.

"Lincoln," he says, shaking her slender hand.

"It's nice of you to help," she says.

"My brother and my best friend are in the cabin," I tell her.

Lois simply nods in response.

"Lincoln's an experienced helmsman. He'll be a better driver than me."

"You sell yourself short," Lois says. "But, that will allow you to stand watch, make sure everything's okay. Here," she shucks off her jacket that I try to shake off. "It's freezing, and I need to help him navigate."

I stop arguing, realizing time is running out.

Lincoln's gaze drifts across me, longing and protests going unspoken as he follows Lois to the cabin. I lift her hood as we get started, the wind turning icy as Lincoln carries us over the choppy waves like a hot knife sliding through butter.

We drive out into utter darkness, the water lapping at the boat as the horizon gets lost into the sea, making an endless backdrop of blackness.

I see the lights of their boat only seconds before I hear the distressed sounds coming from the pod of dolphins, their direction eerily close to the boat.

Lincoln slows as we near, taxiing at a painfully slow rate. I dig through the compartment under the nearest seat, searching for flashlights and headlamps so I can see what's going on as my stomach sours at the distraught calls and whines from the dolphins.

Lois hears them as well, running out before the boat comes to a stop. "What's going on?"

I shine a flashlight on the water in response, catching sight of two dolphins swimming in opposing directions.

"Something's wrong." I rake over the water, trying to see below the abyss, but it's too dark for me to see anything.

"Derek!" I yell, waving an arm.

The music on their boat is too loud, and the laughing is even louder as I scramble for my phone, redialing his number as my heart bangs around wildly in my chest, working to understand the situation and threat.

"Raegan," he says. "I thought I lost signal."

"What's going on? What have you guys done?"

"What?" he asks.

"The dolphins. What happened? Did you catch one of them?"

"How do you see the dolphins?" he asks. "What? Is that you?" His hand goes up like a visor, though it's dark out. "I see you!"

"Derek. The dolphins."

"Oh, yeah. I don't know why they're freaking out. We caught one in this giant fishing net they showed us to use, and the beast went abso-fucking-lutely nuts and broke half of it from the boat. It's going to cost me a fucking fortune—"

"Is the dolphin still in it?"

"What?"

"Is he still in the net?"

"Yeah, we tried pulling it back in, 'cause you said they kill animals when they're loose, but he fights us, and we can't reel it in. It's barely hanging on."

"He's going to drown." My voice is frantic.

"Babe, he's a dolphin. He lives in the water."

"He's a mammal, you moron! He needs to go to the surface to breathe."

I hang up, dropping my phone to the seat as I unbuckle my life jacket, each clasp popping too slowly, my hands aching from the coldness.

I slip out of it, letting it fall to the boat, unzipping Lois's coat.

"Raegan," she says, her voice wary. "You can't. It's pitch black."

"He'll die," I say, tears blurring my vision as I hand her back her coat.

"You might die," she says.

I shake my head, reaching into the next seat where a safety belt lies in a heavy pile that I fasten around my waist, tracing over the knifes before grabbing goggles and a snorkel.

"Raegan," Lois says, her voice as unsteady as my heart. "You can't stay under the water. It's too cold."

I nod. "I know."

She nods in response. "Reach for the net, cut it free from the boat. The dolphins will be able to help get him out and to the surface if you can make a hole wide enough."

"I'll swim to their boat and follow it. I need you to call them, make sure they don't start the boat's engine. See if they can turn on any more lights."

Lois blows out a breath. "Are you sure?"

"I'm positive."

"Raegan!" Paxton's voice hits like a fist to my gut, his fear more contagious than any flu virus. "Don't even think about it."

The boat silences, and Poppy and Lincoln appear.

My heart squeezes, hearing Poppy's questions and recognizing the same fear written across Lincoln's features as I kick off my shoes and grip the railing, swinging my leg over.

"Rae," he yells. "No. Stop!"

But I can't, not now, because if he asks me to stay for him I will, and then it will be too late for Blue.

The water hits me like a million tiny needles, stinging my skin and making my ears burn.

This is a situation we've hypothesized about for over a year, but the conditions are all wrong. The other dolphins don't come near us, their trust low, and as I surface, they begin swimming faster, their paths intentional and aggressive.

"Dammit!" I hear Lincoln's voice even through the commotion, my heart beating painfully with the need to apologize and explain my motives.

I focus on the route to the boat Derek is aboard, on the warmth I'd felt while Lincoln explored my body, the desires to feel him again. I think of everything except for how cold and stiff my body feels, protesting each of my instructions as I swim across the inky surface, my lungs objecting with each stroke that brings me deeper into the abyss.

"Raegan!" Lincoln's voice twines with Paxton's, their pleas hoarse as I continue.

I debate putting my head underwater so I can swim faster, weighing the risk and reward, knowing I might get there faster, which might ultimately allow me to climb out of this hell faster, but I won't be able to hold my breath as long, and the cold and darkness disorient me, which might make it take even longer.

I remain above water, kicking as hard as I can, focusing back on the aquarium. Of Snoopy, and the other animals, of my colleagues who have accepted me as their peer. I think of my time with Maggie this weekend and how complete I feel when she's near.

Derek calls my name, bringing me back to the present, and with it, the realization I'm nearing his boat. "What are you doing? Are you insane?"

I reach the end, feeling for the net while simultaneously reaching for the largest fishing knife on my belt. I pull it free, following the net only mere inches before it sinks too deep for me to reach.

"You need to pull it up," I instruct them. "I'll cut the net, but I can't reach it."

"You need to get out of the goddamn water. What are you doing?"

"He's going to die!" I yell. "Help me!"

Derek hesitates only a second before he yells for two other teammates to assist him. They follow his lead, pulling and tugging, allowing me access to place my blade against the strained threads keeping Blue contained.

"He's just a fish," Derek yells as they struggle to pull the water-logged weight in.

"Keep going!" I yell, forcing myself to tighten the grip on the knife. It feels like my fingers are being cut by the blade, though I know they're not. It's the stinging coldness, a warning that I need to get out of the water.

I slide my mask and snorkel into place, lowering my head in hopes I'll be able to see something as I continue following the net, cutting and slicing my way along the top. It feels like hours and seconds, the pain receding and somehow intensifying all at the same time. Muffled voices echo above me, but I'm so close. I know I have to be.

My muscles protest as I slice through another chink of the net, the blade slipping because I'm not applying enough pressure. The metal connects with the inside of my wrist before falling from my grasp. I barely feel the pain, and the water's so dark I can't examine the cut as I inwardly swear at myself for losing my tool. I surface, reaching for the belt and the next largest knife, my fingers barely managing to bend and form a fist around the handle.

In the background, I hear Lincoln's voice again, warming me, giving me strength because if there's one thing I know for sure, he's my air. My heart thumps in my chest, my breaths still coming out in short bursts, as I dip my face back into the water so I can reach the net, a renewed sense of energy as I cut link after link after link until I come face to face with Blue. I pause, taking in the scar running parallel to his eye, hoping he understands I'm here to help. I cut faster, yanking at the net in an attempt to show him the way out. I think of how the coldness only allows me an average of fifteen seconds without air, and how it has to impact him as well.

He moves, but then something beside me runs into my side, and water pelts me, and I lose the second knife as I lift my arms to cover my face. Water enters my snorkel, making me choke as I swim, losing sight of the surface as I feel the pull of a current nearby, sucking the net in. I work to swim, but the net is stuck, woven through several tools on my belt, tethering me several feet below the surface.

I pull and tug, kick, and twist as my thoughts flash to my mom and dad, to Paxton and Maggie, Poppy, and school. To Blue living, and then to Lincoln, where my thoughts slow, recalling the heat of his body, the weight of his hand. I kick at the net frantically, tears falling from my eyes as my vision grows darker and my thoughts muddled.

I close my eyes, hating this moment. I've rarely considered how I'd die, but the few times I have, it was decades in the future, after living life to its fullest, not when it's only just begun. I consider the things I wish I had said to Lincoln. The chances I wish I'd taken. The little things I wish I'd done, the moments I wish I'd spent with my mom, and how I wish I could ensure Poppy would find peace and remind her she doesn't need any guy to make her happy. Then my thoughts flip, happiness lulling me, so I don't feel the burn in my lungs or the ache in my chest where my heart used to reside. Accomplishments and love opening their arms until I forget the fear and panic as I slowly stop fighting, realizing I've always preferred the darkness of the ocean.

As the end nears, I realize this is exactly where I belong.

Lincoln and Rae's story continues in *Breaking the Rules!*

Breaking the Rules

ABOUT THE AUTHOR

Mariah Dietz is a USA Today Bestselling Author and self proclaimed nerd. She lives with her husband and sons in North Carolina.

Mariah grew up in a tiny town outside of Portland, Oregon where she spent most of her time immersed in the pages of books that she both read and created.

She has a love for all things that include her family, good coffee, books, traveling, and dark chocolate. She's also been known to laugh at her own jokes.

www.mariahdietz.com
mariah@mariahdietz.com
Subscribe to her newsletter, here

ALSO BY MARIAH DIETZ

The Dating Playbook Series
Bending the Rules

Breaking the Rules

Defining the Rules

Exploring the Rules - Coming October 1, 2020

His Series:
Becoming His

Losing Her

Finding Me

The Weight of Rain Duet
The Weight of Rain

The Effects of Falling

The Haven Point Series
Curveball

Exception

Standalones
The Fallback

Tangled in Tinsel, A Christmas Novella

Made in the USA
Monee, IL
10 November 2020